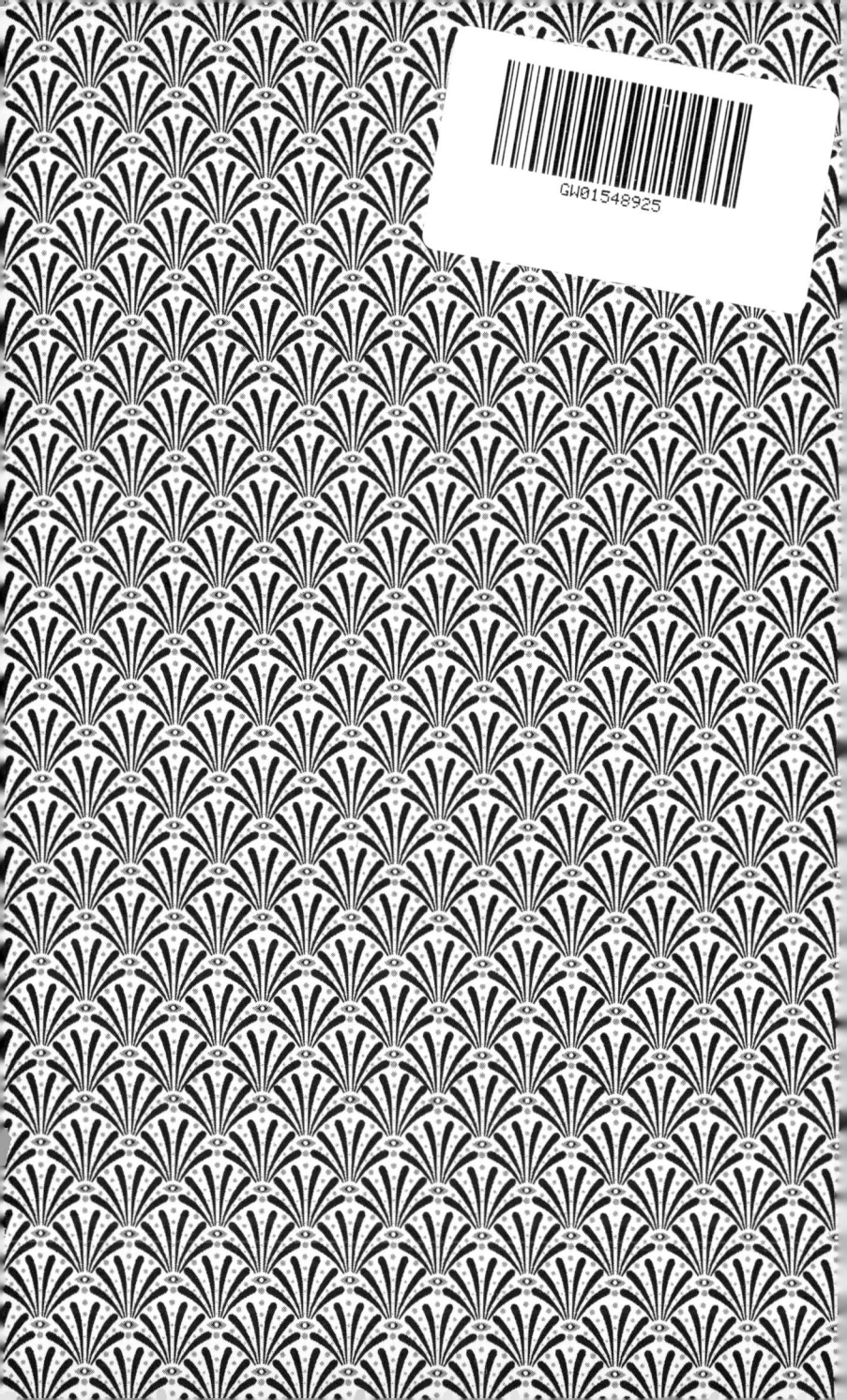

THE INHERITORS

RENARD PRESS LTD

124 City Road
London EC1V 2NX
United Kingdom
info@renardpress.com
020 8050 2928

www.renardpress.com

The Inheritors first published in India by Hachette India
This edition first published by Renard Press Ltd in 2024

Text © Nadeem Zaman, 2024

Cover design by Will Dady

Printed and bound in the UK on carbon-balanced papers by CMP Books

ISBN: 978-1-80447-112-8

9 8 7 6 5 4 3 2 1

Nadeem Zaman asserts his moral right to be identified as the author of this work in accordance with the Copyright, Designs and Patents Act 1988.

This is a work of fiction. Any resemblance to actual persons, living or dead, is purely coincidental, or is used fictitiously.

CLIMATE POSITIVE Renard Press is proud to be a climate positive publisher, removing more carbon from the air than we emit and planting a small forest. For more information see renardpress.com/eco.

All rights reserved. This publication may not be reproduced, stored in a retrieval system or transmitted, in any form or by any means – electronic, mechanical, photocopying, recording or otherwise – without the prior permission of the publisher.

THE INHERITORS

NADEEM ZAMAN

RENARD PRESS

THE INHERITORS

'The secret of great fortunes without apparent cause is a crime forgotten, for it was properly done.'
HONORÉ DE BALZAC

'The course of true love never did run smooth.'
WILLIAM SHAKESPEARE

1

I hadn't been in Dhaka for nearly thirty years. We left Bangladesh for the US when I was thirteen, and except for a few short and dizzying visits in the first couple of years to attend weddings on my mother's side, we'd stayed away. In that time, I lost touch with most of the family I'd grown up with, and I paid little attention to stories about relatives close or distant whenever my parents had one of their immersive moments of nostalgia.

My return happened more as a result of circumstances than being propelled by the growing desire I'd nursed for a while to write a book about the city of my birth.

Since the crash of 2008, my father had been selling off our numerous and lucrative properties back in Bangladesh. He travelled to Dhaka a couple of times a year, and had begun by offloading half of the plot of land connected to the house his father had built some fifty years before. I didn't pay attention. I was living my own life, and trying to mend the fractures from a decision that had caused some tension with my parents. Two years earlier, I'd given in to both my mother's appeals and my own need for steady companionship and let them arrange my marriage. The marriage didn't last a calendar year. Harsh words flew between the families. The connection went back some three or four generations – mothers knew mothers, grandmothers were the best of friends, great-grandmothers had grown up together.

Deep and complex relationships like those do not take slights impersonally.

In any event, we – my parents, and especially my mother and I – found our way back. My father was far less upset than my mother; but over time she too made her peace with it.

Last year, as my father was in the planning stage of another trip to Dhaka, this time to sell off everything that was left, a heart attack stopped him in his tracks. In his seventies now, he had to listen to his body more than he would like. His health had always been robust, but the stress he had put it through finally made a stand. Doctors forbade travel. My mother stood her ground. I happily volunteered.

I was restless – more than I realised. I think I'd been restive for a while. I no longer felt in the centre of anywhere in Chicago. I needed a break from my setting, a release from the heavy slog my life had become. For the last too many years, I'd all but abandoned writing. I considered graduate school, but shuddered at the thought of all that studying. I'd barely made it out the door with an undergraduate degree. Friends I'd had since high school were convinced I'd do better than I gave myself credit for, but they were projecting their capabilities on to me. I've often told my parents that even part of my time after high school should have been spent doing something other than going to college. I could've travelled. Read extensively. Explored my writing with some seriousness. Then, maybe, with a more worldly view on life, I could consider education. To Bangladeshi parents a suggestion like that was a giant gong announcing my detachment from reality. While they nodded along and considered my thoughts in retrospect, they would have shunned me when it mattered.

I was working that year with a midsize marketing firm writing copy. The job had come to me through a high-school friend, and she put in a glowing recommendation to the boss, a former colleague of hers. It was sedate, undemanding work. The salary made it worthwhile, without it being a career I would be in for the rest of my life, and before long five years had galloped into the past. The day I handed in my notice, my boss and schoolfriend took

CHAPTER 1

me out for drinks. They were supportive, knowing I wanted to get back to writing. I'd been doing research and making notes about my possible book on Dhaka, and the thrill of putting words on the page rushed through me like a reviving shot of adrenaline.

I felt restored. I was aware of how lucky I was: to be able to get up and go; to have no money worries, thanks to my father. I'd accepted early on in our new life in America that ours was not the immigrant story of countless others before us. We came here with more than just a dollar in our pockets. We came healthily armed with ancestral wealth. My parents were proud of this fact – so much so that we lived in near seclusion from other Bangladeshis during our first couple of years in Chicago.

Flirting with my forties, I'd reached a sort of morally stringent stance about the world. It had to stand upright, it had to pay unflinching heed to what was wrong, and I couldn't be bothered to understand its wayward, unruly ways, or care about the nuanced tendencies of human nature. Junaid Gazi would prove the exception. Gazi, whom I wished I could've scorned, the kind of person I was raised to see as more of a cautionary tale than a subject of emulation, and who it would become impossible to dislike. He existed in a kind of beauty that was undeniable. He exemplified the mysterious coexistence of opposing forces in one single being. He was as attuned to the universe as much as to his world, like an all-purpose machine, and picked up on the changes that took place miles ahead of others. His state of mind or any grand ability to tackle life with any special creative force towards the creative had nothing to do with it. He went on to prove me wrong on so many fronts, including that of friendship. He was more innocent than the eye at first could see, and this attribute, it may be assumed, made him prey. He handled what was his with, I thought at times, too romantic an eye, a sensibility for ever mired in hope, and a dreamlike faith in the promises of life.

My family on my father's side, the Chowdhurys, were of Yemeni Arab stock. They'd travelled to Bengal in around the fourteenth century and never looked back. As family history goes, down through the ages they were mystics and scholars, gentry and overlords, officials of the Mughals and servants of the Raj. My mother's people were no less distinguished. The Rahmans gave East Bengal, East Pakistan and eventually independent Bangladesh Members of Parliament and Islamic scholars, communist academics and Muslim League stalwarts, old-money elites and new money tycoons, and economic and political advisers to military and civilian regimes. My forebears saw the end of worlds, they witnessed the death of empires. They moved from the shuttered remains of a soon-to-be-forgotten way and launched into their century fresh-faced, trembling and beautifully mad with dreams.

We led a prosperous life in Dhaka, steeped in privilege. We, along with the country, weathered violent coups, two assassinations of heads of state and a long military dictatorship, at the end of which my father had had enough. The country he'd envisioned after Independence had been a heartbreaking let-down. It pained him to admit that we could no longer live there. My mother agreed. Many of their friends also agreed, and some had already taken steps to move away. As was to be expected, being a child, I didn't have a voice in the decision. The more time passed, the fewer our trips became, until they stopped altogether. My father only resumed them to take care of the property sales, then ended them once and for all for his health. My mother never again expressed a desire to go. At the time of my visit, twenty-five years had passed since I last saw Dhaka.

The week of my departure, my father had me on the phone once a day with Mr Ehsan Kibria, his lawyer and long-time employee, getting up to speed. When I wasn't doing that, I was being tutored by my father – which served my budding research quite well. He talked about Dhaka in a way he hadn't before. My mother got into the spirit as well soon enough. We stayed up late every night. They reminisced; I listened and learned. They wondered how much the city must have changed. They wouldn't recognise it any more.

CHAPTER 1

I argued that they would. Places have a way of staying imprinted on our minds – places that are more than where we were born or raised or lived and left. Places that don't go away even when we do.

On a humid, overcast September day in 2017, the gusty air promising rain, I walked out of Hazrat Shahjalal International Airport, and instinctively looked for Mr Ehsan. Then I remembered he'd said he wouldn't be able to meet me at the airport due to other obligations. So I contacted someone else – someone I was much more eager to see.

A small, wiry man, white-haired with a bright orange hennaed beard, beelined over to me through the throngs. With him were four young men dressed in khaki uniforms, who grabbed my luggage off the carts and started loading them into the silver minivan waiting at the kerb; I hoped I was not the reason for it being there, so obnoxiously did it take up the space of three vehicles, leaving a line of cars in an already congested situation in a further clog.

'Just like your father you look,' he said, and drew me in. Rais Ali – Rais Kaka, as I knew him – was a family institution. He held me in a tight embrace. Soon his shoulders were shaking. 'What took you so long? And when will your father and mother let me see them one more time before I go?' He gave his eyes one swipe each with his palm and led me to the minivan. One of the four young men climbed into the driver's seat and the others settled in around us, with Rais Kaka and I centred in the middle row, and we started pushing through the mass of humanity that sprawled endlessly in every direction.

It took about half an hour to navigate the crush of traffic and exit the airport, and then another fifteen or twenty minutes to circle the roundabout just outside and start heading south. Rais Kaka asked me many times during the ride if I was completely struck by the difference between Dhaka now and the Dhaka I remembered. I wasn't. My memories were confined to my cocooned existence back then. Our house, the homes of my grandparents and relatives and friends, school and Dhaka Club were all I knew of the city.

The driver proved a madman, weaving in and out between vehicles like he was riding a crotch rocket instead of a small bus, and by the time we arrived at the house I'd gone through several rounds of nausea. Rais Kaka commandeered the team of servants and my luggage was swept out of the minivan and disappeared inside.

I followed Rais Kaka to my old bedroom. I might as well have been walking through the home of a stranger – or as was the case, one that I was preparing to sell. My old bedroom held no special meaning. In thirteen years, I don't think I slept in that room a total of thirteen days. I was tearfully afraid of the dark, and my parents allowed me to sleep in their room, a habit that I broke within six months of moving to the US, mortified that I'd be ridiculed if it ever became known. I never gave much thought as to why that was not a factor in Bangladesh – probably because Bangladesh was familiar, America not, and in the brutal new days of settling in and getting my reluctant immigrant's footing, I felt I had to grow up.

'You have the whole house, Baba,' Rais Kaka said, throwing open thick curtains that blocked out almost all light. 'But I thought you might prefer your childhood room. I used to sit with you right there – you won't remember – when your parents had guests and you didn't want to be alone.'

'We wasted a lot of your life with our petty demands, didn't we?' I said.

'Baba, never,' he said.

Walking by the window, my attention was caught by what had happened to our once massive lawn that sprawled around the house, now reduced to a patch of ground barely large enough for a sandbox, no longer lush green grass but hard cement. Rais Kaka came and stood next to me.

'I thought it was half that size,' I said. 'The photos Mr Ehsan sent weren't the best.'

Rais Kaka let out a breath and we stared out of the window in silence. Tears were rolling down his face.

CHAPTER 1

'If your father was here today...' he said, but couldn't finish. He broke out of the spell and went to the door and yelled for food to be served immediately.

'We'll eat together,' I said. 'I'll take a shower and put on some clean clothes. Then you and I can sit and talk properly.'

'Baba, I wish I could, but I have to go back to work,' he said. 'I took the morning off for you, but my boss wants me there as soon as I'm done here. Do you need anything else?'

'I can ask those hundred other people if I do,' I said. 'They all work here, for us?'

'No,' said Rais Kaka. 'Mr Ehsan arranged for them for you, just for today. You have the cook, Jatin, the caretaker, Almas, and you have me, once a week, on my day off on Fridays.' He turned to leave, then drew me in and held me. 'Forgive a foolish old man, Baba.'

After Rais Kaka left, I stood looking out of the window at the apartment building, its name brandished on the side of the roof twenty floors up in large neon-green letters – Eternal Complex: a name that fit the temperament my father would be in for the rest of his life over the loss of his family lands.

This was the new Dhaka. More accurately, this Dhaka was new to me. Buildings like this had colonised every sliver of land their developers could conquer, and a new breed of its upwardly mobile denizens, as well as the scions of old-money families, wanted their city to reflect their desires and compete with the world for their wealth.

Dark, heavy clouds moved in over Eternal Complex. Thunder rumbled. The first dots of rain flecked the window, and a gust of wind hurtled by like a gang of fleeing thieves. Then came the downpour, sudden, vicious, obscuring, and it wouldn't let up for the rest of the afternoon, evening and night. Just as I started to turn away from the window, a light came on on the top floor, filling the long window that wrapped around the apartment in the colour of a fiery orange sunset.

2

Mr Ehsan was as I vaguely remembered – maybe with more hair on his head and less flesh on his face: squat, portly, with a handlebar moustache that covered his entire mouth. He bustled in, full of energy, his polished leather briefcase in one hand and a stack of files in the other. His light-grey pinstripe suit was immaculate, as if he'd picked it up from the tailor on his way over. He took off his Oxfords outside, which were also without a spot on their shine, and set his briefcase down to offer me his hand.

'All grown up, my goodness, and a carbon copy of your father,' he said. Looking at him, judging him superficially by his amiable smile, respectful decorum and soft, un-lawyer-like speech, I would never understand the visceral reactions he'd incited in my mother and my father's circle of friends.

'I'm very hungry, Mr Ehsan. Would you like to join me?'

'No, no, I'm fine, you go ahead.'

While lunch was served, he made three separate piles from documents he pulled out of his briefcase.

'Don't fret,' he said comfortingly, seeing my wide-eyed stare. 'This is all for me to tackle, and to explain to you only just what you need to know. Eat, eat. Take your time. You just flew halfway around the world.' He smoothed his moustache with a thumb and sat back, relaxed but still serious. I couldn't eat with him watching, so I finished what was on my plate and

CHAPTER 2

told him he could start whenever he wanted. Outside, the rain lashed on.

Mr Ehsan began, 'Your father said he wants this house, the plot in Dhanmondi and the Gulshan lot sold as a bundle. This house is still pending, except of course for Eternal Complex.' He frowned. 'The thing is, three different developers have made separate offers…'

'Already?'

Mr Ehsan nodded seriously, as though the matter was far graver than I realised.

'One, these are prime, top-notch locations, and two, your family name holds a lot of weight. It's too bad you no longer live here. You'd be living like royalty.'

'So, have you told Dad? About the offers?'

'Not yet.' Mr Ehsan gave his throat an unnecessary clearing, and then seemed to lose his train of thought for a moment.

'Shouldn't we…?' I said.

'Yes, yes, of course. I wanted only to wait for you, so you can see with your own eyes what they are, then tell him. He should hear this from his son instead of me if possible.'

'What's your opinion of the offers?' I asked.

'Top-notch, without a doubt.' He ran a smoothing hand over the papers. 'If you… I mean your father… went with the three offers, my suggestion is to give each a different asset. One asset, one buyer. Three separate buyers for three separate sales.'

He waited for me to show comprehension, then figuring I wasn't that slow, went on.

'That way you maximise on the price, instead of one entity coming back with a reduced lump sum for them all.'

'Makes sense,' I said. Still, there was a 'but' lurking in Mr Ehsan's tone.

Mr Ehsan proved predictable, and his moustache rose and his lips formed a mix between a pout and pucker. 'There is something I haven't told your father yet. There is a fourth offer.' It was almost as if he was embarrassed to mention what it was. 'And it's more than half as much again.'

'Half as much as which one?'

Mr Ehsan leaned forward and said in a lowered voice, 'All of them together.'

He'd said it too low even for me to hear him properly. I brought my head closer.

'Sorry?' I said.

'Only in commercial transactions have I seen an offer of that size,' said Mr Ehsan. 'And he's ready to go higher.'

'Who is it?' I asked.

'You've just arrived,' said Mr Ehsan. 'Naturally you haven't had time to meet your neighbour.' He indicated Eternal Complex.

'No, I haven't,' I said. 'None of them. How many are there?'

If Mr Ehsan was discomfited before, now he burned with embarrassment.

'Just him.'

'So, it's still a new building,' I said. 'Times are probably not the best for people to buy a place.'

'No. The kind of people that would buy a unit in a building like that don't know anything less than the best of times all the time.' Again, his jowls slumped, and he took on the look of a bearer of terrible news. 'The thing is, the owner of Eternal Complex hasn't put any of the other units on the market. And the owner *is* your neighbour.'

'He wants to live by himself in a twenty-storey building?' I said.

Mr Ehsan shrugged, with the futility of someone that had made endless attempts to talk another person out of crackpot ideas to no avail.

'So let me understand. Sorry, I had no knowledge of any of this until recently. He already bought the plot next door back when my father first sold it, and now he wants to buy everything, all of our properties, for more than they're worth?'

There was a knock on the kitchen door. Almas, the caretaker, walked in carrying a gift-wrapped package. Before he could set it down, Mr Ehsan reached for the card attached to the top.

CHAPTER 2

'A welcome gift from the man himself,' he said.

The message in the card read: 'Welcome home. Your friend and neighbour, Junaid.'

'Gazi?' I said.

'The one and only.' Mr Ehsan beamed as if he knew and had planned the surprise of the gift with my neighbour.

'It's quite the welcome,' I said.

'Well,' Mr Ehsan gasped, once I'd stripped away the wrapper and revealed the two-hundred-dollar bottle of Johnnie Walker Blue Label. His eyes enlarged in the hope that I might share some with him.

'Bars in America sell this for twenty dollars a shot,' I said.

'In that case, you should save it for a special occasion.'

'Are you sure?' I asked.

He passed his eyes longingly over the box and nodded. 'Let's have something more affordable for now,' he said. He told Almas to go and fetch a bag from his car.

'I wasn't sure if you drank or not,' he said. 'Maybe you'll like it – I hope you do.'

It was wine – an Italian red that looked fairly pricey – but then I knew precious little about wine, even though I drank it often.

'A gift from an Italian friend, from his own winery,' said Mr Ehsan. He poured, smelled and tasted like an expert, with his eyes to God, as if it was he who would ultimately have to answer to him if the wine wasn't pleasing.

'Delicious,' he said, smacking his lips.

I sipped mine and found it better than any wine I'd had before.

Our drinks quickly finished and another appointment bringing Mr Ehsan to his feet, he gathered up his files and briefcase, leaving on the table the three stacks of papers with Junaid Gazi's offers. 'Your family is a lot older and more distinguished any day than the Gazis. Tell your father, then tell me as soon as you have. Oh, and any time you need the car, just call me. My office is in Gulshan. The driver can be here quickly. Now you get some rest.'

I dialled my parents' number in Chicago, but cut off the call before it connected, and sent a text instead, saying I had met with Mr Ehsan and was tired, and I'd call as soon as I'd slept off the jet lag.

I watched the light in Junaid Gazi's window until it went off some time after ten, and then tried to read myself to sleep.

Outside there was the noise of traffic, even at that hour, and somewhere nearby a beggar with the voice of a Sufi mystic was reciting odes to God. The rain had abated but not stopped completely, pattering pleasingly against the window. I opened iTunes and put in my earphones. Instead of selecting music or a podcast, I opened my contacts and scrolled down to my cousin Disha. I hadn't thought of connecting with anyone else from the past except her. In the flurry of planning and getting ready for my trip, I'd taken a chance and sent her a text asking if it was still valid, and she'd responded ecstatically, demanding where I'd disappeared after our last meeting. She wasn't on any social-media platforms, and anyway I only used mine once every couple of months. When I told her I was Dhaka-bound, she called me immediately and we had a brief chat. She even said I should stay with her. 'We'd tear each other apart,' I joked, 'if we did that for more than a week!' She'd laughed and said that was probably true. We did not play well as a family for long stretches of time.

'I made it,' I texted.

'You're here!!!' she wrote back in less than a minute.

'Just a few hours ago,' I responded.

'When do I get to see you?'

'When you want.'

'After work tomorrow! I'm done at six!'

'I'll be waiting,' I wrote, adding a smiley face emoji.

'I love you, my little brother! Can't wait to see you!'

With very little sleep and startled by the Fajr call to prayers, I got out of bed just before six. I showered, put on a punjabi and pyjama and sandals; it felt as though I was getting into uniform – the dress

CHAPTER 2

for being in Bangladesh. I walked over to Eternal Complex. The humidity was treacherous. Other clothes would have stuck to my skin and made me miserable. The sky was ashen and threatening. Thin fingers of sweat trickled down my sides and back as I crossed the cement path and approached the guard on duty. He was a smiling, frail, affable man, bald with a white beard. A ten-year-old could overpower him. He told me Mr Gazi had already left. He was an early riser, the guard volunteered, and was out of the door before seven to beat the traffic. I don't know why, but I looked up. The window was dark, of course, and I walked back to the house.

I spent some time looking over the documents left by Mr Ehsan, most of which made less sense the more I read them. From the mid-1970s to when we left the country, my father's engineering firm was one of three in the city, and among a half dozen in the country that the government contracted for rural electrification projects all over Bangladesh. Mr Ehsan's documents were full of the jargon I heard my father speak every day when he came home and continued his work over the phone through dinner and on until his eyes closed for the night. The numbers came closer to making sense. One column showed the Chowdhury assets, under my father's name; a second showed the ones that were sellable and what they had been appraised at and the offers they'd received to date; then a third gave the offers, broken down; and the last had Junaid Gazi's all-destroying bid.

'Gazi,' my father said, and fell silent. Rain started falling again while I waited, and came down in a deluge, and then just as quickly restrained itself into a steady shower. 'I should have sold them the whole jing-bang-lot from the start,' he mumbled. 'If your Boro Chacha was alive now...' He was speaking of Disha's father.

'We have time,' I said.

'No we don't!' my father yelled. I heard my mother in the background telling him not to get worked up.

'I'm meeting Disha Apa later today,' I said, hoping to impart a less stressful offering.

'Good,' said my father, as if his mind had switched emotions. He handed the phone to my mother, and she asked me about the house, how it felt, what the city was like – to none of which I could provide a satisfying answer.

I ate a small breakfast and drank two mugs of tea, then opened up my laptop and worked on the outline I'd started months ago and barely touched since. Besides a timeline that began in the early 1600s and trickled down to the present, and a few names associated with the milestone events in the life of Dhaka, I didn't have much.

Jet lag started hitting hard. Jatin brought in a fresh pot of tea and asked what I wanted for lunch. I told him I most likely wouldn't make it that long. He said not to worry: I could eat whenever I wanted, and he'd have everything ready.

I slept through the afternoon, and I'd have slept right on through the evening and night if it hadn't been for the butterfly flutter of my phone next to my pillow that intruded on the strange, unrecallable dream I was having and wrenched me, heavy-headed, to read the message it had received.

'Car is on way to get you!!!' Disha's text announced.

I got out of bed, took a quick shower and put on a different punjabi. For some reason I went through two more punjabis and a few shirts before deciding on the second punjabi, wishing I hadn't sacrificed the very first one I'd put on to the heat and sweat of the day, the whole time stopping myself from thinking I was getting ready for a date. Disha was the family beauty. Elegant, sharp, independent. She was unafraid to be a girl among a legion of boy cousins and keep us in our places, earning our madly crushing hearts in return. I found her radiant. I couldn't speak in her presence. She made matters worse by singling me out. Of all her cousins, she said I was the most well-behaved, on Eid the best dressed, and all-round certain to make the family proud one day. I soared. I dreamed of us as a couple, even though in a remote part of my confused little brain I was aware we couldn't be – not only because we were related, but because she was older. Women were supposed to be younger than

CHAPTER 2

the men they married. This was one of those strange refrains I knew, like a fundamental rule of life, but never found rhyme or reason for. Patriarchy, of course, and medieval notions of gender roles. Exactly the kind of nonsense Disha would tear apart.

The light was on in Junaid Gazi's apartment, the same sunset glow, and for some reason it seemed brighter today – maybe because I'd had some rest and my vision was clearer, the cobwebs in my brain cleaned out. I was about to move away when a figure walked up to the window and slid open the glass. He lit a cigarette and exhaled a jet stream of smoke. If I opened my window and shouted a hello he'd have heard me. I backed away and closed the curtains.

The only time I had seen Disha since we left Bangladesh was about seven years ago. She was in Chicago for a conference and had got my number from my parents. When I saw the unknown number flash up on my phone I ignored it. Her message left no doubt who the caller was.

We hung out all weekend. She brought me to the cocktail and dinner receptions at the end of each day of the conference. I met people I otherwise never would – corporate types whose oxygen was their financial portfolios, with whom I managed conversations only because we were all so profusely drunk.

Disha smirked that Sunday morning when I knocked on her hotel room after making the walk, and elevator ride, of shame from the room of one of her female colleagues. She said our time together had been everything she'd hoped a reunion would be, with a bonus for me.

At brunch, she caught me up with her life. It was a substantial undertaking, but the bulk of the story centred on her marriage, which was nearing an end.

'We met when we were barely twenty-two,' she told me. 'Married fast. Those first two years should have been a warning.'

I asked why.

'Our personalities, our tempers, our prides were identical,' she said. 'It's a bomb that lights itself. Doesn't need outside fire.' She went on to summarise a tumultuous courtship, accentuated by fortnightly break-ups, tearful reunions, promises of never again being apart and hurting each other, a few days of calm and then the next eruption. Jealousy seemed to have set up permanent residence between them. Add to that Disha's zest, her spirit, her lovely brown eyes the size of silver dollars, her wavy hair that bounced around her shoulders with every little move, and a perpetual catch-me-if-you-can gaze. No man could be faulted for having a second and a third stare until the man with her was moved to intercede, with the ingredients in place for just the right spark.

But she left out one detail. I didn't ask for it right away. We talked about other things. Family, our childhood, where other cousins were – and of course she pried out of me my story.

'It's not as romantic as yours,' I said. 'Nowhere near as passionate.'

'Did I hear right that you let your parents choose your bride?'

'Even when I'm nowhere near Dhaka for decades, word gets around,' I said.

'I can't believe you let them do that,' Disha said.

'When you put it that way, it makes me sound like a milk-toothed imbecile. But yes, I did. And we were married for about a year before she decided she was made for a higher standard of life than I could give her.'

'Good riddance. And thank God you didn't have children,' Disha said.

'That was never a possibility or a problem.'

She stared at me while the wheels in her head turned and span.

'How is that... I mean...?' she attempted.

'Without getting into details and spoiling both our appetites,' I began, 'I'll only say that she spent about nine months of that year at her parents' house, and the other three with her sister and friends. The ones she did spend at home she didn't want me in the same bed with her.'

CHAPTER 2

'Sounds like a piece of work,' Disha said, then raised her glass. 'Here's to you getting out of that – whatever it was. And shame on Chacha and Chachi for doing that to their only child.'

'So,' I said after a short silence. 'Who was it? Your guy?'

'You don't know?' Disha was genuinely surprised. 'How could you not know?'

'I heard you got married,' I said. 'Some big shot's son. I didn't find it unusual. I also didn't pay it much mind, honestly. Sorry.' The look she gave me said she read something on my face that betrayed what I'd just said. I used to think she had a clue about my crush on her and that was why she treated me differently from our other cousins, until she had her first boyfriend. He was a tall, ropy-muscled, squash-playing, Greek-god-bone-structured cadet at the air-force academy, and it took one look at a picture of him – not even the real flesh-and-blood person – to end my dreams of romancing my cousin. By the time I was old enough to tell her of my hapless feelings, we'd left Bangladesh. I wondered if we could laugh about it now.

'Also,' I said as casually as I could, 'I used to have a crush on you, so there you go. I didn't care about hearing you got married.' The hangover throbbed in my head. Disha sat serious as stone. 'Come on, I'm kidding. I was a kid. I didn't even know what having a crush meant. I think all of us boy cousins had crushes on you.'

Disha looked out at the river. We were at the rooftop restaurant of her hotel, facing west. It was late spring, the river still green from St Patrick's Day. The sun was somewhere above us, or getting there, our umbrella keeping us amply shaded. We had put away a good amount of food while taking this CliffsNotes version ride through our personal histories. Disha turned back to me.

'Why didn't you say anything?' she said.

In my hungover haze I thought I'd missed a part of what she'd said. 'Say something about what?' I asked.

'You know, the crush.'

'Because I wasn't completely out of my mind,' I said. 'Because my mother and father would take turns throttling me with their bare hands if they knew. Because I was a child. Shall I keep going?'

'Seriously,' said Disha. 'I always thought you were so adorable.'

'Shut up, that's enough,' I said. 'You're my big sister. We're crazy enough as a family without adding incest to the mix.'

Disha's face twisted and contorted, and that was the end of that.

In hindsight, it was amazing that her husband's name was never mentioned. Not even when he bought half our plot. I didn't ask; she didn't say. Some of that boy with the crush on her was still alive in a hidden nook inside me, and he was not interested in knowing who the man was that had captured her heart. We spent a lovely afternoon walking around, going down to Navy Pier, talking about people, family, Dhaka's social scene, of which Disha had become a leading fixture. Her flight was in the evening. I said goodbye to her in front of the hotel and stood watching the lights of the limousine until it made a turn and was out of sight.

On my way out to Disha's car, I inadvertently checked Gazi's window. It was a different side, overlooking the driveway of the house and the main gate, and he was there, smoking, watching me as if he knew exactly when I would come out of the house. The glowing tip of his cigarette moved, like a fly on fire, and he waved. I couldn't see his face; couldn't make out anything other than his outline. I waved back. I almost called out a thank you, but Disha's driver's salaam distracted me. I returned the greeting and climbed into the back seat.

3

'My jaan!' Disha yelled across the room and padded over in her bare feet. She clamped her arms around me and rocked us side to side. 'My jaan, my jaan, my jaan little brother, let me look at you. My goodness, what a grown man you've become.'

'I was a grown man the last time you saw me,' I said.

'You were a baby,' she insisted. 'Now look at you. Grey hair. When did you get all this grey hair? And the beard? Why this look of an old man? And punjabi–pyjama? I thought I'd see that same impish little boy I saw in Chicago.'

'Well, like I said, that was almost ten years ago, and I repeat, I was not a boy then either. You are unchanged.'

'Bullshit. I'm an old hag.' She tousled my hair and wrapped her arms around me again. She smelled of soap and flowers. Her head came up to my chest and I saw the top where the roots of her hair were paper white. The rest was a swirl of burgundy and highlighted streaks of mute gold. I must've been staring, because she pulled a face and gave me a shove. 'See? I can tell how unchanged I am by that look on your face.'

'This is how I look,' I said. 'And I was just looking at you, that's all.'

'Sorry for being in my bathrobe. Come, sit. I'll be dressed in five minutes and then we'll go out. I have you for the whole night.' It was not a question but an older-sister declaration.

'Where are we going?' I asked.

'Opening of a new restaurant first, then to a party. Remember Shahid Mohsin? Dabir Mohsin's son. They used to be your neighbours way back in the day?'

'I do,' I said. 'I think he's a year or two older than me. Dabir Uncle died a few years ago, right?'

'Just a few months before Abbu.' Disha's face fell for a second, and her eyes dropped. Her cheeks had the smallest pouches at the corners of her mouth, and the skin under her eyes was flaky and puffed. She caught me looking and turned her head self-consciously to a more profiled angle.

'I want to visit Chacha's grave before I leave,' I said.

'How long are you staying?'

'Well, I'm not sure. As long as the property stuff takes, I guess.'

She pinched my cheek and gave my facial hair a tug. 'Such an honest boy,' she said. 'Doesn't have to work a day in his life and there he is earning a living. I want to hear all about it.'

'I've been the quintessential rich boy this past year,' I said. 'Working for Daddy. Without pay. Then again, every writer that had the leisure to just sit around and write came from money. Tagore, Tolstoy – even Hemingway lived off his wives after he became rich and famous. Five hundred pounds and a room of one's own is what a writer needs to make it. You know who said that?'

'Why would I know that?' Disha said, scrunching her face.

'Right,' I said. 'I'm already boring you to death.'

'You're not.' She gave my hands a squeeze. 'You're a smart, intelligent man, and you should be proud of it. Now,' she said, standing up, 'I'm going to get dressed. You can have whatever you like right there.' She pointed to a drinks trolley, which was stocked better than most bars.

'Does Dhaka look completely changed to you?' Disha asked in the car. We were stalled in traffic on Gulshan Avenue, which I remembered being open and wide, with houses scattered on either

CHAPTER 3

side, and the mosque, and on both its northern and southern ends opening on to grassland and marshy vegetation – all of which had been turned into paved roads that led to shopping centres, residential areas and housing developments.

'Not really,' I said. 'Just more bling-bling and reaching for the heavens. I guess our own plot is going to add to it soon enough.'

'So,' Disha turned to me. 'Property stuff. What's going on?'

I gave her a summary. She listened without interruption, expressed her wish that she could visit my parents and offer her support, and then asked who the buyer was.

'Gazi Enterprises,' I said.

A strobe of multicoloured lights from shop signs flickered over her face as the car started moving. She was still, not even blinking.

'They've already bought Eternal Complex,' I went on. 'The whole building – and there's only one tenant, way up on the top floor. Junaid Gazi.'

I could sense her stiffen more. The car was frigid with air conditioning and the air freshener was not doing my still-recovering system any favours. I opened the window a crack, and then tried to get a read on Disha's mood. It seemed to have made a downward shift.

The rest of the ride she was quiet, and I left her alone.

'Sorry,' she said, when we reached our destination, then took me by the hand. 'Come, I want you to meet people.'

The restaurant was inside a compound with high walls and armed guards. I had no idea which part of Gulshan we were in, I just knew that it was a street with homes and businesses, one that I was sure I'd visited when we still lived in Dhaka, because someone or other my parents knew lived somewhere on it. The main doors opened on to a spacious lobby under subdued lighting, perhaps forced a tad too much towards ambient. Giant Grecian urns lined the walls. The marble floor alone must've cost in the millions, in dollars, and then there were the chandeliers and the broad staircase plucked straight out of a plantation house in the American South, and we had yet to enter the main restaurant.

'Shahid's done well for himself,' I said. My voice must have been too loud, or my comment uncouth, because I felt Disha's hand brush my wrist. 'Sorry,' I whispered.

But it wasn't me. She was leading me towards a man who was walking in our direction. He'd come out of the side of the open double doors leading on to the restaurant floor.

'About time,' he said.

When he came into view — as best as possible in the low lighting — I saw that his hair was glossy and brushed back, falling into curls at the neck. He wore cologne, something I'd been unused to for years, but my mind shot back to my days of wearing Lacoste, and the tiny crocodile with its open jaw that was its emblem. He gave me a once-over, and Disha, almost as if she'd seen suspicion and unease in his eyes, introduced me.

'Tarek Bashir,' he said, pumping my hand in an impressive grip.

'Nisar Chowdhury,' I said, even though Disha had already told him my name.

We went to the table he had ready for us, and a round of drinks appeared before we were even properly seated. I didn't want mine — some mixed concoction — but I said nothing.

'So, you live in America,' Tarek said. 'Where?'

'Chicago.'

'The Windy City. I've been there. Too fucking cold. I like LA better.'

Disha gave me a smile I didn't understand. It had a touch of embarrassment and leftovers of the sunken mood she'd fallen into in the car.

'I've been to LA,' I said. Neither of them seemed to hear me, or care. Tarek's eyes were hooked on Disha like she'd just slapped him and thrown her drink in his face, and Disha appeared generally self-conscious. I waved over our server and ordered some wine.

'Just bring the bottle,' Disha told him.

Our conversation loosened up after two rounds of drinks, and by the time the main course was served we'd pushed through the

CHAPTER 3

heaviness. Disha cheered up. She and Tarek had been together for almost a year. There were ups and downs, which they left at that, and, like Disha, Tarek had been married before. The difference was he had children, two, whom he adored, and whom, I didn't need to be told, Disha had never met. Tarek's ex had remarried. The new husband had his own ex-family. They lived together in a complex owned by his family in Bashundhara City, one of Dhaka's premier housing developments, and Tarek was welcomed there as begrudgingly as was expected of an ex-spouse in a marriage that had seen a bitter, drawn-out end. Tarek told us all of this as though telling the story of someone else's life, and by the time he had finished, Disha was back to being sullen.

'Your sister doesn't like hearing about my past life,' he said, taking both of us by surprise. 'As if she's as innocent as a newborn. Did you tell him about the jackass you were stuck with for years?'

Disha shot him a look across the table. The Disha I knew would have shocked the room by now with a retort loud and brash.

I recalled our last meeting in Chicago – how she hadn't told me then who she'd been married to, and I hadn't been interested anyway.

'I can't have a past, you see, Nisar,' Tarek said with a martyr's tone. 'Only her.'

She should be flying at him, arms outstretched to grip his throat, suffocate him until an apology popped out of his mouth. I wanted to leave – leave Tarek's company and be alone with Disha. I brought out my wallet and looked for our server.

'Don't worry about it,' Tarek said, waving my wallet away.

'I want to,' I said. I brought out four 500 taka notes, then added four more.

Tarek gave the money a tight-lipped smile. I looked at Disha.

'That's too much,' she said.

'Fine,' I said, leaving the money on the table.

The server asked if we wanted dessert, and after we said we didn't, Disha asked him if Mr Mohsin was around.

'Shit,' she said, learning that he wasn't. 'I'd loved to have given a congrats in person.'

'I'm sure he would have appreciated it,' said Tarek with a sidelong glance, first at her then at me. 'I should go now,' he said, standing. He had another engagement and would meet us in a couple of hours at the party. He said a passing goodbye to me and touched Disha's shoulder on his way out.

I didn't realise how irritated I was until we were in the car, sitting in a cold silence as if Disha and I had had a fight. I had a million questions, starting with where the hell she had picked up a tool like Tarek Bashir. I must've been breathing hard, as was my tendency when I was worked up, because Disha laid a hand on mine and asked if I was OK.

'I'm fine,' I answered.

'He's not always like that,' Disha said after a silence. 'No, I'm serious, jaan. First time I met him I thought he was a prick. Cocky and so self-assured. And then I thought, that's just how I come across to people. Always have. We don't know how other people see us. We're just being us, but others are hearing and seeing how we're really behaving.'

'Well, I'd love to see the side that made you like him,' I said.

'Come on,' Disha said. 'Please? For me?'

'I guess both our records are awful.'

'The Chowdhury bloodline has to keep up its reputation, right?' She took my arm in both of hers and laid her head on my shoulder.

I was not dressed appropriately for a party. People were in shirts and trousers and dresses. There was a DJ booth thumping bass into the room like cannon fire, and the centre of the living room was the dance floor. I stood by the door, feeling awkward, until Disha, not finding me at her side, pulled me in. I met a flurry of people, including the hosts. It was their anniversary. I thought the wife was Latina until she spoke Bangla. The husband reeked of new money, as did their gaudily decorated home. Beyond the dance floor a set of glass sliding doors led out on to a balcony. People were crammed out

CHAPTER 3

there, smoking, drinking, talking. I realised that it wasn't just my attire that I was hesitant about, it was being there at all. I'd long ago given up parties like this, every one of which ended with the sun coming up and reckless drunkenness that led to days of recovery and regret.

'Here,' Disha said, pushing a glass of red wine into my hand and clinking her glass against it. 'You smoke?'

'Not cigarettes,' I said.

'Of course not,' she smiled widely. 'Am I that transparent?' I said.

'I think I can get a sense of my own brother.'

'I'm not even high,' I said.

The smoke I smelled out on the balcony was not from cigarettes alone. Disha introduced me to more people, and one of them, a bald-headed man named Guru, offered me his left hand to shake and proffered his joint with the right.

'How much gossip have you spread about me?' I said to Disha.

'Guru Bhai is smart,' she said.

'Thank you,' I said to my impromptu dealer. He gave me a wink.

I smoked the joint looking out over Gulshan Lake and the row of shops and businesses on the other side. Their lights sharpened, became crisp and brighter. I wished I knew which direction I was looking in, could recognise something from what was once here before the development.

Disha was talking quietly with Guru, their conversation drowned out by the intrusive bass of the music from inside. I had finished the joint and resumed sipping my wine when the well-oiled glide of the sliding door raised the music to a blaring high and just as quickly cut it back down as it was closed, replacing it with the voice of Tarek Bashir. He handed Disha a fresh drink and, coiling his arm around her neck, keeping his eyes locked to mine, whispered in her ear. Disha squirmed and adjusted his arm to her comfort.

I needed to use the bathroom.

I made my way through the dance floor, where the crowd from the balcony had poured back in. Hips were swaying, arms flailing and a few bodies grinding.

I stopped at the bar on my way back from the bathroom and stood behind a woman in a sparkly silver dress that ended just above her knees. Her hair, shiny and straight, fell to her lower back. I felt like a leering old creep, and I knew why – the way I was dressed. I was used to seeing men my father's age in punjabi and pyjamas; people my age only wore them on Eid. Having got her drink she turned around, and, catching me staring, she smiled. I tried to smile back, but paused midway, and heard myself say hi. She held my gaze a moment longer and went off towards the dance floor. I ordered my drink. I tried to be subtle while it was being poured and scanned the dance floor. I couldn't see the woman any more.

I got a glass of wine for Disha and made my way back to the balcony.

Tarek and Disha hadn't changed positions, and they were talking to someone I couldn't see because they were at the other end, behind where the wall of the room partially jutted out.

'My last one,' I said, handing Disha her drink. 'And then your car and driver are taking my pumpkin ass home.'

The person they'd been talking to said something in a low voice that I couldn't make out, and she took a step forward to flick her cigarette over the railing. It was the woman in the silver dress.

'Hi again,' she said, seeing me.

'Hi,' I said.

'Do you know Jasmine?' Disha asked me.

'We go way back,' I said. 'To the bar. What, almost five minutes now?'

'Nice to meet you,' Jasmine said, offering her hand.

'This is my cousin, Nisar,' Disha said. 'Jasmine is an artist,' she said, sounding like her agent. 'Nisar is a writer,' she went on. 'The smartest one in the family.'

'My cousin is biased,' I said.

'I'm aware of it,' Jasmine said, putting her arm around Disha.

Tarek made a sound, and I imagined punching him in the throat. Jasmine went through her tiny purse, which matched her dress, and brought out a business card.

CHAPTER 3

Disha watched me take the card with a wary eye.

'I'm sorry,' I said to Jasmine. 'I don't have one of my own.'

'No problem,' she said. 'I usually don't have any either – haven't used this purse in a while.' I detected an American inflection.

Again, Disha followed my every move when I brought out my wallet and put the card in it, as if she wished I'd thrown it away instead.

'Writer,' said Tarek. 'What do you write?'

'He's writing a book on Dhaka,' Disha answered. 'Jasmine's family has a long history in the city.'

'So does yours,' Jasmine said.

'We're scattered all over the place,' said Disha. 'Not all of us are here. My uncles and cousins all left.'

'I'm one of said guilty cousins,' I said. 'Even though I was a child and didn't have a say in the migration habits of my parents.'

'No, you didn't,' said Disha. 'You were a baby, all right.'

'You're staying for a while then?' said Tarek.

I didn't give him a reply.

'Where do you live?' Jasmine asked.

'Chicago,' I said.

'I love Chicago. I wanted to do my undergrad there, but didn't get accepted where I applied. Ended up in Houston. Bad idea. Texas.'

'I like Texas,' said Tarek. 'It's not cold and the people are chill. Chicago people are fucking stuck up.'

'Who did you meet in Chicago besides Bangladeshis?' said Disha.

'What does that matter?' Tarek said. 'People are people. Bangladeshis have been in the US long enough to be American. Like him.'

'I was born here,' I said, watching Jasmine.

'But you're not from here any more,' said Tarek.

'You lived in Karachi till you were a teenager,' said Disha. 'Does that make you not Bangladeshi?'

Tarek gave her a stare. 'I'm as Bengali as anyone. Bangladeshi too.'

'I stayed way clear of our people in the US,' said Jasmine. 'One dawat was all it took.' When she spoke the Bangla word it was as though English didn't exist in her. 'All they could talk about was marriage, jobs, income and homes in the suburbs.' She held up a slender finger for each item. 'If a cliché was ever true, they're living proof.'

'Same for Chicago,' I said.

'And then there are the ones that are so American, it's like they don't know what Bangladesh is.'

'ABCD. That's what we called them when I was in college,' I said.

'American Born Confused Desis,' we said at the same time.

'Clowns, every last one!' Jasmine said, shaking her head. 'It's sad, is what it is. I mean, look at this. Over there those moms and dads are trying to make good little Bangladeshi children, and here we are trying to be – what, I don't even know. We *are* confused. And we stay confused no matter where we are. I'm sorry, I know it's my friends' anniversary, but seriously.'

The mood turned sombre. For several moments the only sound was of the music from inside.

'Then what are you doing here?' Tarek broke the silence. 'Why do you go to parties then? You're at every single one.'

'Because there's nothing fucking else to do in this town but drink and work.'

'What about you?' Tarek asked me. 'Is that your impression, too?'

'I've not even been here a full day,' I said.

'I'm sorry,' said Jasmine. 'I'll stop being a party pooper.'

I held back from telling her how much I appreciated her honesty, and she had no need to apologise.

'Another?' Disha said, tapping my glass with a finger. 'Or are you ready to leave?'

I started to answer, but Jasmine drained her drink in one swallow and said she had to go. 'Early morning,' she said. She was flying to Chittagong for ten days for work. 'Hey, Tarek, I'm just kidding, man, cheer up.'

CHAPTER 3

'I love Chittagong,' I said. 'We used to go when we still lived here. One of the last trips I remember was to Foy's Lake.' I named people from another life. Jasmine recognised none of them.

'Maybe my parents know them,' she said, perhaps trying to help me save face.

'I'm waiting,' Disha said, holding our empty glasses.

'Not for me,' Jasmine said.

'You're not flying the damn plane, are you?' Tarek said.

'No,' Jasmine replied, without a trace of irony.

'Let's go,' Disha said, and nudged Tarek inside.

In the silence between Jasmine and me, Guru made a cameo. Jasmine introduced us and we joked that we were best buddies and had bonded over drugs. Guru held up a second joint, with the lighter poised to light it. I passed. So did Jasmine.

Downstairs, there was a moment of awkwardness before Jasmine's car pulled up. I wanted to tell her I'd call her when she got back, but hearing it first in my head, in the quiet of the night, made it sound obscenely pushy. She hugged Disha and Tarek, and we shook hands, which felt even more awkward.

'My number is on the card,' she said, and climbed in.

Before Disha, or worse, Tarek, could make a crack, I asked to be pointed in the direction of my house. 'I'm going to walk,' I said.

'Walk?' said Tarek. 'Now? In this bloody humidity?'

'Just point me,' I said to Disha.

'This isn't Chicago,' Tarek said, almost getting up to my face.

'I'll try to remember that,' I said. 'Which way is Kemal Ataturk Avenue?'

Tarek walked off, lighting a cigarette.

'Tonight, please,' I said, snapping my fingers in Disha's face. She was transfixed on something that was neither Tarek nor me.

'This way,' she said, pointing to the next street. 'Gulshan Youth Club will be on your right.'

'Great,' I said, starting to walk. She waited expectantly, either to hold me back or for me to change my mind.

'I'm good,' I said. 'Bye.'

'Be careful, OK?' she called after me. 'I'll be a bad sister if something happens to you.'

I heard their car start. I picked up my pace. I passed the youth club, shrouded in darkness, and kept going.

The three hectic visits we'd made shortly after leaving were barraged with wedding receptions and dinners, home visits, getting stuffed and sick on rich foods and sweets and watching my parents navigate the façades they would later pick off for what they were, like erasing betrayers from the family. My mother may not have been eager to visit Bangladesh so soon, but the moment the invitations arrived, she was calling the travel agent. The trips lasted days and ended hours after the wedding festivities subsided. We did nothing else. We would stay home most of the day, get dressed up in the evening, spend hours at the wedding venue, go to the string of other entertainments, then come home and go to bed. For those brief stays, it felt as though we'd come back home, and leaving again for the US was going back to an extended vacation we pretended was our life. Rais Kaka stayed with us the entire time – the sole person we kept up contact with. I didn't think about it then, but I never once saw Disha on those trips.

One of the wedding receptions took place at Sonargaon Hotel. Like my father, I wasn't much for socialising constantly, and when he ducked out of the reception hall with an old friend, I went with him. They sat down in the lobby, ordered beers for themselves and a Coke for me, and settled into catching up. Maybe it was decorum, but their voices barely rose above a whisper, and my father's friend kept looking around the lobby every so often. The people around us milling about were mostly foreigners, white Europeans and Americans, and there was a stiff sense of secrecy about them too. The upside to the quietness was that despite their low volume, I could hear everything my father and his friend were saying to each other.

CHAPTER 3

'They're leaving no one,' the friend was complaining. My ears were open and my eyes were forward. 'Only last week they arrested…' he named someone who meant nothing to me, but was apparently high up in the food chain – big enough that my father took note with widened eyes and a shake of the head. 'And he's at the Central Jail, like a murderer.' The friend looked over both shoulders. He took a sip of beer. A line of foam stuck to his upper lip. He flicked at it with his tongue before going on. 'Everyone made money – so what? No, it has nothing to do with that. This is about this government and its retribution on people that were friendly to the last one. The next government that comes will make us pay for going along with this one.' He sighed, lowering his head. 'I don't know what will happen. You did the right thing, leaving this hellhole when you had the chance. If you were still here now I don't think you'd be left alone either.'

My father's eyes flicked over to me. I could tell because of the sudden movement of his head, which was amplified in the general motionlessness of the lobby. He would have seen me gazing at the fountain. I didn't break my stare or look back at him.

'I don't keep any more than I need here,' the friend continued. 'They'll say you owe taxes, then rip the clothes off your back. That's what this country has become. What you felt was nothing compared to what's happening now. But that was right after Independence, and you played your cards right.'

I could tell my father was uncomfortable. He tried to change the topic several times, but without success. It was as if he was the man's lawyer, and the man's desperation was on the way to becoming anger.

'The military was far better than this,' the man said, complaining just for the sake of being heard, knowing well his grievance was pointless. 'Men are supposed to run countries, not women. There's no rationality in them. How can hysterical banshees be presidents and prime ministers? Emotional, vengeful bitches, and we are stuck with one of the worst God created.' He drained his beer and smacked his lips. 'The first knock I hear on my door, I'm telling you, I'll be flying out the back. Let them come for me in Europe, in the US. This shit country isn't worth making an extradition treaty with. I'll laugh, and that's the last they'll see of me. What do you think?'

My father sat gravely. His silences could be long, and sometimes that was all they would be. If the friend had asked me what I thought, I'd tell him we should switch places. He could take our house in Chicago and we could move into his in Dhaka.

'I know,' he said. 'There's nothing to say.' He tried to lighten the mood, made attempts at changing the subject, but my father's spirits had been dulled. I didn't recognise the man from when we lived in Bangladesh. He'd never been to our house or been at any gatherings or parties. My father knew everyone there was to know in Dhaka. In our neighbourhood, rickshaw drivers and teashop owners, beat police and beggars knew our house and our family name. I would look out of the window of the car sometimes during a drive, and wonder which of the hundreds of random people we passed on the street were his acquaintances, knew his name, and he theirs.

A few months later my father got a late-night phone call that lasted long enough that my mother grew perplexed and kept motioning for him to tell her who it was. He spoke very little, and what he said were words to offer comfort. Someone had died, I thought, but later I put together from what he told my mother that it was the wife of the friend from the wedding. He'd been arrested. The authorities had raided his house at dawn, pulled him from sleep and arrested him in in his lungi and T-shirt. They'd surrounded the house like a war zone. Even if he'd been awake, he would have had no chance of escaping through a back way.

At home, Almas handed me a folded piece of paper. A handwritten message said: 'Please come up for a drink when you're back. Late is fine. J.'

4

It was a little after ten – an hour I didn't consider late. I went inside to change and from my bedroom saw the lights on in Gazi's apartment. I put on a shirt and jeans. I was tired, I wanted a good, long sleep, and yet I felt a second wind coming on from Gazi's invitation. On my way out I saw the bottle of Blue Label on the dining table and took it along in a plastic bag.

Inside Eternal Complex, the elevator was so smooth it left me light-headed. Another guard saluted me when the doors opened. The hallway floor was shiny marble that had barely been walked on, and it smelled of paint and newly varnished wood. There were four doors on the top floor, and I found myself wondering if all of them led to Gazi's home. But the guard led me to an apartment at the back of a long adjoining hallway that intersected this one at the far end, and the door was completely separate from the others.

'Mr J. Gazi' was embossed in black on a gold plate. The guard pressed the bell. The door opened immediately, before the chiming had stopped. A young man, smartly dressed in khaki chinos and a button-down shirt, led me in. He ushered me into the living room, saying 'Sir, please' at least six times until he saw that I was seated and treated properly as a guest. 'Sir, something to drink?' he asked.

I asked for a glass of water.

'Yes, sir. Sir will be here soon.'

It was after he'd disappeared to the other side of the sprawling apartment that I remembered the bag with the bottle of Blue Label in my hand.

It was a bad idea, I thought, bringing along a gift to the house of its giver. It was uncouth. I was about to hand the bag to the servant, with what expectation I didn't know, when my host made his entrance.

He was an inch or two taller than me, broad-shouldered and on the lanky side. In a loose-fitting shirt and jeans, with day-old shadow on his face, he was just unkempt enough to be ruggedly charming.

'Hi,' he said, coming forward with a smile and extended hand. 'Junaid.'

'Hi, I'm Nisar,' I said.

As soon as our hands met his eyes fell on the bag. I felt my face go warm. If he thought I was returning the courtesy of bringing him a gift, he was wrong, and I was to prove a troglodyte.

'I hope you don't mind,' I said. 'I brought along the bottle you sent so we can share it. It's really thoughtful of you. Thank you.'

'Very well,' he said, almost as though he didn't remember sending it. He motioned for his servant to take the bag. 'Please,' he said, and settled himself into an ornate, high-backed chair across from me. 'You just arrived today, right?'

'Yes,' I replied. 'I'm surprised you know that.'

'Your man, Ehsan, told me your arrival date,' he said, shrugging.

'He didn't mention that he'd told you!' I said.

'You must be jet lagged and exhausted.' He spoke as if this was a self-evident truth, fishing a pack of cigarettes out of his pocket. 'Fag?'

It took me a moment and a skipped heartbeat to understand the offer. 'No, thank you.'

'I have other options,' he said with a boyish grin.

CHAPTER 4

'I'm good for tonight I think,' I said, lamely. 'A drink would be perfect, though.'

His servant rolled in a drinks trolley laden with the Blue Label, out of its box, a bucket of ice and glasses. I asked for mine neat. The servant knew how his employer liked his. We raised glasses and I took two quick sips, thanking him again for the gift.

A portion of the wrap-around window was open, through which I could see a faintly illuminated patch of the night sky. I didn't have a sense of which direction the window faced. I was so turned around I didn't even know which way my house was.

'How is Uncle?' he asked.

'He's OK,' I answered. 'Some health problems, but alive and as well as can be expected.'

'I remember him so well,' he said. 'Handsome and tall, sitting at Dhaka Club with my father.'

'And your parents? How are they?' I asked.

'They're fine.'

I hadn't been looking directly at him when I'd asked, and when I finally did, I found a searching, childishly inquisitive expression pointed at me.

'I hope you find my offer acceptable,' Gazi said, derailing my intention to steer clear of business.

It was a question, but didn't have the inflection of a question, so came across as rather more of a declaration.

'I've told my father,' I said. 'I'll speak to him again tomorrow, and I hope to have an answer for you soon. Sorry for the delay. Dad was hit pretty hard by the recession.' I immediately regretted saying that.

Gazi crushed his cigarette in an ashtray and leaned back with a pensive air, as if he was studying me for a portrait, or a criminal profile. I went searching in my head for the next topic – something, anything to take us off this one – but drew blanks.

'Can I ask, though,' I said, 'why such a generous offer? And why do you want to buy it all?'

Gazi gave no answer. I was wishing for the meeting to end – it couldn't happen soon enough. The atmosphere had the strange tension of a much-anticipated date that had turned out disastrously wrong, and neither person had the courage to end it early. Gazi, though, didn't seem like the kind of person given to artifice. If I failed to open an escape route, he would have no trouble aborting.

'Let's have one more,' he said. He refilled our glasses before I could agree or protest, and the awful date continued. 'Can I ask you something?'

'Sure,' I said.

'Was that Disha's car that came to pick you up earlier?'

'Yes. She's my cousin.' If there was a reason I needed to add that detail, I could not at that moment identify it.

'Cheers,' Gazi raised his glass. 'You think I don't know that. We were family once upon a time. I'm sure you're aware.'

I swallowed a mouthful of whisky. Gazi watched me as someone might eye a person falling ill in front of them.

'Disha didn't tell you,' he said.

'She told me a while back that she was married. Nothing about the… person. No details. I didn't ask.'

'You weren't curious?'

'It was a very short meeting – we hadn't seen each other in years. My head was in a different place in those days. Could I use your bathroom?'

Standing in front of the mirror, I replayed Disha's visit to Chicago, her cryptic hints about who she was married to, my cluelessness, and tonight Disha not giving me the full truth again.

'Are you all right?' Gazi asked as I returned, damp-faced and red-cheeked, to the living room.

'Long day,' I said. 'Sorry. I'm feeling the jet lag.'

'How was it seeing her again?' Gazi asked.

'She's really the only cousin – or relative – I ever liked,' I said.

'I hope she's well,' said Gazi.

CHAPTER 4

'She's fine, I think.'

Gazi's head shook like a regretful parent's. 'I don't know what she's doing with that clown,' he said. 'He's married, and he has no regard for anyone but himself.'

'Married?' I said, as if I'd just been introduced to the word.

'He was married, yes. He has children.'

Gazi finished the last inch of his drink and set it down with care on the glass-topped coffee table. It was the first time I took note of the decor. The table was intricately carved with human-like figures and patterns of leaves, and creations of the mind of its maker that had me lost. The detail was remarkable, spanning every inch of the table. For lack of somewhere else to send my eyes, my gaze stayed fixed on the table for a rude amount of time. Rude because Gazi had asked me a question, and I hadn't answered.

'You didn't know?' I heard him say before tuning out.

'Know what?' I finally said.

'I don't want to overstep boundaries,' said Gazi. 'It's Disha's business.'

'Tell me,' I said robotically.

'I'd rather not,' said Gazi. 'You and I have other things to discuss once you've spoken with Uncle.' He paused, seeming to give his next thought time to play in his head – a rare and precious trait I wished I had – and said, with a dreamy, distant look in his eyes, 'We had good times. I think about her often.'

'When did you last see each other?' I asked.

'Not since the… the divorce,' Gazi replied.

'But that was years ago,' I said.

'Yes, it was. In Dhaka, that's a feat. But I spent a lot of time out of the country. I told myself it was for work, but it wasn't – I couldn't handle seeing her with other people. Other men. And then I couldn't handle seeing her at all.' He smiled and rose to his feet. 'But there's no need for things to get so heavy. You need rest, and we need to make a plan for how we move forward when you're ready.'

The sudden officious tone and bearing threw me off. I thought we'd passed formalities and curtailed business talk, moving on to substance, and despite my torn allegiance between sleep and continuing our conversation, this was a cliffhanger I was not ready to leave until later.

But left for later it would have to be. Gazi was a deliberate man, of that I had little doubt, and before I could speak, he was escorting me out.

'I'm throwing a little something next weekend,' he told me at the door. 'For my birthday. I know, it's silly – birthdays, at my age. But I've always loved them, and loved having people over. I'd like it very much if you came.' He took my hand in both of his. 'Bring someone if you like.'

'I don't know anyone to bring,' I said. It was presumptuous to consider Jasmine.

'Yes, I'm sure you do. Or should I just come out and tell you?'

'I wish you would,' I said. 'I'm not very good with subtlety. Not unless it's in writing.'

Gazi's grip tightened. His smile was big and warm, the smile of a friend and protector, as well as of a shy boy forced to grow up fast and hurled through life to the present in haste, unprepared.

'Bring your cousin,' he said. 'As a favour to me.'

'I'll ask her,' I said.

'I've wanted to reach out to her a thousand times,' Gazi said. 'I guess the timing, as the saying goes, had to be right.'

When I got home, instead of going to bed, I went up to the roof. I looked in the opposite direction from Eternal Complex, aware that the light was still on in Gazi's apartment. My guess was the illuminated window was his bedroom – of course, he could have ten bedrooms in that seemingly endless maze. And then it occurred to me that it was not his bedroom, but the very room I was sitting in ten minutes before. I remembered the way the windows wrapped all the way around. Whatever attention

CHAPTER 4

I'd paid had been delayed – the table only caught my eye after a while, when nothing had been said about it.

My mind played tricks. I heard a sound like the sliding of a window, and after that the tiniest scratch of a lighter being struck.

A long time passed, or so it seemed. The night sky was polluted with light. Houses used to be no taller than three stories, by order of the government, and sitting on the roof after sunset was a favourite pastime in Dhaka. From up here I'd be able to see clear across to the other side of Kemal Ataturk Avenue in one direction, the entrance to the army cantonment on another (now obstructed by Eternal Complex), and Banani Graveyard to the north.

When I looked up again, Gazi's apartment was dark.

My phone buzzed with a message from my father. I called him back and told him about my brief meeting with Gazi. We needed to meet again, with more time to go over everything with proper attention, and then I would visit the properties along with Mr Ehsan.

'As soon as possible?' my father said. 'What else is going on?'

'He's a busy guy, Dad. And I haven't yet been here a full day.'

My father said something to my mother in a tone of impatience and confusion. He's a single-minded, blinders-on type of person in matters of business. I had known this all my life, had seen him electric with energy, not a moment's patience with lags or delays of any kind, day after day, year after year, when he was building his firm in Dhaka and then in Chicago, and had witnessed a revival after the financial crisis, although by then age had caught up with him and slowed him down more often than he liked.

'What's going on?' My mother had taken the phone. 'What did that boy say?'

'That boy is a grown man,' I said. 'I'm so tired I can't think straight right now.'

'Why are you still up?'

'I had dinner with Disha, then met with Junaid, like I was telling Dad.'

'Oh, how is she?'

'Same as always,' I said. 'She's fine, good.'

'Did she ask about us?'

'Yes.'

'Is she really doing fine?'

'As far as I can tell. I don't know what really doing fine looks like. She's a busy, working woman with a healthy social life.'

'Dhaka and its social life,' my mother grumbled. 'It never amounted to any good.'

'Give it to me,' my father said.

'He's very tired,' I heard my mother tell him as she handed him the phone again.

'Listen, I've been telling Ehsan to send me all the documents – not just the one with the offers. Tell him to send me everything.'

'I thought he did. He left it all here for me.'

'No, no,' my father said irritably. 'Those I have. I want the bank statements. There should be statements from three different banks. Bank of Asia, Bank of Dhaka and United City Bank. Damn fool backwards places don't have decent websites, and I don't have time to waste on the computer all day.' He had nothing but time.

'I'll let him know,' I said. 'Maybe you should give him a call too.'

'I did. I left him three messages. I don't know what I pay him for if he's never available.'

My mother had a response to this, which I couldn't pick up, and which was no doubt unflattering to Mr Ehsan.

Dinner was on the table, now cold, which Jatin insisted on heating up, but I said there was no need. I hadn't eaten much of my meal at the restaurant, and the drinks and the weed had worked up an appetite.

I fell on the food and ate until my stomach felt as heavy as my head. I'd had too much to drink, and had mixed whisky and wine

CHAPTER 4

like an amateur. Halfway through undressing for bed, I paused, remembering the Blue Label I'd left at Gazi's place. The thought was fleeting, lasting as long as it took me to get under the covers and close my eyes.

Then all else faded. Nothing was more important, nothing more necessary, than sleep. The night, the day, the airport, the inside of the plane. The one hundred and one thoughts and feelings I'd had from Chicago to Dhaka became a jumble, like scraps of paper with disjointed notes flung into a drawer to be assembled later but made little sense when read again. Disha, Gazi, Tarek Bashir, the drama contained within those lives, the connections, the resentments, the emotions, the truths, the untruths and lastly, before I no longer had consciousness, why Disha had kept from me – and was still keeping from me – that the man she'd been married to was Junaid Gazi.

5

My phone buzzed from messages and incoming calls at hours when I was not capable of distinguishing wakefulness from sleep. They were from Disha, mostly saying sorry for 'last night', which I took to stand in for Tarek Bashir, and I wrote back that I'd be out of commission today and would love to see her as soon as I was feeling human again.

I showered, put on fresh clothes, and asked Jatin for tea. For the time being it was the only sustenance my system could take. Almas came in asking what I wanted him to get from the market. I told him that whatever Jatin felt like making was good for me. Jatin's eyes flashed with encouragement. I asked Almas how much money he needed.

'Ehsan sir has given me,' he told me. 'You don't worry about anything.'

I called Mr Ehsan and left a message on his voicemail. The documents in their piles reminded me of what my father had said about the bank statements, and I went through each piece of paper three times and found nothing that resembled correspondences from a bank. For a transaction this size, there had to be many more reams of paperwork – a prospect that intimidated me and made me leave the documents alone, and try to plan my day, to make it somehow useful towards my book. But my mind kept circling back to one thought:

CHAPTER 5

Gazi's reason for buying us out being connected to his history with Disha.

A little later I felt the need to move around, get some air, so I set out for a walk. I took my laptop along, thinking I'd find myself in one of the numerous coffee shops and work on my book.

The streets were familiar, and yet they were not.

Houses that went back to the era when my grandfather built ours were still there, somehow having survived the way ours had, or perhaps awaiting the same fate in good time. Every plot of earth that once marked the space between neighbours was taken over either by high-rises, storefronts or restaurants. Dhaka was known for its culinary offerings, but had exceeded what it had once been. We made do with Chinese and Thai for the most part. Now there was Turkish and Italian and Indian and a hundred fast-food places within walking distance of each other.

I remembered a house where we'd spent a brief amount of time when my father, who I could best surmise was attempting to establish his own domain apart from the one he had inherited from his father, rented it and moved us out of my grandparents' house. It was on Road 11, a single-storey abode that my memory recalled as being quite spacious. Road 11, needless to say, had gone the way of the rest of the neighbourhood and further. It was a bustling commercial thoroughfare of multistorey shopping complexes, restaurants and shops that sold everything from foreign designer brands and imported glassware to locally made and sourced clothes, handicrafts and other goods. I made a note of Gourmet Bazaar, the grocery store, coffee shop, bookstore as a potential settling spot for working, and made a left.

As I'd expected, there was no indication of our house ever existing. I stood where I gauged the entrance used to be. After a couple of minutes I shook my head, laughing inwardly at my silliness. Further down – where once the street ended in a section of Banani Lake, which there was no way of crossing, nor was there reason to cross at the time – the road curved on to a bridge. Over the bridge was Amari Dhaka, a luxury hotel with a rooftop bar that I would become acquainted with in just a few hours.

At Gourmet Bazaar, I sat distracted for about an hour, looking at my outline with all the fervour of preparing for some awful standardised test. I browsed the books and watched young people and families come and go, swept away again in wondering if this was how life would be if I still lived in Dhaka; or if I would have gone the route of so many of my peers – those that went for degrees in the US and the UK and returned to take up the reins of the family business. In a way, that was what I was doing, for however short a time.

'Are you mad at me?'

Disha's message flashed across the screen.

'Why?' I wrote back.

'I'm sorry,' she replied. 'Let's meet later?'

'Sure.'

I made another attempt at writing, achieving small success in getting out one paragraph and moving on to the next, when Mr Ehsan's call dashed through the making of a sentence. We had a quick chat. He sounded as though he was standing in the middle of traffic – not in a car but on his feet – and his tone, what I could make of it, stiffened when I told him of my father's demands.

'Bank statements, yes, yes, no problem,' he said. 'I sent him already.'

'Give him a call,' I suggested. 'I may have missed something.'

'Call, yes, I'll call. But we shouldn't wait too long.'

'It's fine, Mr Ehsan. There's no rush.'

'I will come Friday,' he said before we hung up, more to fill the silence than to make a plan.

CHAPTER 5

He was harried because he was in a rush, I thought, and let the matter go for the moment. I was fixated on the Gazi–Disha history, and then, as I was paying the bill for my lunch and coffee, Jasmine's business card slipped out and took me down a completely new train of thought. I looked at it and felt that I had something to look forward to that wasn't business or my book, no matter what happened between us. I would welcome a new friendship if that was the extent of it.

And I hadn't been in Dhaka yet two full days.

6

We met in the lobby of Amari at seven. Disha gave me a hug and enough kisses on my cheeks to draw stares. As far as she was concerned, the whole world knew I was her little brother. She was different without Tarek Bashir around. To be fair, I had seen them together only once, but certain things can become evident fast enough. Especially when their opposite holds them in undeniable contrast.

We had drinks and ordered food, and tried to keep our conversation light. After dinner, Disha wanted to smoke hookah. When it arrived and was lit, we took turns taking hits from the same hose, joked about emulating our feudal forebears, and reached a point of relaxed amity that I felt was criminal to disturb.

'Where's Tarek?' I asked, trying to sound casual. We'd been in our own headspaces. Disha was gazing at a spot on the table, steeped in thought, and I was taking in the view.

'He'll be here,' she replied, as if I was the one anxious for him to join us. Seeing my expression, she touched my hand. 'He's really not so bad.'

'I met my neighbour last night,' I said. Despite my intentions, the impact this had set the course for the rest of the night. 'Listen,' I said, leaning closer, getting a burst of her shampoo and a hint of perfume. 'I don't know how things happen in Dhaka, and I know that's the common answer to everything, but we're family

CHAPTER 6

and we need to be up front. It was him, wasn't it? That you were married to?'

Disha leaned back, not so much to get away from me but to give me a studying look.

'I thought you knew,' she said. Whatever compunctions she may have had, or maybe I had imagined, about her personal life, seemed to disappear.

'You told me that time in Chicago that you were married to some tycoon,' I said. 'But you didn't mention any names.'

'I never said tycoon – he'd hate being called that. Your parents knew.' She took a hit of the hookah and held the hose towards me. 'It wasn't a secret.'

'It felt like it was. Last night too. In fact, this is like a whole chapter of your life I don't have a clue about. How did you meet? I mean, was it arranged, your marriage, or what?'

'Seriously, Nisar?' Disha gave me a squinty-eyed look, as if her vision had suddenly gone bleary. 'Arranged? Do I seem like the kind of girl that would get into an arranged marriage?'

'No, right. That was the idiotic path I took.'

Disha reached for my hand and rubbed the top of it.

'Jaan, don't get so worked up. I met Junaid on a professional basis at first. I was new to our firm. Abbu was alive, and he was teaching me the ropes. Junaid had recently taken over Gazi Enterprises, and he wanted to hire our PR firm to redo, rebrand its image. We didn't say a word outside work stuff for a year, at least. He had this way about him – like he was twenty years older than he was. Extremely serious all the time, and he didn't look me in the eye once the whole time we worked together.'

'When did, you know, things progress?' I asked.

'There was no one specific moment,' Disha replied. 'It just happened. You get that, right?'

'Sure. OK. So, then you got married, and the tempest began?'

'You could say that.' Her voice dipped gently. 'My baby brother, we were young, very young, barely in our twenties, when we got married. It was intense, passionate, crazy. Very dramatic. Sometimes the thought keeps me up at night laughing.'

'There was love too.' I sounded simplistically sentimental to myself. But looking back on Junaid Gazi as he led me out the night before, I saw something about him that I recognised. A visage I'd worn a few times and that friends had noted. Hope, the smallest dash of it, in the face of odds we've long known were insurmountably sealed.

'Of course there was,' said Disha, like a celebrity whose life was the casualty of a thousand rumours, all of which she was crushing under her feet like bugs, but not before making it clear how flattered she was that busybodies had made her simple existence so exciting. 'Love, lust, tons of it.'

'Is it still there?' I asked.

This seemed to catch her off guard. 'Why would you ask that?'

'Something so intense can't just go away altogether. Can it?' I said.

She looked at an incoming message on her phone and put it away in her purse. My guess was Tarek Bashir: she tensed up in the way she'd been wound up the previous night, that she only seemed to do in his presence. I sent the phone a dirty look and sat back, hookah in hand.

'It can and it does,' she said. 'I have no feelings for him any more.'

'You're a horrible liar, my dear sister. Horrible.'

'Why are you all worked up about it?'

'Because,' I said, handing her the hookah and feeling a wave of dizziness from the pulls I'd taken too fast, 'I can't figure out why you've not been honest with me.'

'Nisar, stop. If you didn't pay attention to my life, then that's on you. You had no reason to, you had your own life to live, but that's not my fault. And guess what? I don't know the name of the woman you were married to, either. So why have you not been honest with me?'

'Because,' I tried to not sound defensive, 'it was irrelevant. I wasn't even thinking of you or anyone else in the family when that was happening.'

CHAPTER 6

Disha's eyes twinkled, and her mouth made the minutest curve towards a smile.

'Exactly,' she said.

Her phone buzzed in her purse, making a set of keys trill to its vibration. She didn't check it.

'Should it come as news to you, then, that he wants to buy us out?' I said.

'You mean Eternal Complex isn't all of it?' There was a business-like aspect to the question, the kind I'd expect from Mr Ehsan, as if Disha was well-acquainted with the transactions.

'Nope, he wants it all,' I said. 'And Dad is ready to say yes. Although he did say something about... I don't know – it was a little cryptic.'

'Cryptic?' Disha set her chin on her hand and elbow on the armrest.

'He said something like, "What do they want now?" The only thing I can think of is your and Gazi's history.'

Disha looked at me a long time, long enough that I grew uneasy, and she looked stranger with each passing second – someone I did not want staring at me.

'And the thing is,' I went on, 'I think it has to do with you.'

'What has it to do with me?'

'I think he wants you back.' I said. 'And this is his way of doing it.'

'Nisar, for God's sake, do you know how ridiculous that sounds? Seriously.'

'Is it so ridiculous?' I said.

'Nisar,' Disha said, softening her voice, assuming a tone of talking to a child. 'You've been away a long time.'

'Stop with that,' I said. 'I won't accept that trite response from you. If you want more proof then here it is: he's having a party for his birthday and he wants me to bring you.'

I was ready for a range of responses, from laughter to being dismissed. But all Disha did was sit there, looking somewhere, at something, that wasn't me or anything around us.

'His exact words were to bring my cousin, as a favour to him.'

Her phone went off again. She reached into her purse mechanically, read the text, sent a response and settled on me again, back from wherever she'd been a moment before.

She tried to be upset, boring her large eyes into me, attempting outrage, offence. None of it worked. I saw a glimmer where she was working hard to hold severity. Her mouth wanted to break into a smile, making her facial muscles twitch comically.

'His birthday,' she said, quietly, to herself. 'He's a such a child.'

'So... you're going?' I said.

'Are *you* going?' she asked.

'Why not?'

'His parties are fun,' said Disha. 'You'll meet a lot of people.'

'So you're saying no?' I wanted a direct answer.

'Nisar,' she started. 'Nisar, I... can't...'

'Because of Tarek?' I asked.

'Well, yes, for one,' Disha said. 'It wouldn't be fair to him. It wouldn't be fair to me, either. Or, for that matter, to Junaid.'

'Do you *want* to go?' I asked.

'Doesn't matter,' she said, and looked away.

'Tarek and his wife,' I started.

She slowly turned back to me.

'Are they divorced?'

'Already Dhaka is sinking its teeth into you,' she said.

'I don't know what you mean by that,' I said.

She got distracted by people coming out on to the roof. A group of women and men walked by us, led by a server to a table on the other end.

'I think you do,' she said. 'You know how the rumour mill of this city operates.'

'You're saying Junaid Gazi is trying to spread rumours about you and Tarek?'

'I... no. That's not like him. He said something about Tarek's marriage? To you?'

CHAPTER 6

'I don't like talking about people behind their backs,' I said. 'But you're here, and I'm talking to you. You're my family. So I'm asking you: Is the man you're seeing still married to his wife?' Disha was silent, and still, for a long time – long enough that I sat back, pulling on the hookah, and feeling this trip had already become too intense. My hope was for the business part to be swift. Mr Ehsan and I would spend a few stressful days, there'd be back and forth with my father over the phone, meetings with Gazi to finalise details, and we'd be done. Then I'd work on my book, do some research, get reacquainted with Dhaka – or acquainted in a way I'd never been.

The fact that things got complicated was no one else's doing but my own. I could pinpoint the outcome of certain decisions to that moment at Amari, as Disha and I sat in our silences, unknowing of each other's minds, not thinking about what the other believed we were thinking – that determined how the tumultuous next few weeks would go.

'They've filed,' Disha said. 'These things take time in Dhaka. It's not as simple as in America. And they have children.' Her attention was swept once more to the door leading out to the roof.

She waved. I looked in time to see Tarek making his way over. He and I gave each other cold, stiff nods.

'Some serious talking going on,' he remarked with a grin I was beginning to resent. 'I thought you lost your phone or something,' he said to Disha. He took up Disha's hose and gave it a pull. There wasn't much left, and he gave the hose a dispirited look and tossed it on the table.

'Just catching up,' Disha said with perfect calm.

Tarek ordered more drinks and then set his sights on me. 'How far along are you with your book?' he asked. I didn't think he'd paid me enough regard to remember.

'Not very far,' I answered. 'I still have a lot of research to do.'

'What do you need?' he asked. 'For research? Do you want to do interviews, find books, what?'

I looked at Disha. 'Both would be great,' I said.

'You should come with me next week,' he said. 'Meet some people, talk to them, ask them questions.'

'He's right,' said Disha, a little too eagerly.

'Sure,' I said, despite my plan to keep disliking Tarek. 'That's nice of you to offer.'

We had our drinks in silence, and then I stood up to go. Disha barely said goodbye. It was Tarek who shook my hand and walked me to the elevator.

'Tuesday,' he said. 'Call me when you wake up and I'll send a car.'

Halfway through my walk home it started raining. In seconds the drizzle became fist-sized drops, which turned into a downpour. The wind howled, gusting and pushing.

I didn't rush, didn't seek shelter. A long line of cars sat stalled on Road 11, their brake lights hazed with rain and steam. People cut between them, running the way people do in the rain even after they've been sufficiently soaked, and I thought about how one of the biggest scarcities in this city was space. It was why the smallest inch, the tiniest, most impossible opening, had hordes racing for them all at once. I passed a motorcycle and two rickshaws trying to wedge through between the front end of one car and the rear end of another, none of the parties willing to back down. A little further down, a drenched policeman's whistle screeched like a tortured monkey while he blocked a CNG scooter with his body from moving forward and obstructing the intersection. Horns blared tone-deaf symphonies.

The rain finally started letting up, leaving the air cool and bearable. My clothes stuck to me like they were glued on, and I felt chilly.

I felt a tug on my sleeve; there was a boy of six or seven with a distended belly and a missing arm looking up at me, holding out the palm of his hand. I gave him a 100 taka note. His eyes dropped on the money like it had sprouted magically out of his palm, then jolted up to me again, flashing disbelief. Before I'd taken another step, a small gang of boys and girls crept out of corners I'd never know were there. I took out some more notes, all the cash I had,

CHAPTER 6

and gave them away, then held my wallet upside down to show that it was empty.

I'd pushed my key into the door when a shadow to my left startled the beating heart out of me. I guessed it was the night guard, but then realised he was at his station at the gate, where I'd just received a salute from him on my way in.

'Hi, boss.' Gazi stepped partially into the light of the portico. He'd come around the back of the house from Eternal Complex, which kept him unseen to anyone at the front. 'Didn't mean to scare you.'

'It's fine,' I said, unlocking the door.

'You're soaked, boss,' Gazi said. 'What have you been doing?'

'I walked home from...' I didn't know where to take the rest of it. And the 'boss', now spoken twice, was strange. 'From being out,' I said.

'You should get dry before a cold takes you. And a drink to warm you up good.' He held up the Blue Label.

'Thank you,' I said, accepting the bottle a second time. 'Would you like to join me?'

Gazi didn't respond. He stood just a few steps short of being under the portico, his face lit only from the nose down.

'Did you ask her?' he said.

It occurred to me, watching him stand outside the cover of the portico, dry as I was wet, that the rain had stopped at some point during the last leg of my walk. Now there was just the wind rising and falling.

'Please come in,' I said. 'I really want to get out of these clothes.'

'Did you?' he repeated, as if I hadn't spoken.

'Not exactly, no,' I replied.

Gazi stepped fully into the portico's light. He was wearing a salmon-pink, short-sleeved shirt, cream-coloured khakis and tumbled calf-leather moccasins, either brown or black. His posture, gait and general bearing reminded me of a Hollywood icon from the era of silent films – Valentino, or Errol Flynn; all he was missing was a cigarette in a slender, expensive holder to finish the picture.

'Will you?' he asked.

'I'm not sure she thinks it's a very good idea,' I answered.

'Did she say that? Herself?' He took a step forward, and his eyes came into view. I thought I noted menace in them. It didn't stay long, if it was there at all, sent on its way with a smile that rounded off the portrait of the matinée idol.

'I guess she didn't have to – not in so many words,' I said.

'But she didn't say no,' said Gazi, eyes aglow with hope. 'Boss, I'm counting on you. Please.'

With that he was gone. His exit only heightened the cinematic figure he'd drawn, walking backwards, meshing soundlessly with the night.

7

Friday morning, following Fajr prayers, Rais Kaka came over. He let himself in with his key and sat in the living room, without turning on the TV or so much as asking for a cup of tea, and if it hadn't been for the last strains of jet lag in my system rousing me, I wouldn't have known he was there for several more hours. And he wouldn't have disturbed me either – he would have waited all day if need be.

'Baba, did you sleep good?' he asked, jumping to his feet.

'Yes, finally,' I said. We embraced and he held on to me. I could tell he was tearing up.

He pulled away and wiped his eyes. 'I can't tell you what I feel deep down in my soul on seeing you, Baba. Deep down. Where I loved your mother and father. I'll probably never see them again, but you're here now, and thank God for it.'

I hadn't seen this hour of the day's beginning since I worked with campus security for a year in college, and that was because I did the third shift from eleven at night to seven in the morning.

'You wake up this early on your day off?' I asked.

'The habit of the lifelong servant, Baba. The other thing was, if you want to see the city, now is the best time. Before traffic gets started in a couple of hours.'

Instead of being hunched over my laptop for hours, then going out to a coffee shop to do the same, I could be out in the city.

Jatin had just brought out tea, and he asked if he should serve breakfast.

'No,' I said. 'We can take this tea with us and get something to eat outside.'

'Baba, have something here quick,' Rais Kaka suggested.

'I'll make some eggs and toast,' said Jatin.

'No, I'm not hungry right now,' I insisted. 'I want to get going right away. I'll call for Mr Ehsan to send the car.'

Mr Ehsan was up. He asked what I was doing awake so early, as if I'd broken a rule. I told him Rais Kaka was there and that we were going out.

'Out?' he said. 'At this hour? Where?'

'Mr Ehsan, please just send the car,' I said. I could see Tarek Bashir or Junaid Gazi putting their father's employee in his place far quicker than I was, telling him to do as he was told. 'I'd like it to be here as soon as possible,' was the best I could manage, adding, 'otherwise we'll just take an Uber.'

Mr Ehsan cleared his throat and exhaled a frustrated sigh. 'No, no,' he said. 'Why will you take Uber when you have your own car?' He yelled an order to a servant. 'Any place in particular you're going?'

'Just around the city,' I said, trying to sound curt. 'When do you need the car back?'

'Keep as long as you want, no problem.'

Before hanging up, I reached for the upper hand by the low tactic of pulling rank.

'Did you prepare those bank statements for Dad?'

'Well, the thing is, it takes time,' Mr Ehsan replied.

'Then maybe I should go myself later today,' I said.

'Go? Where?'

'To the banks. See management, tell them what my father wants. It shouldn't be that difficult.'

Rais Kaka was watching me with large, unblinking eyes and an expression I would not define as amiable. He was among those that

CHAPTER 7

Mr Ehsan had rubbed the wrong way from day one. My mother, in fact, had commiserated with Rais Kaka the most, while my father responded to her reservations with refrains about finding one good and honest worker in a country infested with crooks. She wasn't the only one. His best friend from boyhood, a colonel in the army, said he'd blast Mr Ehsan out of a cannon if he came within smelling distance, and some of my father's most trusted colleagues confessed they didn't appreciate the liberties Mr Ehsan allowed himself, being a subordinate. I understood none of it. Mr Ehsan was another adult in the forest of adults that surrounded my life. He smiled, said hi, I returned the greeting, and that was the extent of our exchanges.

'No, no,' Mr Ehsan pressed. 'You already are busy. Car will be there very soon. Enjoy yourself.'

After hanging up, I considered the point about the liberties Mr Ehsan took. It was clear he felt he had authority over me, and I had no problem with that – not in the sense of being his superior and expecting him to bow to me as he would to my father. It was something about his tone, the condescension that crept in, whether he intended it or not, because once he'd spoken intention became beside the point.

Rais Kaka had something to say, but with the same practiced patience, and a lifetime of knowing his place, kept his thoughts to himself.

We set out for Old Dhaka. I'd start where Dhaka had been established and work my way back. There were places that were must-visits, an airy term I coined on the fly as the car sped through the open morning road, and each would require multiple days to be devoted to them. It was a daunting task, however I imagined the book turning out.

The sights unspooled like an old film. Childhood memories resurfaced in glorious black-and-white, here and there with a stylistic dash of colour. The railroad crossing at Mohakhali brought to mind my tingly anticipation of the train, especially at night when the metallic mass of it lumbered like a mythic beast through darkness.

We reached the series of streets leading to Ahsan Manzil, and the driver, with great hesitation and hope that he'd be told to not make the attempt, aimed the car up ready to enter the first of the impossibly narrow lanes.

'Sir, it will be very tight,' he said.

'How far in do we have to go?' I asked.

'Just a few minutes,' the driver answered.

'Then let's walk,' I said.

The driver's relief filled the rear-view mirror. Rais Kaka and I got out and I told the driver I'd call his cell when we were ready to leave. He declined the money I offered him to get tea or breakfast, saying Mr Ehsan had seen to it. The mention of Mr Ehsan's name brought me to ask Rais Kaka about what I'd noticed in his demeanour after my call.

'Baba, what do I say that hasn't been said a thousand times already?' he said. 'He's no good. But don't tell him I said so. If your father and mother were still here it would be different. Now, I can't trust anyone.'

'I have to tell my father something,' I said, 'and he won't like hearing it. But I don't know what else to do. No one besides Mr Ehsan knows the property business.'

Rais Kaka looked at me blankly. 'Property business?' he said.

It didn't occur to me that he would have no idea, that Mr Ehsan would have no reason to tell him. I brought him up to speed as we walked, and after I was done I felt as though I'd delivered news of a death.

'So,' he said with a catch in his voice. 'Whatever was left of you all is going to be gone.'

'I'm going to tell Dad that we should keep the house,' I told him, the decision occurring to me on the spot. 'There's no reason we can't, even if we have to get tenants. You can be the landlord.' This cheered him up, and a smile smoothed out some of the sadness. It was a good place to let the matter stand for the time being.

The way the lanes were used by every form of traffic – pedestrians, motorists and animals – had to be seen to be believed. Three grown people standing shoulder to shoulder could cover the width of the lane and block it end to end. Ten feet ahead of me was a truck bumping along at an unwise speed with precariously stacked uncovered produce on its back. A man leading two cows, street vendors and passengers headed for the launches at the port of Sadarghat. Every walk of life that needed to use that lane all at the same time did so like a miracle. I bumped into a huge metal barrel of bubbling oil with chicken pieces sizzling in it, overseen by a boy who could not have been more than ten, and felt someone run into me from the back. Rais Kaka, an expert in navigating any part of Dhaka, was a few paces ahead. Over my shoulder I saw a young man, eighteen or nineteen, with a stylish pompadour, a black button-down shirt and black jeans rolled up several inches above his ankle for fording water, glowering at me.

'Have to stand right there, do you?' he scowled. 'Now I'm going to get it.' He was addressing me, no doubt, and a policeman was standing right there, a few steps away, watching him. It had to do with the manoeuvring of the truck. The young man was guiding it through a turn that no amount of skill I had could undertake, and the policeman was apparently waiting for a violation to occur. I apologised and tried to move out of the way, but on the other side of the chicken barrel was the man with the two cows. Rais Kaka had made his way around them and was waving at me to join him as if I was stalling on purpose. Just to make sure the young man with the truck wasn't ready to attack me if that was what it took to get rid of his obstruction, I looked over my shoulder. The policeman was standing at the truck driver's window. In the time it took for my head to turn and to turn again, a hand-to-hand exchange flitted like a bird between the driver and the cop, the cop walked away, the driver shouted at the young man to get back on and the tricky turn went forward without incident.

We got two of Old Dhaka's specialty: bakarkhani – the crumbly, baked hybrid of a pita bread and thick pie crust, savoury, buttery, gluey once bitten into and chewed, and best eaten piping hot – and washed them down with sweetened tea as we continued on our obstacle course along the edge of Ahsan Manzil, the mansion of the Nawabs of Dhaka, and the birthplace of the All India Muslim League in 1906. The grounds were barricaded from the street by corrugated tin fencing, and I imagined the unimpeded, breathtaking view the Nawabs would have had of the Buriganga River from their front steps at the height of their palace's days of splendour. I'd never visited Ahsan Manzil. We finished our breakfast and I told Rais Kaka we should go inside.

It was a museum now, time locked inside its walls, history preserved behind glass panelling through which visitors were able to catch its essence.

From the front veranda I looked out at the river. Despite the obstructions, the raucous humanity and jangling commerce, I could envision the sight the river would be to behold at night. The sprawling lawn, freshly watered by the rains, with more to come, was filling up fast with visitors. Young couples, families, groups of friends, the occasional foreigner, generally white European or North American, snapping photos with cameras fancier and more expensive than a tourist's, and here and there a lonesome wanderer that looked as though they'd kept on walking and ended up here without rhyme or reason. Rais Kaka and I strolled the outer edges of the lawn. Rainclouds were gathering over the river.

Rais Kaka didn't talk about himself, not even when asked questions, which I did, realising how single-mindedly self-absorbed I'd been. I knew his wife had died two years ago of complications from a stroke. They'd been married since I was one or two years old. They'd met at our house when he worked as my grandparents'

CHAPTER 7

driver and his wife as kitchen help and maid in the house. They had two children. I vaguely recalled the son, a miniature copy of his father, but not the daughter. His wife, too, no longer brought a fully formed face to mind. Rais Kaka and his son hadn't been on good terms since Mintu had invested a majority of the family's savings into a business scheme that went bust before it took off, when his associate disappeared with the money and any more word about the venture vanished with him. Ever since then Mintu had stopped speaking to his father. Rais Kaka didn't bother him, didn't demand restitution of the money. Going to the police was pointless, because there too he had to produce money to grease the system to come to his aid. When his wife was alive, Rais Kaka implored Mintu to set aside his pride for his mother's sake. It was to no avail, because that pride was everything. Mintu had lost face. He was mad at himself. Unable to blame anyone else, he closed up, and his shame had curdled into hatred of himself he couldn't handle or vent on others.

Consequently, Rais Kaka's daughter's marriage had been stalled, as a portion of the savings were part of her dowry. Eighty-thousand takas, a flatscreen TV, and a bedroom set were the demands of a prospective groom's family.

'Where will I get even a tenth of that?' he said. We sat down near the bottom of the entry steps.

'What about your boss?' I asked. 'Can he help?'

'Baba, if bosses were that good there'd be no need for God.'

'I can't believe that in this day and age people still want dowries,' I said.

'In this backwards place nothing will ever change. But Baba, this is not your concern. How fortunate I am that you even asked.'

I felt helpless, embarrassed, guilty. I shouldn't have pried. There was no point in asking if there was nothing I could do to help. We sat in silence for a few minutes. The wind blew in gusts. A shelf of clouds loomed over the lawn.

'Let's go, Baba, before it starts.'

We managed to make our way back to the car without me getting into further tangles with the locals. We bustled in just as the first drops of rain pelted us.

'Sir, do you have hundred takas?' the driver asked me.

'For what?' said Rais Kaka, cutting in.

A uniformed man was at the driver's window peering past him at us in the back seat.

'Sir, parking is very hard to find,' the driver said, to me, not appreciating being questioned by someone who was not his superior.

'Start driving,' Rais Kaka said. 'Right now. It's about to rain and traffic will be hell.' He glared at the uniformed man, then seeing that I had my wallet out waved at me to put it away.

'And next time you offer someone a bribe, do it with your own money,' he said.

8

There were three text messages and one voicemail from Disha, all of them riddled with ellipses and cryptic, hanging thoughts. I called her back after taking a nap following the Ahsan Manzil outing, and what she told me was the last thing I expected. There was even a touch of nervous excitement in her voice, as if she was asking to be introduced to a friend of mine that had caught her eye. She had conditions, though. 'Instructions' would be more apt. The meeting had to happen the next day, between three and five in the afternoon – not a moment before or after – and the place had to be mine. Her place and Gazi's place were out of the question for obvious reasons, as were the countless public locations within walking distance.

'Why those specific times?' I asked.

'It's when I'm free,' Disha replied irritably.

'Free? From?'

'Nisar, will you help me or interrogate me?'

'Don't get defensive, sister. The last thing I need is to get banged around in the middle of a lovers' drama.'

'Yes or no, just tell me,' she pressed.

I was going to agree anyway, but her seriousness made me anxious about my upcoming day with Tarek Bashir. I said nothing, hoping that he'd been kept out of the loop altogether.

'What do you think?' I said.

'I don't know, Nisar, all I know is you're... please, can you not give me a hard time? Please?'

'I'm not,' I said. 'I'm just trying to understand.'

'You can't understand everything,' Disha exclaimed, like evidence arrived at after scientific rigor. 'Not even a brain as smart as yours understands everything.'

'I'm pretty dumb,' I said.

'Right this minute, yes, you are.'

'Don't hold back now.'

'Yes or no?'

'That's a trick question,' I said, enjoying ruffling her. 'If I say yes—'

'You're impossible,' Disha yelped.

'Why did you wait till now?' I asked. 'To see Junaid? Or should I call him Junaid Bhai?'

'Call him whatever you like.'

I waited for an answer to the first part of my question. I got the feeling she was searching for one, or, having arrived at it, was trying to put it into words. Disha's silences had that quality. You could draw the difference between her wanting to just be quiet and the quietness being put to use by the way the air felt between you, even over the phone – it was almost bristling with electric charge.

'He never asked to see me before,' she finally said. 'Not once. So I could also ask, why now?'

'Is that why you're accepting?' I said. 'Because you want to find out?'

'Wouldn't you? Yes, you absolutely would, so don't try to bullshit me,' she said, before I could answer.

'In all seriousness,' I said, 'I'm telling you right now that I'm not going to be your errand boy and facilitator.'

'You're the sweetest boy, Nisar,' said my cousin. 'This tough-guy routine doesn't suit you.'

'If I was a real tough guy, I'd tell you both to get a room on your own and fuck off.'

'But not to your favourite and best sister.'

CHAPTER 8

'Wouldn't matter,' I said. 'Because the best and favourite sister doesn't know how to not have her way.'

'I'm not that bad!'

'No. You're not. But my attempt at a joke clearly is.'

'You're a good boy, Nisar. A very good, decent boy.'

'I'll change your mind soon enough, just wait.'

She gave a soft, breathy laugh, and we ended the call.

That evening, Gazi was a like a boy blown away with a surprise in the middle of his uneventful day.

'Boss, this is the best thing I've heard in... I don't know how long. Did she say anything about the party?'

'No,' I said.

We were in his living room, which I could now took in more clearly than the first time, having had proper rest and sleep. The furniture was all of the same intricate craft as the coffee table, and paintings by Bangladeshi artists – village scenes and national monuments, crowded streets and daily life – covered the walls. Between where we sat and the adjoining dining room hung three chandeliers, all of them lit, which no doubt aided me in seeing the place better, and the dining table was a long, hand-carved piece of solid wood that seated twelve. It reminded me of the banquet scene from *Macbeth*.

I hadn't come prepared to talk business, as I hadn't expected my call to last more than a few minutes, but my host was who he was, and people like him had an innate talent of steering the courses of meetings and conversations their way if they chose. I could stand at his door all night saying I didn't have time for a drink, and it wouldn't matter. He would leave the door open, go inside and make two drinks, and not wanting to be rude I would inevitably walk in.

'Did you ask her?' he asked.

'I did,' I said. I wanted it to be clear I wasn't going to jump to his cues and read his mind, and so said nothing more.

'I guess one thing at a time is the best I can hope for,' Gazi said.

'It's a good place to start,' I said. 'If you don't mind, and this is more for my curiosity than anything, why do you want to buy us out?'

'Is there a problem with the offer?' he said, not missing a beat. 'Did Uncle not like it?'

'No, nothing like that,' I said. 'I mean, you have history with Disha—'

He cut me off. 'Boss, this has nothing to do with that.' I found that hard to believe. 'Business in my family stays where business belongs,' he said. 'It never mixes with friendships or social circles.'

'Must be difficult in a place like Dhaka,' I surmised. It occurred to me to ask then, 'What made you change your mind in this case?'

Gazi threw me a look made up of sharp scepticism and a sort of damning charm, the kind his rivals in business, and maybe associates too, must have found disarming as well as respectable in a man whose dealings on a slow day moved millions, in US dollars, through channels local and far and wide, and which women found alluring.

'Boss, why don't you tell me what's on your mind?' he said, crowning the look he gave me with this perfectly timed selfless inquiry.

It was difficult not to trust his concern, his decency, no matter if it was practiced veneer or genuine.

'And,' he smiled. 'I'll tell you what's on mine. Answer any questions you might have.' He lit a cigarette, blew the smoke out of the corner of his mouth, and said, 'I'd rather you hear the good and the ugly all from me. If anything is difficult in this city it's avoiding trash gossip.'

'I'm aware of that,' I said. 'I know the difference. What I'm asking is not gossip, it's fact.'

Gazi tapped his cigarette into a standing ashtray.

'Of course there's a personal stake, boss. I'd be an idiot if I thought you didn't get that. But I also respect Uncle. I respected Disha's father. I loved him and he was so good to me. I want to honour his family and hers. What would you rather have – a stranger buy the

CHAPTER 8

place and treat it without any personal attachment, or someone who understands its real value?'

While he waited for my reply, I got distracted thinking about him and Disha locked in battle, neither giving an inch, compromise a concept unknown, as damnable as accepting defeat.

'Well, boss?'

'I appreciate how much you care about it,' I said.

'And so? That's it?'

'I think so,' I said, disappointed with myself for being so easily derailed, even if, in fairness, I hadn't come prepared for a weighty talk.

'Bullshit,' Gazi said and wagged a finger at me. 'You quiet ones are the dangerous ones. No wonder you're a writer.'

'You are far quieter than me,' I said.

'So, are you saying I'm dangerous, then?'

'By your logic it would seem so.'

'See, that's what I mean,' he said and winked. 'I want to show you something.' He crushed the cigarette in the ashtray and started out of the living room, and only when he was out of sight did he call out. 'Boss, bring your drink, come on.'

I followed his voice down the hallway he'd gone down and discovered there was a second level to the apartment, up a set of stairs that led to an entire living suite furnished even more lavishly than downstairs. Gazi was holding open a door that went out to a balcony. A metal ladder was affixed to the wall a few feet from the door, going up to the roof.

The view did not disappoint. On one corner of the roof were a reflecting pool and a fire pit, both covered against the extreme heat and days and nights of rain. They'd be better enjoyed, anyway, in a few months, when winter brought perfect temperatures and the awful humidity abated. Gazi went to a corner on the other side. He leaned on the stone balustrade and looked straight ahead. He stayed that way for a long time. I stood next to him, fidgeting with my hands in and out of my pockets, and finally settled on doing what he was doing. We were facing north and east. Dominating the view was a sign over a building, lit by a single floodlamp mounted over it, casting a green wash over the name of the tower. It was a name I recognised because we were looking at my cousin Disha's building.

Gazi must have sensed the miniscule change in the air around me, even though I was still, like an animal or bird feels shifts in the atmosphere and tremors on the ground that humans don't, because he straightened up and regarded me for a second as if I'd asked a question to which the answer needed long consideration.

'It's not an accident,' Gazi said. 'Not a coincidence either.'

I understood he meant being able to see Disha's home from his roof. If I should have been disturbed by this, it didn't occur to me then. If anything, I found it endearing.

'I've only been there once,' I said. 'I can't tell if we're looking at her window… are we?'

'No.'

Gazi walked over to the reflecting pool and fire pit, to the bench built into the wall facing the pool, sat down and lit a cigarette. 'You want that refreshed?' he pointed to the empty glass I was carrying. Before I could ask, I saw the small fridge to the side, on top of which were bottles of liquor.

'I'm good,' I said.

Gazi smoked quietly, gazing at the covered pool as if it was his reflection in water.

'It's not about money, boss. It's about connection.'

I was walking around the pool and stopped. 'Connection? As in business?'

'No, boss. Human. Disha is the only person on earth that I've ever felt like a human being around. Maybe that sounds stupid, but I don't care. It's true. This world – this city, for sure – doesn't let you be honest, and when you are it spits on you. And if it can't do that, it ruins your name. My father dealt with it. My mother too. That's why they left.'

CHAPTER 8

He didn't clarify, left unsaid where they'd gone, and I didn't press.

'We,' he went on, 'Disha and I, couldn't go anywhere without the paparazzi hounding us. She hated it, hated not having her freedom. You know how she is. Doesn't like anything getting in her way. Hated the attention and hated when it took me away from her. And I reacted, calling her jealous. Our fights were the saddest things I've ever gone through.'

I was facing away. Crying made me as uncomfortable as not knowing what to do with myself. Gazi wasn't in tears, and I didn't think he'd break down, but I still took the cautious measure to keep my eyes off him, which had me facing the view looking west. An airplane was rising in an arc, completing take off, and lights from the army stadium to the right had erased part of the night sky with their glow.

'Are you married, boss?'

'Not any more,' I answered, without turning to him.

'So you understand.' Gazi walked over, smoothed out of the deeply personal place he'd wandered off to, and joined me. 'Since we're being honest, boss, I want to ask you, out of respect for Uncle and your family: this Ehsan fellow – is he trustworthy?'

'What makes you ask that?'

'Sorry, boss, I just, I know how long he's been with you, and he's Uncle's long-time man, but Uncle isn't here any more and, well, Ehsan has a bit of a reputation about town.' He saw my budding reaction and said, 'No, this isn't gossip, boss, I promise. We're talking strictly business now. Well, business in the sense that it has no personal angle. Personal reputations are nowhere near it. I couldn't care less about his or anyone else's private life.'

'Can you be more specific?' I asked.

He took a last drag of his cigarette and dropped it to the ground.

'We, my family, we're one of the owners of a Premier League cricket team. I don't know how familiar you are with the league, but it's become popular in recent years. Anyway, about three years ago, there were allegations of matches being fixed, with players involved in the scheme. It went on for a while before one of the players blew the whistle – who knows why. Didn't get his fair share, got disgruntled, maybe a guilty conscience. Then other players came forward, and there were inquiries made – an investigation took place. And the money trail led to your Mr Ehsan.'

'Investigations?' I said. 'Meaning it became public knowledge?'

'Yes.'

My stomach fluttered and my heart rate went up.

'I'm sorry, boss,' he said.

'Why?' I said.

'It's a lot to take.'

'It is,' I said. 'I'm just looking back on his behaviour since I got here. Makes sense, given what you're telling me.' When anger strikes me, it leaves me numb, and the immediate rage I felt at Mr Ehsan was so sudden it left me out of breath.

'Boss, I'm sorry to have upset you,' Gazi said.

'You don't mind if I help myself, do you?' I asked.

'Be my guest.'

I walked over to the fridge and poured myself a whisky. I held up the bottle, but Gazi declined.

'How much money?' I asked, returning to his side.

'Let's leave it for another time, boss.'

'Tell me. I can't leave this hanging.'

'Will you tell Uncle right away?'

'That's not your concern.' I said it abruptly, but I didn't apologise.

'Enough that the Anti-Corruption Commission got involved. I think Ehsan cut and run early in the game, paid back what he owed and found his way out. But I do know he was questioned by the ACC.'

I threw back my drink. Gazi touched my shoulder.

'I promise you, boss, I don't know any more details. If I did, I would not hold them back.'

It didn't matter. Impatience went hand in hand in me with anger. I wanted answers, I needed explanations, regardless of whether I shared them with my father right away or not.

CHAPTER 8

'Boss,' Gazi said turning to face me, 'take what I said as the concern of a friend. Even of family. Please think through things before acting on them.'

The way he looked at me made me question whether he'd digressed from the conversation to get the upper hand. He hadn't given a straight answer to my question about why he wanted to buy us out, and had managed to manipulate the discussion in a way that left me on the defensive. I took some deep breaths, pushed my anger aside, saving it for Mr Ehsan, and repeated my question.

'Why the buyout?'

'I've already told you, boss,' Gazi answered with a quizzical glance.

'And that's it? Your respect for Disha's father and our family? That's all?'

'You have my word.'

I left with a pounding in my temples. It got bad enough that I took two Advil and closed my eyes to calm myself. I told myself Mr Ehsan must have a good explanation. We could talk it through. I didn't want to put more stock in Gazi's tale than taking it for what it was and give Mr Ehsan the opportunity to have his say. I held back from sending my father into a panic with messages about Mr Ehsan's antics. I hoped the worst of my suspicions weren't true: that he had used my father's money, and that whatever mess he'd created would fall upon us.

As for Gazi's word, I didn't know how much of it to trust. I was still of the mind and troubled by the prospect that owning us was his way of getting Disha back. He could be sincere about his feelings for Disha's father – my uncle was a well-liked man – but he could just as well be pulling me in, snaring my faith, using my friendship for ends I couldn't conceive. The more answers I sought, the more questions I aroused. It made no sense that Gazi and Disha would choose now, of all times, to reunite, if getting back together was what they wanted. If Gazi was so keen on acquiring our holdings, he could have initiated the effort at any time. My father would probably not have agreed, and it was true that sometimes things just happened the way they did at the time they did, no matter that they seemed unbelievably coincidental, their confluence leaving us with a range of emotions we can't pin down from one moment to the next.

I spent part of the late morning and afternoon at Gourmet Bazaar, futilely writing sentences and entire paragraphs only to delete them and waste time on the internet or browsing books. I had lunch there, and at two, with a touch of resentment, started for home. I could be out in the city today. The weather was decent – the sky clear, the day sunny. There would probably be rain at some point, but I didn't mind. Instead, I was babysitting two people that had been married and divorced without the hint of my presence in their lives at the time and now wanted a rekindling.

Disha called a few minutes into my walk and, hearing the telltale noise of traffic in the background, demanded why I wasn't at home.

'Sorry, Mom, I wasn't aware I wasn't allowed to go out,' I said.

'Nisar.' She was in no mood for jokes.

So I kept joking. 'Am I in trouble?'

'If you break your promise, yes.'

'What promise? I didn't make any promises.'

'Where the hell are you?' she asked.

'Old Dhaka. Stuck in traffic on my way back. It's bad. We haven't moved in an hour.'

'Bullshit.'

'Why do you say that?' I asked.

'Because you wouldn't do that to me.'

'You trust my innate goodness too much, sister.'

'I'm serious, Nisar, please.'

'I'm a terrible man, a liar and a betrayer.'

'Goodbye.'

'You hang up first.'

'Nisar, I'm serious.'

'So am I.'

CHAPTER 8

'You're seriously in bloody Old Dhaka?' she said.

'It's so much better. I could live here.'

Disha exhaled a tired, dispirited breath. 'Are you done?'

'I just got started,' I said. 'You think you can trust your good little brother, but he's not little any more, and you haven't seen him in years. What makes you think he's not rotted to the core in that time? Become some devious, double-crossing shit?'

'My God, Nisar, you better not be having a stroke.'

'What if I told you,' I said, 'that Junaid Gazi is through with you, and it was all a play of power, this charade he put us both through?'

'I think,' Disha started and paused. 'That is really mean.'

'Who, me or him?'

'Both of you.'

'Why did you get divorced in the first place?' I asked.

'Why do you do the things you do, Nisar? Does everything you do make sense?'

'Nothing I do makes sense. I never claimed otherwise. I'm a mess.'

'If you weren't OK with it, you should have said so in the first place.'

'OK, so it's off, then.'

Crossing the street, I splashed into a puddle. My socks grew heavy, cold and wet. A mangy dog ran over and started lapping up the water. On the other side of the street an SUV and a sedan had gotten into some kind of accident – not at all serious as far as I could tell – and the two drivers were standing guiltily to the side while their employers were in hushed conference. Passing them I saw in the back seat of the SUV two women wearing an enormous amount of make-up and jewellery. They were sitting with their heads locked forward, as if on pain of punishment if they looked this way or that. They reminded me of my mother and aunts, on the way to a wedding or some other function, dressed and bedecked in finery and jewels, paranoid out of their minds that robbers would ambush the car on the way, and praying for the journey there and back to pass with God's special attention seeing it through.

'Why are you being like this?' Disha said.

'I just got wet,' I said. 'I'll be home in five minutes. Your date is still on.'

'It's not a date.'

'I don't care.'

Disha took a breath to speak again, but I ended the call.

Ten minutes before their appointed hour of meeting, Almas brought word that Gazi was out front. While Gazi made his way in, I thought I picked up a scent of his cigarette. I didn't take him for someone that would presume such a liberty in another's house without permission.

'Hi, boss,' Gazi said, stopping at the door.

'Hi, come in.' We shook hands as if we were meeting for the first time. He wore a light-yellow polo shirt and blue jeans, and indeed he must have smoked an entire pack back-to-back not long ago. The room was soon suffused with the odour smokers carried on them like skin. Fortunately, I kept up the habit of opening windows first thing in the morning here as I did in Chicago, so it wasn't long before the smells of rain and wet leaves took over.

Gazi was harried. He couldn't sit still for ten seconds. He looked like he didn't sleep much the night before. His face was sunken into his cheeks, and half-moons of ashen blue hung under his eyes.

'Boss, do you mind?' he held up his cigarettes.

'Go ahead.'

'Good day?' he asked, lighting one.

'Not bad,' I replied.

'This shit weather, right. I can't wait till December.'

'Do you travel in the winter? Around the country, I mean.' I asked.

'Used to. Now, not unless it's for work.' A long minute of silence passed. 'Hey, boss, I hope what I told you about your guy, Mr Ehsan, you take in the spirit of goodwill. I had a hard time after you left.'

'I appreciate it,' I told him. 'I haven't said anything to my father yet. But that's my problem, not yours.'

CHAPTER 8

Gazi checked the time on his phone. 'Did she say why this time?'
'Not in any detail, no,' I said. 'But she was adamant about it.'
Gazi smiled, as if at a fond memory, and he was calmer. He took his cigarette to a window and finished it there with his back turned to me. For the last few minutes leading up to three o'clock, he almost did a countdown.

'Boss,' he said, at the stroke of three. 'This was a bad idea. I'm sorry. It doesn't look like she's coming, anyway.'

'Traffic, maybe,' I said. 'It's only three now.'

'You know your cousin better than that.'

Five more minutes passed. Gazi was pacing, close to the window that looked out on the driveway.

'This is silly. She's not coming. Why should she? She's with... she's moved on.'

Ten minutes had passed. While Gazi battled his conscience and his will, I grew mad at my cousin. I'd give her an earful, tell her to arrange her own clandestine meetings, that her activities weren't my problem, and her name and reputation among snivelling Dhaka guttersnipes wasn't my headache, and while she was at it, she could think about kicking Tarek Bashir's ass to the kerb.

A horn blared in the quiet afternoon. Gazi stiffened at the window, like an explosion had stunned him. The watchman came out of his shed, released the padlock on the gate and revealed Disha's car. The car crawled into our cramped driveway, once as wide as Kemal Ataturk Avenue, with Disha at the wheel. Only my cousin, I thought, only she would do such a thing in a city where people of certain standing wouldn't be caught dead driving themselves around.

Almas scurried over, greeted her, and opened the door for her. Disha said something that drew a bashful smile on his face and he showed her in.

I wanted to make an escape before becoming a third wheel, but stayed, if only to say hello to my cousin, play the bare-minimum host and avoid having to hear later that I'd chickened out and run, or some such mocking Disha judgement.

I may as well have not been there. The moment she walked in they locked eyes and the rest of existence dissolved.

'Hi,' said Gazi.

'Hi.'

I slipped out unnoticed. I didn't, however, leave them to their privacy just then, but stayed in the hallway, out of sight but within earshot.

Nothing passed between Disha and Gazi for a while. It was so quiet that I could hear my heartbeat in my ears. I kept saying to myself there was time yet to walk away, to let them have the privacy I had promised them, including from me; but then a competing urge would hold me back, wanting to hear a word, a syllable, an intake of breath, a breath exhaled.

There was movement, footsteps, a whisper of clothes, of fabric meeting fabric, and then the tiniest whimper. I couldn't help myself. I peeked in.

To say they were holding each other would understate what I saw. The two were in an embrace so complete that neither calamity nor death could pry them apart. The moment I turned to leave the doorway, Disha opened her eyes. Her face was pressed to Gazi's shoulder, his back to me. It was momentary. Our eyes met, she shifted to Gazi, and I walked away.

I went up to the roof, even though the sun was hot and it was not the time to be in it. As children, we were forbidden from being out in the afternoon sun because it would make us 'dark'. The same went for drinking tea. Our complexion would suffer the consequences of skin colour handed down by God to lesser mortals. Shade and milk were the superior options – one with its protection against our skin being maligned and the other's whiteness keeping us 'fair'.

I stood at the railing looking down at the street, which was still in its afternoon languor but not as empty and quiet as I remembered it being between lunch and before tea, after post-prandial naps. Four men in shirts and lungis were in conversation, hunkered on their haunches, a fruit-seller scratched himself for want of something to

CHAPTER 8

do between sales, young people huddled at the tea stall across the street – possibly students with Saturday classes at one of the private universities. Then from somewhere directly ahead of me came the pinging of a hammer on steel, interspersed with the high-pitched torque of a drill, and Kemal Ataturk Avenue supplied its constant tangle of impatient car horns. I walked to the side overlooking the driveway.

Disha driving herself here today meant she wanted no witnesses – none. If I was supposed to do the same, it was too late. She'd said nothing to me, and if Disha wanted things to be a certain way, as she did with their meeting place, she'd leave nothing to guesswork, mind-reading or chance. The watchman was sitting in the cool of his shed with the fan blasting him from an inch away, listless until he had to open the gate again. Almas had left for the market, and Jatin was probably in the kitchen. Neither seemed to me as the gossiping type, if there was a quality that gave them away. They were known only when they opened their mouths.

I brought out my wallet and looked at Jasmine's card. Maybe it was Gazi's upcoming party that made me reach for it, or maybe it was the thought that her time out of town was up in a day or so, as far as I could recall. I sent her a few lines asking if her trip went well and if she was back in Dhaka, and if she was would she like to get together some time. I deleted and rewrote the last part several times, ultimately deciding to keep it out in the final draft, and sent it off.

The watchman jumped to his feet. He hustled out of his shed and started opening the gate. I looked down, and heard Disha's heels click-clacking out of the house. Her car door opened and shut, almost in one fluid sound. She was out of the gate before I could reach the stairwell.

Gazi was in the chair where he'd first sat down before Disha's arrival, and he looked as though their meeting had never taken place – as if he'd been stood up. He was hunched over with his elbows on his thighs and his clasped hands supporting his chin, cutting the figure of someone begging forgiveness, or in deep contemplation.

'What happened?' I asked. Time couldn't have been the issue: it was barely four thirty.

My neighbour beamed an impish grin at me. 'Not a thing that I expected,' he said.

I had no idea what that meant. It must have shone off me like an SOS signal, because Gazi burst into laughter.

'Well,' I said, 'whatever it was, I'm glad it left you in a good mood. Disha ran out like she was—'

'Like she was…? Fleeing a secret rendezvous?' he said.

'You could say that,' I said.

'Boss, you have no idea how shy your cousin really is.'

'No, I don't, because it's not true,' I said.

My phone received a message. I brought it out, expecting it to be from Disha, but it was Jasmine. She was back in town, and wanted to know what I was up to. I put the phone away, catching Gazi watching me just as I dropped it into my pocket.

'Thank you, boss,' he said, getting to his feet. 'I couldn't tell you exactly what I feel, but it's better than I thought I would. Or maybe worse. You're a good man. I hope business doesn't get in the way of our friendship. Ever. And I look forward to seeing you both at my party.'

'So she's going,' I said, following him out.

'Unless she changes her mind, boss, in which case I'll hold you responsible.'

'Seriously?' I said.

'I thought you had a better sense of humour than that,' he said jovially, with a spring in his step as he started out.

'Good for you for asking her yourself,' I said. I wish you'd done it in the first place, I thought, watching him almost float to his building, which seemed an ocean's distance away, till he disappeared inside.

9

I got out of Tarek Bashir's car and checked in at the reception desk, where two employees remembered my father well and asked after him and wondered where we'd gone and when we were returning. I guess there were some who had no idea back then about our plans to leave the country, or when we left, which made sense, as my parents had kept the decision strictly under wraps. Tarek Bashir wasn't there yet, nor were any of his other guests, and the rules were for members to accompany their guests into the club. One of the veteran employees insisted I go in and not wait in the lobby. My father, he said, had had a standing among members that 'makes this your home – you come and go as you please'. I thanked him and said I'd like to walk the grounds and the tennis courts while I waited.

During our last year in Dhaka, anti-government protests were at a peak. They'd been relentless throughout the 80s, since the military regime had ousted the sitting civilian President and declared martial law. Dhaka University, a few minutes' drive from the club, was the source and the centre of the protests. Student activists hadn't let go of the bone of contention in their teeth since day one, and no amount of police fire, clubbing by soldiers or staring down tanks had deterred them.

One afternoon, in the middle of a tennis game, I started coughing and struggling to breathe, and my eyes burned as though I'd touched them with pepper on my hands. I noticed my friend on the other end of the court keel over, gag and spit. Soon everyone around us was experiencing some level of similar distress. Smoke was rising above the walls of the club from the street on the other side. The ground picked up a low rumble like a passing tremor.

'Tear gas!' someone yelled.

'We need to get inside!' shouted another.

Next thing I knew we were gathering our things in a mad rush and bolting into the club. The main gates were closed and padlocked, as were the doors of the club once the tennis courts were emptied out and every one of us herded in.

I don't remember how long we waited inside, or when – or if – we went back out to resume our games, but it must not have been longer than the time it took the tanks and guns to shoot their way through, clearing the protest, before we were back to 'normal'.

Some months before our planned departure, I saw the newspaper on the floor of my parents' bedroom one morning reporting the end of the military government and saying the President had 'absconded'. That word got thrown around a lot over the next several weeks. I assumed it was a special way reserved for presidents to leave the country after their time in office.

There were grainy black-and-white photos of him with entertainment-industry people, which in and of themselves were nothing extraordinary, except for the many liaisons he'd had with actresses and singers, all of them married, and the lifestyle he funded by exploiting the national coffers. The last I'd heard of the President had, in fact, to do with my own family: the daughter of a distant relative on my mother's side had married a nephew of his.

Tarek Bashir was genial to the extreme. He ordered a big spread, rounds of drinks, and introduced me to his colleagues Majid Uddin and Gowhar Wasim as a 'friend of the family'. Majid's family business was in the garment sector, and Gowhar's family owned car dealerships around the country. Gowhar was an enthusiast and collector of classic cars. He showed us pictures of a line of vintage

CHAPTER 9

models he kept at a location outside the city in Savar. They'd both gone to university in the US but, from the sound of it, held no special love in their hearts for America.

Gowhar's dislike was perhaps a few degrees higher than Majid's, and he decided that, since I represented America in the group, it was my lot to bear his disdain.

'I always knew you guys were a crazy country,' he said. 'I never liked being there. But my father, he had to have his way. Thank God I left before this new madness started.' He looked askance at me. 'Who did you vote for?'

'Not the one that became President,' I said.

'The thing is, it's a good country,' said Majid. 'I always thought so. I met wonderful people there that I still keep in touch with. The problem is that it's a young country, and it's grown so much in a short time that it doesn't know what to do with all that power.'

'It's an ignorant country,' said Gowhar. 'You may not have voted for the guy,' he said to me, 'but millions of your people did, and that's bad enough.'

I was not keen on going down this path, however much I agreed with him. I was weary of politically charged fights, and did not want to enter into one here, thousands of miles from the US, about the state of the depraved American union.

'Nisar is a hundred per cent Bengali,' Tarek volunteered. 'No doubt about it.'

'The man must be doing something right if that many people wanted him to be President,' said Majid. His eyes closed completely when he smiled.

'Majid likes dictators, you see,' Gowhar said. 'His family is army, so what else would you expect?'

'That was another generation,' Majid said casually. 'My last uncle retired more than ten years ago. We're all civilians now.'

'After causing all the damage, you took off your villain suits,' said Gowhar. His voice echoed in the mostly empty lounge. Majid seemed used to the treatment. He'd probably always been that person, genial to a fault, never objecting to the ridicule of friends.

'I understand both your families are long-time residents of Dhaka,' I said.

'Not really,' said Gowhar. 'We're from Faridpur. Only been in Dhaka one generation.'

Dhaka, like Chicago, was a city of transplant. It was rare to come across someone that didn't trace their roots back elsewhere, and the move to Dhaka had been the story of millions who had left ancestral homes to start over, not always willingly.

'We're from Cumilla,' said Majid. 'Although, if you went back to my grandparents, they're from West Bengal. Left during Partition. Everything they had they lost to India.'

'And stole from Bangladesh to make up for it,' said Gowhar.

Tarek sat detached from the conversation, as if he had nothing to do with the rest of us.

'There was no Bangladesh at the time,' said Majid.

'And if it were up to people like you, there wouldn't ever be,' said Gowhar.

'Meaning what?'

'Meaning we, all of us, are opportunists. Whichever way works best for us, that's the way we go, and then pretend we did it for our country or some great bloody national cause.'

'You just summed up the entire human race,' said Majid.

'Hell with it all. And hell with politics!' Gowhar opened the photos on his phone. 'Look at this beauty: 1962 Porsche Roadster, fully restored, and on its way to me. It's going to be the crown jewel of my collection.'

'Are you ever going to drive these things, or do you just leave them to rust?' Majid asked innocently.

'What would you know about fine taste in anything? Collecting is an art. Isn't it, Nisar?'

'Sure,' I said. 'I've never collected anything other than stamps when I was young, but it can be a passion.'

CHAPTER 9

'You see, Majid. That's the sound of refinement, which you will never have.'

'Still collecting dust in Indonesia?' said Tarek, leaning forward.

'Don't worry, it's being very well taken care of. Owner moved there from Italy a long time ago,' Gowhar confided. 'Said he was looking for the perfect home for it – someone who'll know what it's worth.'

'That is dedication,' said Majid.

Gowhar raised his glass to him. 'You can be a connoisseur of good things and a real friend. Even if we give you shit for coming from a family of thugs.'

A split-second's irritation passed over Majid's face. Tarek had gone back to being distracted, though I caught him staring at me several times, and when I looked his eyes darted away.

'Where's your family from?' Majid asked me.

'Sylhet on both sides. I was born in Dhaka.'

'Sylhetis are a tough bunch,' said Gowhar. 'No one is good enough for you people.'

'I won't argue with that,' I said.

'Nisar's interest is in Dhaka,' Tarek added. 'He's writing a book about the city. I'm sorry, Nisar. I couldn't get hold of the others like I wanted, but I still thought you should meet some people while you're here.'

'You're a writer,' said Majid. 'That's got to be such satisfying work.'

'When it's happening properly, it is,' I said.

'I hate reading,' said Gowhar. I thought he would spit in my face to emphasise his point. 'I read two headlines in the news and my head starts hurting.'

'There's a name for people like that. Gondo-murkho. Ignorant illiterate,' Majid jokingly chided.

'I don't give a damn,' Gowhar said proudly. 'I read what matters.' He finished his drink and went to use the bathroom.

'So how long have you been in the US?' Majid asked me.

'We moved there when I was thirteen.'

'Long time,' Majid said pensively. 'How is it being back?'

'I'm still trying to figure that out,' I said.

'Dhaka has changed, and it also hasn't,' said Majid. 'I've felt that way for at least the last ten, fifteen years.'

'Guess who bought his family's property?' said Tarek, as if suddenly remembering it. Before I could stop him, he said, 'Gazi.'

Majid's eyes opened wide. 'Eternal Complex? That's yours?'

'Yes,' I said.

'That place went up in no time. Of course it's Gazi Enterprises. They are not wasters of time. And Junaid, my God, he never stops working. I have no idea when he finds the time for all the parties. So you still have connections here?'

'My father wanted to keep them,' I said. 'Mostly sentimental reasons. It's not really practical.'

'If you no longer live here, it's a complete waste. This city just keeps getting more expensive. That is not only a change, it's a fact.'

Gowhar rejoined us.

'Guess what?' Majid said. 'Gazi built Eternal on his property.'

Gowhar had brought out his phone to send a text and stopped. 'That's you?' he said. 'Junaid never told me what was so special about that location. It's not very good. That area is too congested. I tried talking him out of it, but he was adamant.'

'Where do you think you are?' Majid said with a horsey snort. 'Where isn't it congested in this city?'

'Plenty of places,' Gowhar said. 'If you go out of the city. Junaid could have had his pick, but he built that place where no one wants to live in.' He tapped out the text and set the phone on the table. 'What's your father's name?' he asked me.

Tarek answered. 'Nisar is Disha's cousin.'

Gowhar gave him a look, then turned to me.

'Isn't that just like Dhaka?' said Majid. 'The further you go, the smaller the circles become. You can write a book just about that,' he chuckled, his face filling with a smile.

CHAPTER 9

'He and Junaid were family,' Tarek felt the need to point out.

'And I had no idea when we were,' I said. 'I've been out of touch with most of my relatives for many years.'

'You're lucky,' said Gowhar. 'What a fiasco that was. I've known Junaid since we were in school, and it was like he was possessed by demons when he was married to her.'

'Junaid is no angel either,' said Tarek.

Gowhar's phone buzzed before he could respond. I was close enough to unwittingly see the name Maisha on the banner. So did Tarek. Gowhar sent off a reply.

'No, he's not, but Disha,' he said, eying me, 'is a piece of work in her own category. You take that how you will, Nisar, but it's God's honest truth.'

'OK,' said Tarek, holding up a hand to quiet him.

'Shady family,' said Majid. We all looked at him, thinking he'd meant mine. 'Unfortunately,' he went on, without noticing our intrigue, 'no one in this city, this whole country, can do business without him being everywhere. Gazi Enterprises, they're a mafia. But at least Junaid is trying to turn over a new leaf. At heart he's a decent man. But I don't know how far he can go to undo their damaged reputation.'

'How does that make him different from every other family in this city?' said Gowhar. 'Who is so clean?'

'It's not about clean,' Majid argued. 'It's about...'

'About what?' said Gowhar. 'Putting on a face? Showing you're one thing and being another?'

'Who exactly do you mean, who does that?' Tarek wanted to know.

'You're too sensitive, Gowhar,' Majid said.

'Next time you hear shit talked about you behind your back, tell me how well you take it.'

'OK,' said Tarek. 'We have a guest here, after all. Let's not all make assholes of ourselves.'

It was too late for that. And I felt like the biggest asshole of all.

'Sorry, Nisar.'

'Anyway,' Gowhar said pushing to his feet. 'I have to pick up Maisha. My wife.'

Tarek gave him a look, but Gowhar was angled away, his back to him. He held his hand out to me. 'Nice to meet you. I'll see you again soon, now that you're Junaid's neighbour and business partner.'

'Nice meeting you.'

After he left, I thought about taking Tarek aside, but abandoned the idea. He would deny any ulterior motives for bringing me here today. Then there would be Disha to deal with if he told her.

'Thank you,' I said to Majid.

'For what?'

'For your candour.'

'I told you already what a bastard Gazi is,' said Tarek. 'Your cousin never stopped being hypnotised by him.'

'I think I'll go now,' I said.

'What's the rush?'

'I have work to do.'

'Stay, stay.'

'No, Tarek. Thank you for the meal and the drinks.' I shook Majid's hand.

'Just send my driver home after he drops you off,' said Tarek.

On my way out I recognised another one of the staff from when I was a child. He was old then, and he looked decrepit now. I walked up to him, gave my name, told him whose son I was. His rheumy eyes lit up. We embraced. He asked about my parents. I gave him a thousand takas. He smiled a smile with the three teeth left in his mouth and clasped both my hands in his gnarled fingers.

I left the club and made a right, going towards the Shahbag traffic circle. At the intersection I asked three CNG drivers before one agreed to take me to Banani at a rate that would be extortionist to locals but to me was less than what I would have paid as a tip.

10

Mr Ehsan didn't arrive until six on Sunday evening, and when he did, he tried his best to put on a show of how much of a rush he was in – a busy day behind him but not yet over. He made a fuss of settling into his seat as if the couch wasn't good enough, then touched his briefcase several times as though he was on public transportation or feared it would fly away.

'Is your phone working properly?' I asked, maintaining calm.

He frowned, and touched his moustache. 'Why do you ask that?'

'I'd double check it, since I haven't had a call back or a text from you,' I said.

'It's with me always,' he said sharply, 'but sometimes I have to turn it off for appointments.'

'I understand you're a busy man, Mr Ehsan.'

'I think so you don't.'

I took a breath and relaxed my clenched jaw.

'You don't check your messages when you're not in appointments?'

'Some days it's very late when I finish and I don't have the chance,' he said, as though delivering a well-prepared line.

'How long does it take to send a quick acknowledgement, Mr Ehsan? You don't have time to do that before going to bed?'

He crossed his arms and pursed his lips. I had a vision of him as a teenager, facing a parent with the same stance, the same resentful eyes. 'You have time to do that on your busy days?' he asked.

'Mr Ehsan, I'm not going to sit here and play one-upmanship with you. I'm talking to you on behalf of my father.'

'Your father, he can talk for himself,' he said quickly. 'It is not possible for me to return messages, no.'

'Not even to my father?'

'I have a wife and I have a home to attend to.'

'Mr Ehsan, I understand you can't sit around texting and talking with me all day, but you also can't just disappear.'

'Listen,' he began.

'Never mind,' I interrupted. 'I heard you fine, and I respect your life outside of your work for my father and me. I just want communication. You don't have to get back to me right away, but I do need to hear back from you the same day. I don't care what you do with your personal time, Mr Ehsan, but I'm here on my father's time, which is also your time.'

Caught off-guard by my temper, he stared blankly at me, the steely callousness shaken. I controlled myself.

'You shouldn't be so angry like this with me,' he said. 'I knew you when you were a child. I see you like my own son.'

'Then I want you to be honest with me, and with Dad.'

'Honest? About what? What have I not been honest about?'

'When can my father expect to see the bank statements?' I asked.

'As soon as I can get them, I have said to you. Maybe in America you get what you want in seconds – not here.'

'Bank statements are that hard to get?' I asked.

'Do you know how much work and time it took to prepare those other documents?' he said. 'If Chowdhury Shaheb was my only client, it would be one thing. He's not. And I have to make a living still, as grateful as I am to his years of generosity. I still do more work for him above and beyond any of my other clients, on my own time, too. If I have to explain everything I do, you'll be stuck here many years.'

In an argument with a lawyer, I wasn't going to get far with decorum.

CHAPTER 10

'Is there something in those statements that will bother my father?'

'Something?' Mr Ehsan slid forward. 'Such as?'

'Three bank statements cannot take the kind of time you're making it sound, Mr Ehsan. It makes no sense.'

His eyes narrowed. 'And you know this better than me all of a sudden?'

His phone rang in rising and falling scales. He stopped himself from saying what he was about to as if a blade had entered his rib, his eyes wide and defensive.

'Go ahead, answer it,' I said, relishing the moment. 'Might be a client.' The phone rang several more times and went quiet.

'Someone has said something to you? Filled your ears with lies?' said Mr Ehsan.

My terrible capacity for hiding what my face gives away must have been on glaring display. Mr Ehsan was no novice. Like Gazi, he also waded the many and varied fickle currents of Dhaka.

'Who?' he demanded. 'Tell me. If my integrity is on the line, I want to know.'

My heart was going too fast for me to talk. I was angry, but at whom I wasn't sure.

'Mr Ehsan,' I said through the hammering in my chest. 'Don't disappear. I want you to stay in touch, that's all.'

'Be careful who and what you listen to,' he said, shaking a finger. 'This is not the Dhaka of your father's time, and you are not a child any more. Friends are few in this town. Keep the ones you have close.'

'I have no interest in your business, Mr Ehsan, just in the part that is my father's business too,' I said.

Mr Ehsan let out a long breath, deflating into himself. Before he could speak again, I picked up my phone.

'Since you're here now,' I said, 'Dad should hear from you himself.'

He made a movement, maybe to stop me, but I had already dialled my parents' number.

'Dad, Mr Ehsan is here with me,' I said, before even greeting him. 'Hold on.' I put it on speakerphone.

'Sir, hello, sir,' Mr Ehsan managed to get out before needing to swallow. He became a different person, stooped and subservient, his voice softer.

'Where have you been?' my father asked, as if talking to a lost child. 'And where are the bank statements? You know I can't be up day and night over here dealing with them. My health is not good.'

'Sir, it's just coming,' Mr Ehsan said. 'I've been busy and Nisar has been also busy.'

'How long does it take to get a few statements from the bank?' Mr Ehsan went mute. He stared imploringly at me.

'Are you there?' my father said so loudly the phone vibrated and made a miniscule anti-clockwise turn.

'Sir,' said Mr Ehsan. 'I'm here only, sir, yes. Sir, I'll send them to you this week.'

'You send them to me tomorrow, Ehsan, not a day late. Nisar?'

'I'm here, Dad.'

'Go with him. I want you both to walk into the branches, give them my name, and stay until every page of every statement is in your hands. If there's any issue you get me on the phone, I don't care what time it is. You hear me?'

'Yes, Dad.'

'Ehsan, is that clear?'

'Sir.'

'Talk to your mother.'

I took the call off speakerphone and went to my bedroom.

'Are you next to Dad?' I asked.

'No, I'm downstairs, why? What's going on over there?'

'Too much. I'm sure Dad will get you caught up.'

'I knew this would happen,' said my mother. 'I knew nothing left to that man would come to any good. What is he saying? What's going on with these bank statements? Is he stealing?'

CHAPTER 10

I almost told her that that was exactly my suspicion. And that it didn't stop there. That he might have gambled with our money. Possibly very large amounts. Large enough to send his boss back to the hospital.

'I can't figure Ehsan out,' I said. 'I know you don't like him. I'm seeing why. The man doesn't know how to be straightforward about anything.'

'I've been trying to tell your father all my life,' my mother said. 'But he's been hypnotised by him since the day he met him.'

I sat down on my bed and gazed out of the window.

'Is he stealing?' she repeated.

'I don't know,' I said. 'But don't get Dad worked up. I can't do any of this alone. If Ehsan isn't here, nothing will get done.'

My mother lowered her voice. 'Serves your father right.'

I couldn't take more of talking about Ehsan, but my mother didn't sound ready to hang up just yet.

'What do you remember about the Gazis?' I asked, changing the topic.

My mother was quiet for a beat.

'I met them but didn't know them that well. Your uncle, Disha's father, was the one that knew him, Mohammad Gazi. That's how we met them.'

'I'm finding out many things about our family,' I said.

'You should,' said my mother. 'I'm happy that you've taken the interest. You should know what's happening with everything.'

'I can't help wondering how it would've been if we'd stayed and not moved to the States. Do you ever think about that?'

'Back then it didn't look very good. Now – well…' she trailed off. 'How is your book?'

'Neglected,' I said. 'But I've been seeing a lot of the city.' My father's voice rose in the background.

'Be careful,' said my mother.

'There was something else I wanted to tell you,' I said. 'Rais Kaka needs money for his daughter's dowry. I'm going to give it to him. I'm just trying to find a way to tell him without hurting his pride.'

'Good, good – that man can have anything this family has.'

I hung up and went back out to the living room to find Mr Ehsan sitting like a suspect in a crime awaiting interrogation.

'We'll go tomorrow,' I told him. 'All three banks. I'd like you to come get me first thing in the morning.'

'Nisar, please listen,' he said, trying to be placating – a different persona entirely from our previous rounds. 'Please. I've eaten your father's salt longer than I ate my own father's. But I'm only one man. I can't make do with the salary I make with him any more. I work from 6 a.m. till late, sometimes past midnight. My one daughter is in Australia in university, my son thinks he's male heir to a kingdom and lives like it, and my youngest daughter needs medical attention almost around the clock. I'll spare you the details – you're not here to hear my sob stories. I just want you to understand what your father can't see from far away.' He gave his moustache two strokes with his thumb.

'Then you tell Dad tomorrow when he asks,' I said.

'This is what will happen if I go in, just walk in and demand such sensitive documents to be processed like that: nothing.'

'If we go together—'

'Believe me, nothing will be different.'

'Are you saying we can't get our own bank statements?'

'No, of course not,' said Mr Ehsan. 'I'm saying everything needs time and process, ten times more in this country. When the sales are final, all documents have been signed and the transaction is complete, I will personally deliver everything by hand to you. Hard copies, multiples, of everything. In the meantime, you must speak with your father and ask him to be patient. Sit. Your father's money, these properties, the government doesn't just leave them alone for nothing. In any other civilised country, sure. Not here. Here everything is about keeping the right people happy.'

CHAPTER 10

'What does that mean exactly?' I said. 'You're bribing people with Dad's money?'

'I promise you,' he said, 'I'm not doing anything your father wouldn't order me to do. You're sitting here in this house today because of it. You have the properties and the funds intact because of it. Your father gave me responsibilities when he first hired me, and I've devoted myself to them like religion ever since. I'm just doing my job.'

Mr Ehsan waited triumphantly for my response. I had none. I wished I didn't care about any of it myself, that it had been all for the sake of my father, and then I could abandon the whole thing to Mr Ehsan, let him deliver whatever was left of the debris to his boss.

'When Dad asks tomorrow, I tell him what?' I asked. Mr Ehsan stood up.

'Tell him there is no reason to worry. You are here, I'm here, and we will get everything done. Also, Nisar, he has not made a final decision yet, has he? About the Gazi offer? That has to happen too.'

He was right. And the truth was, I was beginning to feel conflicted about selling everything. I wanted us to keep the house.

Maybe being here again at an older age, with a regard for history, was playing a part. Not the history I didn't have in or with the house, but the house's place in our family's past. For a time, that was how it had happened with my mother's parents' property. They'd sold part of it and overnight the front lawn where I'd learned to ride a bike and played cricket with my cousins was turned into a ditch for the foundation of the high-rise built by the new owners, a multinational bank. It was sad not having that beautiful lawn to look at from the veranda, and not having it to wear us children out, whether it was games or swinging on the branches of the jackfruit and mango trees that lined it – and moreover dispiriting to see the ugly cement façade growing on it day by day like a giant canker. Eternal Complex was done; there would be no surprises. If Gazi ever sold the other units there'd be that traffic, but that would be manageable. If needs be, some kind of boundary could be built between the two buildings.

I made one last attempt. 'When do you think it would be possible to get the statements?' It was without conviction, and he answered by first putting on his best condescending face.

'You leave that to me. Do you need anything else? The car? Are the servants behaving?'

'I'm fine,' I said. 'You worry about what you're doing.'

He took the jab, picked up his briefcase and showed himself out.

I sent a message to my mother to keep my father calm. Nothing was going to happen by tomorrow, or the day after.

I went up to the roof. The sky was draining of light and dark, and voluptuous rain clouds loomed in the east. Looking up and down the length of our street brought to mind the flood of 1988.

The first drops of rain tapped my neck and the backs of my hands.

11

Cyclone Bhola massacred half a million people in November 1970. There were reports of corpses hanging from trees, entire villages rendered extinct, and there were aerial views of the Bay of Bengal that showed the waters dotted with debris, which on closer inspection were revealed to be floating bodies. It was a chilling prologue to the killings that were going to end another three million lives at the hands of the Pakistan Army the following year during the Liberation War.

The flood of 1988 was the worst in the country's history since Cyclone Bhola. Kemal Ataturk Avenue was undriveable for weeks. The only way to travel it was by boat, and boats were what I saw one afternoon from our roof, cruising both ways, ferrying passengers back and forth, and life going on because it had to.

On Friday morning, a storm ripped through the city, flooding roads and grounding vehicles where they were caught in the squall. Rais Kaka called and said he was on his way, but the bus broke down and it would take him hours to reach the house. I told him not to worry, not to risk the journey. The news showed footage of water up to the windows of smaller cars, rickshaws and CNGs fording lakes, and people wading water for dry land and going about their day as naturally as if the drowning waters were mere puddles.

I sent Disha a message about Gazi's party, and she wrote back an hour later saying she'd be there, but probably not till after ten.

I was looking forward to it, more with curiosity than excitement. It was a sort of experiment: I wanted to see how the same people that stabbed Gazi in the back in his absence would behave at his party, on his turf, in his home.

I had asked Jasmine if she was interested in joining me. She was, of course, already among the invited, and was a long-time friend of Gazi – even before he and Disha were a couple. Jasmine had friended me on Facebook, and as I looked at the few pictures she had on a page she clearly rarely used, I realised I didn't remember her well enough to be able to recognise her at the party. It was a good thing she'd agreed to meet me at the house for a drink before we went.

My phone lit up. 'Boss, I hope I see you tonight.'

His text came in just as I was looking out of the window at the clearing day with the hope of getting out of the house for a while. 'This one is a memorable one for me,' a second text followed.

'I'll be there,' I responded, and added: 'I look forward to being part of it.'

I took a chance and went out. The years since the last flood had brought some progress – or it could just be that I was getting a closer look now than I was able to back then, because Kemal Ataturk Avenue was going on with business as usual, cars stalled both ways in a jam? I crossed to the other side and went into Ahmed Tower. I sat at Second Cup Coffee and drank two mochas back to back while trying to write.

The rain started again but didn't last long. It had stopped by the time I reached my gate, and the sun came out. There was a flurry of activity at the entrance to Eternal Plaza. Cases of liquor and beer and wine were being taken in by men in T-shirts and lungis, and a catering service was arranging the evening's menu. A small crowd with nothing better to do had banded across the street as an audience. Gazi wasn't home yet, and I wondered who was overseeing the preparations for what appeared very clearly to be more than a casual gathering. The doorman I met the first day salaamed me and answered that a 'madam' was up in Gazi's apartment, in charge.

CHAPTER 11

Disha, I thought. But she wouldn't go around me like that. I asked my watchman if Disha had come by. She hadn't. He had seen the woman in Gazi's apartment before, but didn't know her name.

There was no way of finding out who she was without creating a situation potentially damaging to her, to me and to Gazi if I paid her a visit. It wouldn't matter that the place was swarming with people, including Gazi's servants, and that everyone was aware I was Gazi's neighbour. The scene would be what the eyes saw, and from it determine the story: a strange man and a strange woman of the upper class meeting in a home that wasn't theirs, alone, in the absence of the owner.

I was in the living room distractedly watching TV when Almas brought word that the 'madam' next door was outside.

'Here?' I said.

'Wants to see you.'

For the same reason I didn't go up to Gazi's apartment; I didn't ask her to be shown in. Given certain circumstances and the consideration they required, courtesy had to take a back seat to reputation in Dhaka, the paradox being Bengali hospitality sharing the back seat with it.

She was wearing an olive-green salwar kameez, head covered in the orna, and stood with her back to me, looking at my narrow, unlovely driveway, as if she was contemplating giving it a makeover.

'Hi,' she said, turning around as I stepped out on to the portico, and held out her hand.

'Hello, I'm Nisar.' Her palm was clammy, and I might have jerked my hand back too fast.

'Maisha. Nice meeting you.' The name rang a bell.

'Maisha Wasim,' she said, seeing the blank expression on my face. 'You met my husband, Gowhar.'

'Yes, of course. It's nice to meet you.'

'I just wanted to come by and introduce myself.' She plucked a business card out of her purse. 'This is my company.' The card was pink with ornate black cursive script announcing in all caps

MAISHA'S CATERING & EVENTS. 'Junaid is one of my best clients, and a friend. Are you coming to the party?'

'Yes, I'll be there,' I said.

'He said you're Disha's cousin.'

'That's right.'

'Their wedding was my first job.' I noted a touch of longing and a twinge of regret. 'It wasn't even a full-fledged business yet. I did all the cooking in my mother's kitchen.' She smiled fondly. 'My friends helped with the deliveries. Uncle – Junaid's father – paid me more than I deserved.'

Her orna had slid back, and she adjusted it. There was a patch of blond at the front of her hair about the size of my palm. On the left side of her neck, just below the ear, was a birthmark. As birthmarks go there was nothing odd about the shape – in fact, this one seemed too uniform, almost as measuredly square as a postage stamp. I looked at it long enough for her to become aware I was staring, but she didn't seem to care.

'You met Tarek, too,' she ventured.

'I have,' I said.

'It's nice to meet you,' she said. There was a sadness about her, a trace of the tragic, and I found myself unable to send her away without anything more than a sheepish nod.

I heard her speak with her employees, then get into her car and drive away. Still holding her card, I gave it another look while trying to ward off a notion that under any circumstances would be none of my business. Her birthmark was not a birthmark. It was something else entirely.

12

Gazi's light came on early, before the sun had fully set. He wasn't home yet, and for the rest of the day people came and went – under whose supervision I couldn't tell, and if it hadn't been for Maisha Wasim I would not have thought about it. A group of three young men and a young woman arrived and unloaded two minivans of musical instruments and sound equipment.

At seven I was waiting for Jasmine more eagerly than I cared to admit, and reminded myself not to make a big deal of it. She was going to be one among the many people I'd meet while I was here, no more, no less, and once I was gone she would fade to the recesses of my mind, confined to social media. I sent Almas out for ice and tried to create as best a presentation of Gazi's gift, the bottle of Blue Label, as possible. The half-empty bottle, two glasses, an ice bucket and tongs and a corkscrew, just in case, sat on a silver tray I had fished out of the china cabinet in the dining room that my mother would once have screamed bloody murder upon seeing used.

Almas came in with a grin on his face and bloodshot eyes. He was high. I asked him if he could get me where he was, offering him a finder's fee on top of the cost of the stash. He didn't take the money, but went off and returned fifteen minutes later asking if he should roll one for me.

'And one for yourself,' I said.

We went up to the roof with the joints, Almas holding a small cup of the Blue Label I'd forced on him.

'You can go home for the night,' I told him after the drinks and the joints. 'Jatin too. I won't need anything.' I gave him a couple of thousand takas, which he refused, until I held the money over the balustrade, threatening to drop it to the ground, and chuckled as I pushed the notes into the pocket of his shirt.

Jasmine didn't arrive until a little after nine. She didn't explain her lateness or apologise. My irritation went away when I opened the door and saw that she was nothing like I'd remembered, or how photos captured her. She was elegantly dressed in a long-sleeved floral print shirt, palazzo trousers and open-toed heels, her silky black hair framing her face in an oval. Added to the ensemble was a bottle of red wine. My little presentation of a pathetic drinks cart must've charmed her, or touched her pity, because she gave it a warm look in the way a parent would at the best efforts of her child, knowing full well it was garbage, before sitting down and asking if she could smoke. She took her cigarette to a window.

'You can never be late to one of Junaid's parties,' she said, blowing a jet of smoke.

'I wasn't worried about that,' I said.

'You're getting the perfect intro to the Dhaka scene.'

'What about the one last week?' I asked.

'Nothing – not even close. One-time thing.'

'I see. Wine or whisky?' I asked. 'A gift from the man himself,' I said, holding up the Blue Label.

'Of course it is,' said Jasmine. 'Junaid has the one thing none of these other assholes have in this city: he has class. But I think I'll stick to wine.'

I opened the bottle, poured the wine and brought it to her. She took the glass and held me in a look that I couldn't read.

'Texas wasn't your thing, huh?' I said.

'Is it anyone's?' she laughed.

CHAPTER 12

'I guess not,' I said. 'Though I know some pretty good people that live there.'

'But not from there.'

'A couple, sure. Right now, though, with the country gone completely deranged, I'm not too crazy about a Texas vacation any time soon. But you know, Chicago can be bad too. So can New York or California. Really, the whole country's fucked.'

'Just like this one,' she said.

She finished her cigarette and stayed by the window. I wished she'd come over and share the sofa with me.

I learned that Jasmine's family owned a chain of restaurants and bed-and-breakfasts in Chittagong, where both her parents were from and spent a good portion of their time. She had two sisters – one lived in Malaysia with her husband and children and the second, the baby, in Canada with a woman twenty years her senior. Jasmine was always the one assumed to take over the family business.

'My father even talked about me like I was a son.' She wanted to study art and art history, but her father decided on the degree he was paying for: business.

'I remember Disha mentioning you were an artist,' I said.

'She exaggerated. I wanted to *study* art. And literature, too, in fact. Islamic and Renaissance. Tell that to a Bangladeshi father, right?'

'Mine wasn't crazy about an English major either.'

'And here you are living to tell it – and writing a book.'

'Did you even need a degree?' I said.

'What do you mean?'

'You'd take over the family business anyway, so you could've studied whatever you wanted.'

'Must be nice having your parents,' she said. 'Maybe you're right. I must not have wanted it bad enough. Like you wanted to be a writer. But that was how it was going to be. Anyway, it was a long time ago. I don't think I could even find my diploma anywhere in my house without turning it upside down. Or maybe I threw it out with the trash when I left Texas.'

'So you live alone?' I said.

'Alone with a houseful of my parents' most trusted servants, all from Chittagong, with a long history of serfdom with my family, of course,' she said.

'Of course.'

She drained her glass.. I started to bring the bottle over but she said, 'No, stay.' She sat down beside me, leaving about a foot between us. I refilled her glass. 'How's your book going?' she asked.

'Nowhere.'

'That can't be true.' She angled her face and gave me a look both fetching and scrutinising.

'I can prove it,' I said. 'The work I haven't done is right there in the dining room.'

'You seem like such a hard-working, smart guy.'

'Seem: the operative word. What I take the greatest pleasure in is laziness.'

'I don't believe that,' she said seriously. 'Writing a book isn't easy. I liked writing papers, but twenty pages was my limit. For classes.'

'I promise you I have far less than that.'

She dropped her shoes and tucked her legs under her.

'Why Dhaka?' she asked.

'Why Dhaka – like why do I want to write about Dhaka?'

'There are so many more interesting places. You could be a travel writer, visit places no one visits, write about them, have adventures. Not be stuck here.'

'I've always wanted to write about Dhaka,' I said. 'Probably because I left when I was so young – there's unfinished business, if that's the word.'

'Like what?'

'Getting to know the city – you know, really getting to know it.'

She considered my answer with a sip of wine, and reached for her cigarettes.

'No need to go to the window,' I told her.

'Sure?'

CHAPTER 12

'No one stays here year after year. A few cigarettes won't bother anyone.'

'It's you I care about bothering.'

'No worries there.'

She lit the cigarette and took a long drag, which she turned away to blow towards the window. 'Dhaka isn't an easy place.' A better first line for my book I couldn't think of, and it hit me in the profoundest depths of composition, and there lay its magic. She'd said it without thinking, without ambition, and hence made it worth a hundred books.

'Never was,' I said.

'You're lucky you left. Whatever you remember of it, it's worse.'

'How?'

'The question is how *isn't* it,' she said. 'The bitch of it is...' She paused, looking for something to drop her ashes in. I handed her an empty glass. 'Thanks.'

'The bitch of it is?'

'I love this city,' she said. 'I love this country. It's corny as hell, but I do. I'm from here, I belong here, and I never got the same feeling anywhere else.'

'That's something I'll never be able to write,' I said.

Strains of music floated in from Gazi's party through the window. There were also the sounds of cars and people arriving. I was in no hurry to bring our time alone to an end.

That she was accompanying me to the party suggested she was unattached, but making such an assumption was still risky – and shouldn't matter, in any case, because soon I was going to be gone. I gestured at the wine bottle, and she accepted the offer of another round.

'Disha and Junaid had quite the marriage,' she said. 'I'm sure you're well aware.'

'Actually, no,' I said. 'I knew she'd been married. I didn't know who it was until a few hours after I landed in Dhaka.'

'Are you serious?'

'Completely. We weren't in touch for a long time, and I was tuned out of family affairs.'

'You know,' she began, and paused. 'I was wondering what the deal is with that place.' She meant Eternal Complex – she tilted her head in its direction. 'I was surprised that he was so determined to buy that cramped little space. Sorry, no offence. I know it's your family property.'

'No worries. It *is* cramped. I'm surprised there was even enough room to put up a building.'

'Junaid gets what Junaid wants.'

'Why do you think he did?' I asked.

'Clearly to be close to Disha. Now it makes sense.' She sat forward with her glass in both hands.

'How so?' I said.

'You're her family, and being in business with her family keeps him close to her. Are you related to Shahriar Chowdhury?'

'He's my father,' I answered.

'Oh my god, now I make the connection. OK. So, Rajib Chowdhury…'

'Disha's father, my eldest uncle.'

'He was such a lovely man,' Jasmine said. 'I loved Rajib Uncle.'

'I didn't know you and Disha were so close.'

'Once upon a time. Then, well, our lives diverged. She was married, I wasn't. You know how that can go.'

'I do.'

I wasn't sure whether to be glad or worried about this history. My cousin continued to be an enigma – not in a romantic way. I wanted her to be honest, to know everything I needed to know from *her*, not pick up pieces from strangers all over Dhaka.

It was after ten and I said we should probably make our way to the party. I was certainly intrigued, even looking forward, to an extent, to a Junaid Gazi – I felt I should call it based on all accounts I had heard – event. People were drinking and talking and eating, and they were spread out throughout the apartment,

CHAPTER 12

sitting draped over sofa arms, on the floor and in the many furnished rooms that I would need a tour of to know my way around. Jasmine took my hand and led me in. I couldn't see Gazi or Disha. I'd texted her on the way up, but hadn't yet heard back. Jasmine led us to the bar, and we took our drinks with us around the floor to meet and mingle.

Jasmine knew everyone. She introduced me around, and for the first half hour or so I went along with being her sidekick. The first face I recognised was Guru's.

Seeing me, he pressed two fingers to his lips, and I accepted the invitation.

'You're becoming my own personal dealer,' I said, taking hits of his joint. He gave me a wink and smiled. 'I really should pay you something. I feel bad.'

He double blinked, like he was playing peek-a-boo, and waved at me to keep enjoying myself.

'Thank you. I assure you I do go through part of my life sober,' I joked, but he may not have even heard me, because he was walking away.

I rejoined Jasmine, and found her with Gowhar and Maisha Wasim and Tarek Bashir.

Seeing me, Tarek resumed the cold, distant eye with which he held me on our first meeting. The warmth he'd shown me at Amari and at the lunch at Dhaka Club was put back on ice. My eyes wandered to Maisha Wasim's neck, but I couldn't see the mark.

Tarek seemed out of place, uncomfortable, in that group. Even his posture said he was a misfit – standing a little way off, keeping his distance, as if he'd been shoved out but refused to leave.

'Is Disha here?' he asked me quietly.

'If she is I haven't seen her,' I said.

Tarek huffed off. He refreshed his drink at the bar, and went down the hallway I remembered following Gazi through to get to the roof. Maisha Wasim excused herself. Gowhar and Jasmine were in a discussion about things I couldn't keep up with, and I followed with my glassy eyes and light head Maisha Wasim going the same way Tarek Bashir had.

I tried to pay more attention to Jasmine and Gowhar.

'The birthday boy isn't anywhere to be seen at his own party,' I heard Jasmine say. I moved closer to her. My hand brushed hers. She didn't mind.

'You know this is the start,' Gowhar said. Then, turning to me: 'Enjoying yourself?'

'Just got here,' I said.

'Don't worry,' he said. 'If you don't like this one, there are going be plenty more.'

'Great,' I said, my sarcasm lost to the general hum.

'From here to New Year's Eve,' said Jasmine, nudging me with her elbow.

'And you come to all of them?' I asked.

'Don't make it sound so miserable now,' Jasmine said. 'They're not that bad.'

'No, that's not what I meant,' I said. 'I hardly ever go to parties in Chicago. And never to Bangladeshi ones.'

'You'll get your fill here,' said Jasmine. 'Especially now that you and Junaid are business partners, and buddies.'

'Hardly,' I said. 'It's a one-time transaction.' I didn't know how to respond to the part about being buddies.

'Junaid's birthday is kind of like a launch,' Gowhar said.

'All other parties fade away to the lights of his,' Jasmine added.

'He starts with this one, and every weekend after that,' said Gowhar.

'All the way to New Year's Eve,' I said.

'Welcome to the scene,' Gowhar said, clapping my back.

I couldn't bear the thought of being part of 'the scene' every weekend – not even once a month. I'd take it as exaggeration if only I hadn't had the sense in person that Gazi did nothing half-heartedly or didn't deliver what he was known for above and beyond expectation, whether it suited his personal preferences or not.

CHAPTER 12

I checked my phone. Still nothing from Disha. When Gowhar went to refresh drinks, I asked if Jasmine had heard from her.

'She's fine,' was her reply. 'Are you having a rotten time?'

'It's not that,' I said. 'Just, you know, I was expecting to see her here.'

'Disha does what Disha wants,' she said, with the same cadence she'd used for Junaid.

We got food and joined people at Macbeth's banquet table.

'What's funny?' said Jasmine, seeing me grin to myself.

'I'm high,' I said.

Across from us sat two women and a man who were all talking loudly about Gazi. One of the women had a crew cut, and the man's face was pocked with the aftermath of severe acne. The other woman was very drunk. Her eyes were wayward. She kept looking from one end of the table to the other, as if making sure everyone present was hearing everything the three of them had to say because they were critical instructions and would not be repeated.

'What's the point?' the man said. 'Buying all this land when the market is so bad.'

'Everyone knows that's why he's buying it,' said the crew-cut woman. 'He couldn't care less about the land or what he does with it.'

'It's stupid,' said the man.

'It's romantic,' said the second woman, her speech remarkably steady. She'd straightened up, her eyes had stopped roving and she had even sent a smile Jasmine's way and given me an eye of curiosity.

'How about you guys leave the man's business alone?' Jasmine remarked.

The crew-cut woman and the man paused like a remote button had been pressed.

'Seriously,' Jasmine said, 'does it matter to you that much? And you're sitting here at his table, eating his food, drinking his liquor.'

'Jas, come on, don't be a bore,' said the crew-cut woman. 'Junaid is like our brother. We can say whatever we want.'

'You're talking shit, and that's not cool. You wouldn't talk like this about your own brothers, so don't give me that crap.'

'My God, what a mood to bring to a party,' said the drunk woman, meaning it as a joke, and getting a scorching gaze from Jasmine in return.

'Calm down, Jas,' said the man.

'I'm calm. I just think it's cheap to talk behind his back. To his face, you all fawn like the hangers-on you are.'

The crew-cut woman seemed to laugh and sigh simultaneously, then rubbed her eyes.

'Jas, Jas, Jas,' she said.

'I'm just pointing out what's not right,' Jasmine said.

'Without us hangers-on Junaid would waste away like an old relic,' she said. 'Pining for that… that… woman.'

Disha was *that woman*. My jaw was stuck. I couldn't utter a word in defence of my family, or I'd embarrass them by revealing who I was.

'It would be a lot healthier than dying from being stabbed in the back.'

'No one is stabbing him in the back. We're telling the truth up front, like we always have done.'

'How about respect?' Jasmine said.

'What next – are you going to lay down your prayer mat for a few rakats of namaj?' the man said with a cackle. 'I know he's your best buddy too, but what Junaid needs is good counsel.'

'And you three are it?' Jasmine snorted. 'Good luck, Junaid.'

'We're still better than that ex-wife of his,' said the drunk woman. 'We all had to endure that, and now…'

'Go ahead,' Jasmine said. 'Now what?'

I could hardly take the next breath. The drunk woman leaned in.

'She's here, you know,' she said.

My chest grew tight. I had a sip of my drink. I could kiss Jasmine for not telling them who I was to Disha. I didn't care to be introduced to these three to begin with, and now my nameless, context-free presence was bearing fruit.

CHAPTER 12

'So what?' Jasmine said.

'So what?' said the drunk woman. 'Are you serious? After what we had to put up with for years with that spoiled bitch? Junaid had to leave the country to get away from her.'

'Don't talk about things you don't have the first clue about, OK? Just don't,' Jasmine said, apparently ending the conversation.

The drunk woman's wandering, fluttering eyes looked briefly at me. I kept mine on my food like an obedient child.

'It's a party, Jas,' said the crew-cut woman, pushing to her feet with her plate in her hand. 'Lighten up.'

'Hey, bring me back a couple of egg rolls – the meat ones,' the man called after her.

The drunk woman thought she heard her name and left.

'I'm going to go to the roof for some air,' I told Jasmine.

'Let's go.'

'Why so distracted?' Jasmine asked as we reached the roof.

'Sorry,' I said.

'Mr Serious Writer.' She smiled over her shoulder.

The band was going back and forth between covers of American songs and their own. They were in the corner of the roof that looked towards Disha's building, and the sign with the green lighting distracted me, no matter how much I tried to avoid it and pretend it wasn't there.

'I'm sorry about that,' Jasmine said.

'You have nothing to be sorry about. Right now I'm pretty pissed at my cousin, too.'

'Do you dance?' she said, taking my hand.

'No,' I said, cheekily adding, 'Go ahead without me – please, I insist.'

She pulled me in, slid her arms around my waist and tried to give me rhythm, only to learn within seconds that I was horribly deficient in that regard. She tried harder, until I begged my way out and stood back, watching her join the others on the floor.

My younger, twenty-something self would have smacked me. A beautiful, forceful, slightly haunted woman that I'd wanted to accompany me to a party had said yes and was giving me the loveliest looks while dancing and mouthing Janis Joplin, and I was disengaged as a restless child at a mosque. I pointed at the other side of the roof to indicate where I'd be. She blew me a kiss.

I wasn't pissed with my cousin, I was furious. I walked towards the reflecting pool and fire pit, where there were fewer people, my last visit there feeling like years in the past. My hunch told me I needed to go back downstairs and search for Disha.

'Not having fun?' Maisha Wasim was making her way over along the edge of the pool. Behind her, on the bench cut into the wall, was Tarek Bashir. He was by himself, and he was watching Maisha as if he'd sent her over to me to chat me up.

'Hi,' I said. 'The food is excellent.'

'Thank you.' Her voice had a warmth of sincere appreciation.

'I don't imagine you still do all the cooking yourself?' I said.

'Not such a big amount, no. But if you had the chicken korma, that's my specialty.'

'I did, and it was special. Took me back to my childhood.'

'I take that as a compliment.'

Tarek approached us. He was weaving, and I feared for a moment that he'd fall into the waterless pool and crack his skull. Up close he was not that drunk.

'Those three idiots,' he said. 'What garbage were they saying to you and Jasmine?'

As if the mention of her name conjured her, Jasmine appeared next to me. Her scent of soap and sweat was sweet in the warm night air. She was drinking from a plastic bottle of water and her hair was up in a ponytail. Her neck was remarkably slender, almost pencil thin, and her ears protruded at an angle that made them seem bigger than they were.

'Same shit,' she answered.

'Are you two staying much longer?' Tarek asked.

CHAPTER 12

Jasmine looked to me.

'As soon as I find Disha,' I said, 'I'll probably leave.'

Maisha's eyes made the faintest move towards Tarek, but he didn't react to Disha's name either way.

'We're leaving soon,' he said. 'Might get a drink at Westin, then…'

'…then home,' Maisha finished the thought.

'Where's Gowhar?' Jasmine asked.

'He left,' Maisha said. 'You know him. One drink, two max, and he's ready to sleep all next day.'

A few more awkward moments later they took their leave, abruptly, as Tarek made an impatient move and gave Maisha's sleeve a tug, as if he couldn't stand being there any longer.

Jasmine started talking to some other people. I excused myself.

I didn't know where to start, where to go looking in the maze of Gazi's hallways and rooms. One floor down, on the second floor of the apartment, a few people were scattered about, lounging, talking in whispers, but paid me no mind. I checked the floor as best as possible, then headed downstairs.

No one could tell me where Gazi was. I didn't ask about Disha. I hadn't met more than ninety per cent of the guests, didn't know their estimation of my cousin, and felt it was better to keep her name and my search for her to myself. Down the hallway from the stairwell were three rooms with their doors open. They were furnished with beds, chests of drawers, entire bedroom suites, akin to a hotel. Guests were hanging out in them in various states of drunken half-waking, and in one of them I saw the crew-cut woman, the other woman, who no longer seemed as drunk as before, in the midst of so many others in far worse condition, the man with the pockmarked face and Guru, all in a hushed but intense discussion.

At the end of the hallway I made a left into a smaller passage, and on the other side of it I came to a closed door. It opened on to the master bedroom. Inside it was cold, institutionally clean and sparse. The furnishing was modest. The room stood out like a misfit, a forgotten nook, compared to the rest of the place. The most indulgent thing was the flat-screen TV mounted on one wall. Gazi's bedroom, I guessed, and the last place they'd go off to be alone.

Passing by the bar I saw Gowhar Wasim. He was staring into his empty glass as if reading the dregs, of which there were only melting pellets of ice. A lot of the party had thinned up to the roof, and some to the second floor, but not enough to drain this main part of it completely. People's energies were subdued with liquor and pot, and I suspected other substances too, which Gazi may not approve of, but I had no proof to substantiate or refute this.

I'd lingered too long. Gowhar came up and wrapped an arm around my shoulder. 'Leaving?' he said.

'Not yet. Just looking for someone.'

'You won't find them in this goddamn place,' he said absent-mindedly.

'I thought you had left?' I asked.

He held me in a long, searching stare, then said, 'No, just my wife.' I couldn't reconcile this version of him with the endlessly cocky one I'd met at Dhaka Club. That Gowhar did not come across as a pushover – certainly not one that would speak so casually about his wife leaving a party with another man. Tarek and Maisha must've made a covert exit – or maybe not. Maybe they walked right by Gowhar.

He put away his glass. 'Can I ask you something?'

'Sure you can,' I said.

'Do you pray?'

'You mean like five-times-a-day pray?' I asked.

'Sure, but not that formal. I mean like' – he positioned himself to face me – 'like really talk to God.'

'I can't say that I do,' I said.

'You do believe in God, right?'

'Well, I've gone back and forth. I don't know yet.'

'Prayer is only one way to talk to God. Five times, six times, a dozen times, doesn't matter. It's only one way. Not even the most

CHAPTER 12

effective. The kind of prayer I'm talking about is – it's like looking Him in the eyes, like I'm looking you in the eyes right now. You know. His eyes that are always seeing, always watching, always knowing. You can't do that in a five-minute prayer five times a day. That has to be a constant, lifelong practice. Devotion. The real kind.' He led me to a window. It was the same one Gazi had opened to smoke on the night of my first visit.

'Look up.' He was pointing at the night sky. 'You see?'

'What am I looking for?'

'God's Eyes. You have to look, man, really look.'

My brain was undergoing enough altering chemical states to believe in the power of Gowhar's suggestion.

'I just see the sky, I'm sorry,' I said.

Gowhar chuckled and patted my back. His breath was minty, his cologne a bit much.

'You see what you know to be the sky,' he said. 'I see God's Eyes. And He sees us all, everywhere, all the time, no matter where we go to seek cover. From now on, every time you look up, believe that the largest pair of eyes you've ever seen are looking down at you. Watchful, protective, but also taking note of every move you make.'

I felt bad for him. But his contemplation of the omniscience of the divine gave me an idea.

Out in the hallway, the guard at the door saluted me and then watched warily as I made my way over to the other units. Why I suspected they'd be behind one of the doors of those unoccupied apartments was as good a question as what God's eyes looked like to Gowhar Wasim, or why he didn't show the unease of someone whose wife had left the party with a man that wasn't her husband.

'Sir, no one's in them,' the guard's voice echoed. I ignored him and went from door to door. After finding them all locked, I went back to the first, this time knocking loudly as opposed to the discreet turns I'd given the knobs. The third door I knocked on stirred up movement on the other side. I knocked harder, feeling at my back the bristling discomfort of the guard.

'Disha?' I called. The hallway boomed my voice like a public announcement.

'It's open, Nisar,' came her answer, as naturally as if she'd been expecting me.

She was stretched out on a divan with her head on Gazi's lap, her hair covering his legs. Gazi had one hand on the top of her head, in the middle of stroking her hair, the other laced through her fingers.

'Hey, boss.'

'I told you he's that smart,' Disha said.

'How's the party?' said Gazi.

'It's fine. Happy birthday, by the way.'

'Thanks. Having a good time?'

'Sure.'

'Maisha's food is spectacular, isn't it?' he said.

'It's very good.'

'Jasmine is a darling, isn't she?' said Disha.

'She's a great girl,' Gazi added.

'Hey,' Disha said, turning her head. The only light in the room was the floor lamp next to the divan. It had a big shade with frills and the bulb was not powerful, the combination of the two casting just enough of a glow to keep them hidden. Disha's eyes still penetrated the murk, bright as searchlights. 'I wasn't ignoring your messages, OK? I just didn't answer them.'

'That's called ignoring his messages,' Gazi teased. 'Hey, boss, it was my fault. Really. I didn't let her step foot inside, and hijacked her here.'

'Well, if I don't see you again tonight then...' I couldn't finish the thought. More than that, I couldn't stand being there, facing them while their smugness looked back at me.

The door made a blasting, reverberating sound, and I hadn't slammed it. The guard eyed me as I walked back into the party.

Some time later the first of the guests started trickling out. It was almost 3 a.m. The band had stopped playing a while back, and the crowd had mellowed into conversations in small groups around the

CHAPTER 12

roof. Jasmine and Gowhar were on the ground next to the pool. Gowhar looked like he'd been crying. I sat down behind Jasmine.

'I'd do it myself, but I can't – I can't even think about it,' I picked up from Gowhar.

'You're a good guy,' Jasmine told him. 'Maisha is also good. You two just need to trust your hearts and forget what people say.'

Gowhar gave a hard, mucous-loosening sniff, then cleared his throat and spat on to the tarp covering the pool.

'I'm done,' he said. He pushed himself to his feet like an injured man and gave his clothes a few smoothing strokes. He didn't see me – or pretended not to – because he didn't include me in his goodbye.

'So did you find Disha?' Jasmine asked, turning a full circle.

'You could say that.'

'Don't worry. Those two never made sense.' She reached over and gave my arm a squeeze.

We sat there for another half hour or so. Sounds of drunk people talking, laughing and leaving were replaced by the catering crew and Gazi's servants cleaning up.

'Are you ready to go?' I said.

'You are, it seems,' said Jasmine.

'Unless we plan on sleeping on this roof, I'd much prefer my own bed.'

'What's your story, Nisar?' She leaned back on her hands and stretched out her legs, crossing them at the ankles.

I'd not been asked that question in those words before. I had asked a few women something like it, phrased differently, and received answers that were everything from evasive laughter to hours-long dissections of every relationship they'd stepped in and out of, generally bad, largely unsatisfying and in some cases deeply scarring.

'Nothing exciting,' I said.

'Doesn't have to be. Life isn't exciting.'

'It seems to be here in Dhaka.'

'Oh dear God, you poor thing if you think *this* is exciting.'

'It isn't?' I said. 'Look at all this. Living like this every weekend? It's exhausting, but how can it not be exciting?'

'I think you've seen why.'

'I don't know what you mean by that.'

'Yes, you do.'

'OK, well, maybe it's not the best setting for a healthy marriage, but I wouldn't know a healthy marriage if I was... married to it.' It was a terrible joke that rightfully did not get a laugh.

'Marriage isn't everything, is it?' Jasmine said.

'Not even remotely.'

She held out her hand.

I walked her to her car and when she reached for a hug, I didn't bring my hands out of my pockets fast enough, and she'd already reached around my neck, kissed my cheek and pulled away.

'Thank you,' I said.

'See you again, I hope,' she said. 'You're here for a while, right?'

'A little while.'

After her car pulled away, I stayed outside on my driveway, unable to go inside, despite how tired I was. I felt calmer, but not less angry at Gazi and Disha. I couldn't pick between them. They'd become one. Junaid–Disha. Disha–Junaid. Gazi–my cousin.

I heard voices at the guard's station and walked over. Almas and the nightwatchman were chatting and drinking steaming cups of tea.

'What are you doing here so early?' I asked Almas.

'Couldn't sleep at home,' he said. 'Wife's brother and sister are visiting, and they fight all the time. If they want to fight, they can do it in their own home, I told them. My wife got mad at me. So I left.'

'Do you have...?' I wanted one last hit.

'Go upstairs, I'll bring it up,' he said jumping to his feet. 'I'll make you fresh tea.'

Disha's voice stopped me in my tracks, and after it came Gazi's. I told Almas to go ahead.

CHAPTER 12

'Disha, just wait one minute,' Gazi said, as she strode away, sniffling and panting.

'Have the life you want, Junaid, just have it,' she cried. Then she was outside. Car doors opened and closed, the engine cranked and awoke and she drove away.

Gazi watched, helpless. He lingered briefly then went back inside.

13

I spent part of my Sunday morning trying to reach the managers at my father's banks. The sum of the experience was anger and yelling at underpaid clerks and leaving messages for management that would never reach them. Mr Ehsan didn't answer his phone, and I couldn't leave a message because his voicemail was full. Texts sat unread all day. I told my father that Dhaka was being efficient at Dhaka speed, and he found nothing funny about it. He knew too well how Dhaka worked and what got it and kept it working. I assured him I'd keep trying.

With the day before me, I planned an outing somewhere that was on the must-visit list, but not in the chronological order of events in the outline of my book. Keeping to such a strict timeline didn't seem practical, and it wouldn't be manageable either. Even if it were, it would be joyless.

Almas knew how to get there, and once again I said we didn't need to bother with Mr Ehsan, or the car.

I'd seen pictures of the monument built on the site where more than two hundred intellectuals were murdered in December 1971, just as the war was ending and the Pakistan Army scrambled desperately towards surrender. The disappeared men and women were found at the bottom of a brick kiln at Rayer Bazaar within days of victory, blindfolded, bound, pierced with bayonets and riddled with bullets.

CHAPTER 13

On the way there I couldn't help taking note of how easily Dhaka was coming back to me. It had been since my first walk by myself around my neighbourhood. I'd never visited Rayer Bazaar, and it took some asking around to get proper directions, which Almas handled expertly around the neighbourhood, but the way there was familiar as soon as we were en route. Once we reached the end of Manik Mia Avenue, going past the National Parliament, we went to Dhanmondi, where we took a right at Road 27, took the first left, then another left, and the monument came up on the right.

The moment I stood in front of the reflecting pool, the city and its clamour faded away. There was no need for sentimentality. All I had to do was listen: the silence was enough.

After making their rounds, the Pakistan Army had held their captives at a location in nearby Mirpur, a place that has come to be known as Jalladkhana – loosely translated as a place of execution. People were imprisoned there for weeks or months over the course of the nine-month-long war, and were tortured, raped and brought to their ends in the final hurricane of slaughter at the war's bloody end.

Three nights before they saw the Bengali and Indian forces entering Dhaka shouting 'Joi Bangla', my mother's parents' house received a late-night visit from a death squad. Dozens of men, not all of them uniformed soldiers, entered the house in a 'routine search' for contraband weapons and Bengali freedom fighters, who to the army were terrorists. My grandmother challenged the young captain to defile her house where her unmarried young daughters were living, and then doubled down and charged them to find guns and ammunition in the home of a retired civil servant who had dedicated his life to the service of his country and his wife, whose own life had been devoted to social work. 'Just the same as you,' my mother recalls my grandmother telling him. The captain in his turn assured the headstrong, belligerent woman mouthing off at him in front of subordinates that he was doing his duty and sometimes that led him to acts he didn't believe in as a man. 'You people tell us you're doing God's work,' my grandmother fired back. 'Tell me which God wants you to murder innocent people.' She had her Koran, and held it between the captain and herself. 'Show me where it says jihad is about killing innocents.' Then she addressed the Bengali mullah behind the captain. 'A religious elder like you, you should be ashamed, Maulana Shaheb. May God forgive the sins you commit for your sake.' My mother spoke sparingly about the months of the war, but her recollections were as clear and detailed as pictures.

Around the back of the wall that stood above the reflecting pool was fencing and a kind of empty lot. It was the most open space I'd seen in Dhaka. Out front, a group of boys had a game of cricket going. I watched them for a while, even catching one of the batsman's hits, and the bowler asked if I wanted to play. Years stood between me and the last time I saw a cricket bat up close, let alone held one. I took him up on his offer and the batsman passed me his bat. It was a full-sized bat, with a thick handle wrapped in rubber, and a heft that took me several missed balls to get used to, and still I was clumsy. In half an hour I made contact with the ball five times, and scored as many runs. The workout felt refreshing. I bought them soft drinks and snacks, and Almas watched with trepidation as I brought out a 500 taka note and handed it to the oldest boy, the bowler, and got his assurance that he would share it with the rest.

During the drive home I received a message from Tarek Bashir – there had been nothing yet from Disha – telling me that a journalist friend of his was interested in meeting me. I didn't respond. Five minutes later he informed me in another message that he'd passed my number along and I should hear from her soon. He gave me her number as well. I wrote back a one-word response: 'Thanks.'

I looked up the name Tarek had given and found that his friend *was* a journalist, and a widely published and respected one at that. She'd written a series of features on Dhaka and the prominent families of the city, from the Nawabs to the current new-money

CHAPTER 13

elites whose pedigree was creations of their wealth and its power. Her name was Asma Ferdous. Instead of waiting for her to call or text, I reached out to her.

These days her base was the office of the *Dhaka Gazette*, the paper she wrote for most regularly, and we set a meeting for the next day at a coffee shop in Dhanmondi.

I was watching TV after dinner when Almas brought word that Gazi was outside. I was not in the mood for him or his woes about my cousin. I stopped short of telling Almas to say I was already in bed. It really was the cheapest, most insulting excuse for turning away a guest, however unwanted, and I doubted Gazi would buy it. I went outside to meet him.

'Hi, boss.'

'Hi.'

A melancholy Devdas pining for Parvati, without the alcoholism.

'You must be mad,' he said.

'About what?' I asked.

'Not seeing me at the party.'

'It's not a big deal,' I said.

'I hope you had a nice time,' he said. 'You were in great company with Jasmine.'

'I did, thanks.'

'She's a sweetheart, isn't she?'

'Yes.' I was not in the mood for small talk but caved to curiosity.

'It's so nice out here,' he said, looking up. The weather had made a turn for the better in the evenings. The humidity had loosened its treacherous grip and the cool wafts of air made it easier to breathe. 'Has she said anything to you?'

'I haven't talked to her since the party.'

'This is it, boss – this is how it's always been.'

'I don't know what that means,' I lied. I kept to myself that I'd seen their tense parting. I didn't think telling him would matter or serve any purpose he'd find helpful.

'It means, boss, that we can't get it right, no matter what, and we can't stop once we start either.'

'Did something happen?' I asked.

'Something like that,' he said with a wistful edge.

'That's too bad. Did you have a fight?'

'It was a flashback. Years coming together in minutes.'

'I wasn't aware you two were trying to get back together.'

'Do you think we're crazy?'

'That's not for me to say.'

'Come on, boss. Don't give me that American answer. You're better than that. She's your family. So was I. You can judge, say, do whatever you want.'

'I really don't want to,' I said.

'I'm sorry, boss, I've offended you. I can tell. Now you see why I lost so many good friends from my corner because of…' He trailed off.

'Then why go through it again?'

'That is the definition of crazy, isn't it?'

'I guess, but this is real life, not a movie. You two are grown people with lives and careers. You can be perfectly happy just moving along.'

Gazi searched my face for signs of intelligence, or imbecility. 'You really believe that, boss? You've never had something with someone that tore you apart to lose?'

'Well, sure, but if something doesn't work out it doesn't work out.'

'And so you quit?'

'You two divorced. Isn't that quitting?'

'It's a piece of paper,' Gazi said, 'And it's people talking. It means nothing. I can have it overturned tomorrow.'

'Maybe check with Disha first,' I said in a mistimed attempt at levity.

But Gazi went along with it. He punched my shoulder playfully, brought out cigarettes, and offered me one. 'Look inside – there's something special just for you.'

CHAPTER 13

I took out the joint and pulled on it while he held the light.

'Thank you.'

'It doesn't take long for people of a certain kind to get to know each other, does it?'

'What kind is that?' I asked.

'The special kind – the kind that is real. That don't hide who they are or what they've done, and they're not ashamed of living their lives by the only standard that matters: their own.'

'I'm not so sure any of that applies to me, but I'll take the vote of confidence,' I said.

'I bet you break as many hearts as you win with that modesty,' Gazi said.

'No, not that I've kept note of.'

My phone fluttered in my pocket. Afraid it might be Disha, I was hesitant to check it in Gazi's presence.

He finished his cigarette, but there was more of the joint left, which I did not plan on finishing right then.

'I'm going to be out of town the next couple of days, boss,' Gazi said. 'Be my eyes and ears while I'm gone.'

Before I could say I had no idea what that entailed, Gazi bid me goodnight and walked away. The message I'd received was from Jasmine, asking me to join her for an art exhibition and a musical program on Saturday.

14

If Tarek Bashir was vying for my good side against Gazi, his strategy was certainly strange. I didn't know what to make of him, and even if I wanted to, I wasn't sure it was worth the time. This was a world to which I was too alien to ever fully fit in – a world I didn't understand. I wouldn't understand it if I lived in it for years, or all my life. It wasn't a matter of judgement or discomfort or thinking I was better than them or was living my life on a higher plane of morality or principle. It was the remove that no amount of time or effort would minimise – I could call it 'distance'. It's the same as when two people disconnect, go their own way, then years later think they'll pick up right where they left off, then be stunned into reality by time. It doesn't happen. Old times are just that and no more. They're no longer the living, breathing present, they're dead, not to be revived.

I took an Uber to Dhanmondi an hour before my meeting with Asma Ferdous, and had the driver drop me off near the Pilkhana military cantonment on Satmasjid Road. It was one more place of absolute importance I had to visit, although there was no chance of going inside. The former police barracks were the current headquarters of Border Guard Bangladesh, and it was one of the centres of fighting at the start of the war in March 1971 when it was the headquarters of the East Pakistan Rifles. I couldn't do more than stand outside and imagine what had

CHAPTER 14

happened that night in March. Being there was unlike anything I could reconstruct in my head to serve my purpose on the page. A crowded, noisy sidewalk with chicken throats being slit at roadside stalls on wheels and dropped into plastic buckets to thrash and flail to death, and freshly caught fish laid out on newspapers on the ground odorising the air that only the seasoned denizen could endure – these details up close were richer than reading a thousand first-hand accounts.

The day was hot but endurable. I walked part of the way on Satmasjid Road, up to the Abahani Playground, and from there took a rickshaw to Crimson Cup Coffee. It was the first rickshaw ride of my trip, and one of less than a handful of my life.

Asma Ferdous was thirty minutes late. I'd brought along my laptop, so I spent the time reading her work. There was one series she had done some years ago that gave me an idea of the kind of blood she went after. It was an exposé of a Bangladeshi family that had to flee the country to evade authorities after a scandal involving bribes to high-ranking political figures, at least one known killing of a businessman and the abduction of a movie star, whose glamour shot was one of the pictures attached to the story. I knew journalists in Chicago. I'd worked with a few on small-time local stories, more to learn about the city than journalism, and any one of them would have given their arm for a scoop like this, which was what made me sceptical. This story was too good to be true. But a fabrication of this proportion would be a bigger scandal, and could fold the paper, disgrace the writer and the publisher and end careers.

I recognised Asma Ferdous from her picture when she walked in. She was at least ten years older than the photo, and as many years older than Tarek Bashir, who I guessed was closer to my age, give or take a few.

'Hello,' she said, walking up to me without hesitation.
'Hi. I'm Nisar.'
'Asma. And please call me that. No seniority nonsense, OK?'
'OK.'

She was sweating and kept touching her face with her cotton shawl.

'What can I get you?' I asked.

'Iced coffee.'

While I waited for our order, she made calls and talked loudly. She'd been in the crosshairs of those with a lot of power in this town. She said in an interview to a Turkish journal that she'd received death threats for a year after the publication of the series on the scandal. The interview was widely circulated in Asia and Europe, but didn't cause the stir that later instances of journalists being jailed by the government would. Such an experience would toughen anyone's skin. It wouldn't matter what they said or how loud they said it if someone was going to come after them either way.

'This heat must be awful for you,' she said when I returned with our drinks.

'It would still be pretty bad in Chicago,' I said.

'Chicago, right. Tarek mentioned you live there. I was there many years ago. I did two intensive summer courses in journalism in the US. One was at Northwestern.'

'Medill,' I said. 'It's one of the best. That's what I hear.'

'Yes. The other was at Columbia. In New York.'

'You didn't want to get a degree in the US?' I asked.

'No. I was in political science at Dhaka University,' she said. 'I started in journalism in my first year. Everything I learned, I learned from doing. Getting a degree in something I was doing already seemed – I don't know – frivolous? Those summer courses were just right. Mostly, though, it was nice meeting the people. Americans put a lot of faith in their journalists.'

'Maybe once upon a time,' I said. 'It's the not the same any more being a journalist in the US.'

'The world seems to be falling apart with us standing in it,' she said.

'I looked up your work,' I told her. 'Really impressive.'

CHAPTER 14

'In this country, impressive doesn't mean much.'

'Can I ask, if you don't mind,' I brought my voice down to a whisper, 'about the...'

'Death threats?' Her face had the flattened roundness of a chapati, and when she smiled it expanded even more.

'Yes. But I understand if you don't want to get into it. I wouldn't.'

'That's really it. There were threats. Calls to my house. Messages at work. They went on for a while. I didn't back down. It was that or not living my life.'

'That's courage,' I said.

'No, it's not. It's being really stupid by most standards.'

'It's admirable.'

She took a second to appreciate the comment.

'So then,' she said. 'Are you and Tarek good friends?'

'I'll be honest, I don't know Tarek that well. He's a friend of my cousin's.'

'Disha Gazi – Chowdhury, I mean,' Asma said. 'She's your cousin?'

'Yes, first.'

'So then your father is...?'

I told her.

'Rajib Chowdhury is your uncle,' she said. 'Then you should know all there is to know about the Gazis.'

'I don't understand,' I said. 'All I know is that Junaid Gazi, my neighbour, has made an offer to buy us out. All our properties. He already owns part of our land in Banani.'

'Eternal Complex,' Asma said.

'Right,' I said. 'Other than that – and the fact that he was married to my cousin – I don't know anything about his family.'

'I knew your uncle,' Asma said. 'He was a good man, and he had a spotless reputation. And that's saying a lot for the moneyed class of this city. Which was why I was floored when I heard he went into some business venture with Mohammad Gazi. Lucky for your uncle it didn't last long, his end of it. He was a smart man. The moment he realised what sort of man he was getting into bed with, he walked out.'

'What kind of business?' I asked.

She gave it a moment's thought and said, 'Mobile-phone company, when it was still new in this country and there were only a few.'

'What happened?'

'Mohammad Gazi swindled the three other investors, vanished their money overnight to a place none of them could trace it, then blamed it on bureaucratic corruption. The problem was that these men spoke the same language. They knew about Gazi, what his family was like, and they nailed him. In fact, if it hadn't been for Rajib Chowdhury, Mohammad Gazi would have gone to prison for a long time.'

Her knowledge, I learned, was impressively thorough. She had enough history of the Gazis going back to Junaid Gazi's grandfather for a tell-all book. I guessed if I asked how she came about such comprehensive information that she would not reveal her sources.

Rahim Gazi – Gazi not being the original family name but the name of the merchant that had adopted Rahim as a boy and mentored him in his trade – inherited his adopted father's fortune upon his death under circumstances no one believed at the time were accidental. The deceased having no heirs made Rahim, just a boy scarcely in his twenties, a rich man overnight. He paid off the authorities, befriended public officials and married the daughter of a rich man as crooked as himself, and then when his father-in-law died (of natural causes, surrounded by his family at home), Rahim consolidated their wealth.

Junaid Gazi's father, Mohammad Gazi, was the third of eight children, and the one that emulated his father the most in his singular ruthlessness of character when it came to business. None of his siblings stood a chance at a fair share of the family wealth. Mohammad kept close to his father in life and, by the time of the old man's death, held powers of attorney over every last cent to

CHAPTER 14

the Gazi name. He wore his siblings down, gave them no more than he decided was theirs, which he measured by the time and devotion they'd shown their father in life. By those standards, it was Mohammad that came out on top.

Asma had had no luck reaching out to Rahim Gazi's other children – not even Mohammad, for that matter – and Junaid had given her the brush-off numerous times at social gatherings. This was when he and Disha were still married. I asked if Disha had been approachable.

'On a social level, yes,' Asma said. 'I didn't want to put her in a bad situation with other questions about her husband's family.'

I suspected even if she did, Disha would not have answers.

'I also think,' she went on, 'that it's unfair to judge Junaid by what his father and grandfather did.'

'I agree,' I said, 'but I would still like to know.'

'Oh, Junaid knows, I'm sure of that,' Asma said. 'He's too smart a guy to be that ignorant. I just mean he's an only son carrying the burden of an entire family. Not even the children of his uncles and aunts are there. It must be a heavy load.'

'If you don't mind my asking, what are you going to do with this information?' I asked.

'I just did something with it,' Asma said. Seeing my confusion she went on, softer this time, 'This kind of thing is the story of too many people in the upper echelons of Dhaka. It's not news, and it's nothing that people don't know a thousand and one times over. Telling you is the best use of it. Otherwise I would've forgotten it a long time ago. Sensationalism isn't journalism. That's one reason I didn't want to study in America – too much over there these days is cheap and insulting to the profession. Woodward and Bernstein are the last of the great ones – and Sydney Schanberg – what a loss. Any Tom Dick and Harry with an internet connection can call themselves a journalist these days. I don't want any part of it.'

'I appreciate your time,' I said. 'And your candour.'

'Tarek is very dear to me,' Asma said. 'He's a bit of a louse and a fool, but his family and I are close. He tries to do good, but can't keep his brain from dropping into his pants all the time.'

'He and my cousin are more than friends,' I blurted.

Asma grinned. 'That is the furthest thing from being news to anyone.'

'Can I ask what Tarek told you about me?'

'That you're a writer and a friend and I should meet you. I get the sense that you don't believe me.'

'It's not that,' I said.

'If you don't trust him, you don't trust him. You don't have to.'

'I can't get a sense of what he really thinks of me one way or another,' I said.

'Do you care what he thinks?'

'I guess not,' I said. 'My cousin being in the mix makes it even more confusing.'

'Disha Chowdhury is a lot more than just your cousin in this town.'

'I'm seeing that.'

Asma's sincerity was refreshing, her boldness reassuring. 'How are you finding Dhaka?' she asked.

'Alien.'

'Really? How long has it been since your last visit?'

'If you don't count the short ones for weddings, almost thirty,' I said.

'You don't seem really fazed by the changes.'

'I'm not. Nothing's really changed, has it? Just time that's passed. But that's a long distance, too, isn't it? Time?'

'It is – it very much is.'

Asma spent the rest of our meeting telling me about her family. She was estranged from most of her mother's side except a few cousins, and on her father's side she had once been close to her ten uncles, aunts and profusion of cousins until everyone started scattering, some within Bangladesh, others elsewhere.

CHAPTER 14

We walked out together and she got on a CNG scooter.

'Thank you again for meeting me,' I said. 'I guess I should thank Tarek.'

'You too,' she said. 'But we will see each other again.'

It was a lot to process. I had time on my ride back home, stuck as the Uber was in a massive jam just before the turn on to Manik Mia Avenue, and I tried to balance the Gazi I'd met with the one connected to the history Asma Ferdous had shared.

Later that night I received an email from United City Bank. Someone I'd spoken with had done their job and relayed the message to a superior, and up the ranks it had gone, my father's name leading to the managing director. It was his assistant that had sent me the email. Mr Sadek wanted to meet with me at my earliest convenience, with the option for the meeting to take place the next afternoon or evening, as it suited me. I accepted the earlier time. I didn't tell my father about it. His tutorial about what questions to ask and what information to cull would be exhausting, and then if what I reported back didn't meet his satisfaction, it would plunge us into an argument.

It was a little after 1 a.m. I opened my laptop and wrote out what amounted to a diary entry of the day. As I was halfway through re-reading it a message arrived from Disha. The gist of it was that she was bored, couldn't sleep and wished I was there to help her kill the time.

'Do you think I'm horrible?' she asked.

'No,' I replied.

'Tell me the truth – you're my little bother.'

The irony in the typo was too much. I *was* telling the truth. I wrote back: 'Sure you don't want to come over? My driver will be there in ten.'

If I were being honest with myself, I too would not be able to sleep any time soon.

'Fine, I'll be ready.'

Disha was in the living room, in her silk nightgown, halfway into a bottle of wine, with only a small table lamp casting a stained-glass glow in a corner. Flamenco music was playing faintly out of unseen speakers.

'My jaan,' she said throwing her arms around me. I'd brought along the last of the Blue Label, but didn't tell her who it was from.

'Are you sure you want to mix?' I said, when she asked me to pour her a glass.

'I can mix it all,' she said airily. It was as I was handing her the drink that I noticed she'd been crying.

'What's the matter?' I asked.

'Everything, jaan, every bloody thing.' She stretched tiredly on the sofa and propped her feet on the coffee table. 'Do you know how happy I am you're here? Not like here now, but here in Dhaka with me when I need you so much.'

'Why's that?' I said.

'Jaan, do I have to give my own brother a reason why I need him?'

'No,' I said.

'Because we are the only ones in this family that are only children,' Disha said. 'We get it. We get *each other*. I don't care that we spent half our lives apart. There's still a… a connection. That's why Junaid… he gets it too.'

We drank in silence for a while. I admired the lamp. She shrugged as if things like that fell into her lap all the time. The music, too, was good. Andrés Segovia, she said, whom she'd gotten into after a trip she and Gazi had taken to Spain.

'Are you OK with Tarek running around with Maisha?' I asked.

She was rolling her glass between her palms, and stopped – or rather, paused to give her reply. 'I don't care what they do.'

'But you and Tarek, you're still what? Together?'

'Sure. He was here earlier. Said you two are getting to know each other better.'

'He did, did he? Well, it's the least I could do for my big sister, right?'

CHAPTER 14

'Nisar, my jaan, I know how odd all this seems to you. Did you think Dhaka was ever different? It was exactly the same in our parents' time. They just lied about it better.'

'I'm not *that* naïve,' I said. 'You're right, though. I did buy into Dhaka's civility and all the clean and respectable family reputations for a long time. It's easy to maintain a story if no one challenges it.'

Disha raised her glass and pinched my cheek.

'When will you shave off this beard?' she said. 'I want to see those smooth baby cheeks.'

'They don't stay smooth too long,' I said. 'Remember? Tagore and Tolstoy?'

'No, but as long you're not becoming a mullah, I'm fine,' she said with a one-note laugh that was more a yap.

'Only the best kind,' I said, clinking her glass with mine.

'I know how idiotic I seem,' Disha said. 'What feels right doesn't always make sense, does it? And it doesn't even feel right at the right time, like when it's supposed to. Our marriage was a pile of shit most of the time, but the good was really good. We were just too damn young to appreciate it, to work for it.'

'Will you get married again?' I asked.

'God, who knows? No... I don't know. Who the hell will marry me in this city?'

'Should I state the obvious?' I said.

'Do you think we should?' she said, facing me.

'I'm the last person on earth to answer that question.'

'Why? You're a good guy. Everyone has bad experiences.'

'I don't plan on marriage again, so I'm not the best guy to talk about it,' I said.

'Never?' Disha said.

'Never any time soon – how about that?'

She touched my leg just above the knee, then laid her head on my shoulder. 'Can't we just do what feels good?' she said. 'Just because it feels good?'

'Sure.'

'There's too much talking always, not enough feeling.'

'You're right.'

'And whatever is felt is a lie. No wonder people are so unhappy all the time. My God, if you knew half the things about people in this town, you'd have enough material for books for ever.'

'Not my thing, really.'

'Good.' She hugged my arm.

'I haven't told you the full story of my marriage,' I said. One song ended and in the interval before the next, my voice filled the room. 'She didn't just go and stay with her parents and friends out of nowhere.'

'She wasn't good enough for you,' Disha said.

'Beside the point,' I said. 'I've cheated in every relationship I've had. Every single one. Going back to my first girlfriend in college. With her, there were times we'd go out and I'd drop her off at home then go meet up with someone else. We'd have sex in the afternoon, and later that night I was hooking up with another girl.'

'It was college,' said Disha. 'You were young. You're supposed to play, have fun.'

'College never ended for me. That was the problem. And then I turned around and got jealous of her and other girlfriends. Accused them of things I was doing.'

'Jaan, don't be hard on yourself.'

'I'm not,' I said. 'I thought getting married would change things. It wasn't Mom and Dad, it was me – I told them to find me someone.'

Disha raised her head and looked at me. 'Are you serious?'

'As a heart attack,' I said. 'She was a really nice, good person, too. Our marriage wasn't a week old when I was connecting with an ex and sleeping with her.' I hadn't told this to anyone before. Facing what I'd done, what I was, would have been the loss of a story I'd been telling myself.

'Was she horrible in bed or something?' said Disha.

'That's the point you take from the story?' I gave her a shove and she fell back laughing. 'You're biased. I get it. But I'm

CHAPTER 14

telling you, your little brother is a pig and has the receipts to show for it.'

'You two didn't even do it, did you?' Disha laughed on, clutching her stomach. Her gown had slipped back, showing her thighs and underwear. I looked away.

'You're sick, sister, sick in the head, and that is proof positive we're blood.'

We finished the bottle of wine, mostly in silence. I set a cushion on the floor and laid my head down. Disha kept dozing off and waking up, at times with a start as though she'd heard me say something or had something to say to me.

'Goodnight,' I said.

'My little brother, you're a good boy,' Disha mumbled.

No, dear sister, I'm not.

Seconds later she was snoring.

The music had stopped. I left the lamp on.

15

Mr Sadek came out of his office to greet me personally, asked if I wanted lunch, then insisted I have tea or coffee while we talked. 'How is your father?' he asked once we were settled in his uncomfortably air-conditioned office. 'He had some medical issues, he told me.'

'That's right,' I said, although I was unaware that the two of them had spoken. 'He's doing better.'

'Good, good,' he said thoughtfully. 'I wish I knew who you were sooner. Your father, your whole family, I've known for years. Your uncle Shahjahan and me, we were batchmates in university. He's in Canada now, I think?'

'I think so,' I said. 'I'm very bad about staying in touch with family.'

'We all are,' Mr Sadek said with a smile. 'I keep in touch with strangers more often than I do with my own children. So, Uncle, what do you do?'

'I was working in marketing in Chicago, but it's writing that I'm focusing on.'

'Writing – how nice. You studied it?'

'English.'

'Your uncle Shahjahan was in English. He's the youngest, no? Yes. I was in economics. Runs in the family. That's great. He was a brilliant student, your uncle.'

CHAPTER 15

There was a light knock on the door and his assistant brought in a folder. Mr Sadek placed his hands on it and leaned forward. 'I'm sure you're busy,' he said. 'Let's take care of important matters first, then we can talk more.'

'You're doing me a favour, Uncle, thank you.'

'No, it's fine. It's why I'm here.' He seemed to consider how to say what was on his mind, then asked, 'Do you have any idea why your father made Ehsan Kibria a co-signer on the accounts?'

'I didn't know he had,' I replied.

Mr Sadek nodded, gave the folder a look and slid it across the table.

'The amounts highlighted in yellow,' he pointed, 'were withdrawals Kibria made over a period of three months two years ago.'

They were in the lakhs, which I had trouble translating into dollars.

'In US dollars,' said Mr Sadek, 'it was a total of one hundred thousand.'

'Why?' I said.

'That's the question I had as well, but since he's a legal co-signer there was nothing I could say. Nothing anyone could say. We had to give him the override, and he walked out with the funds as he wished.'

'Did you tell my father?' I asked.

'I've been wanting to, Uncle,' he said with a sigh, sitting back. 'But then I thought it would be intrusive. After all, there's nothing illegal about it, and I know you still have property in the country. Which I understand is being sold?'

'Yes. That's why I'm here,' I said.

'The thing is, Kibria did the same thing at the other banks where your father has accounts. I don't know if he's an idiot or forgot where he is – this is Dhaka. We all know each other. My cousin is married to the President of the Bank of Asia, and I'm related to Bank of Dhaka's managing director. When they told me of similar activities at those places, I knew something was up.

But I couldn't do anything. And I didn't know how to bring it up with your father.'

I didn't either. He would erupt. His heart would launch another attempt at killing him.

I asked if he could help me get appointments to see the people at the other banks.

'Consider it done, Uncle. Call and say my name. Anything else you need, I'm here.'

He was ready to order lunch, but I thanked him and took my leave. I was too furious to eat. I left shaking so hard I could hardly type a message to Mr Ehsan.

'Call or text immediately or I will tell Dad things I've found out that he won't like.'

Within hours I'd spoken with the other banks. Mr Ehsan had made withdrawals, though in smaller amounts. He had also been more detailed in his communication with them, saying the withdrawals were being made at my father's specific instructions. Medical bills, household finances – he could go into details, or they could check with him themselves if they didn't believe Mr Chowdhury's most trusted employee and his lawyer. He knew no one would challenge him, even if they were suspicious, and it worked. Mr Ehsan Kibria, the consummate employee, trusted long-time confidante of a respected family, signed for the funds, and walked out with the money to do with as he pleased.

I hadn't heard back from him even an hour later when I got home, so I called but got through to his voicemail.

'Mr Ehsan,' I began, my voice trembling. 'I don't like doing this any more than you like hearing it, but I'm getting really tired of your behaviour. I don't want to upset Dad and I don't want him to get angry with you. If I don't hear from you by tomorrow, I'm going to tell Dad what's going on and about your withdrawals, and other things he should know. Then I'm going to find you.' The voicemail beeped and cut me off.

CHAPTER 15

I texted my mother and asked her to call me when my father was asleep. Half an hour later, I was fuming about Mr Ehsan to her and asking why people didn't intervene and wrench my father out of his blind belief in such a callous, unprofessional prick.

'Everyone tried,' said my mother. 'But you know your father.'

After hanging up with her, in a final surge of spite, I wrote to Mr Ehsan: 'I also need the car more regularly!!!' even though I didn't, and I was much happier riding Ubers and rickshaws and scooters.

'Received your messages,' Mr Ehsan's reply finally popped up on my screen. 'Stay calm. Things take time.'

'How much longer?'

'Soon.'

My hands cramped up from typing and then I erased what I'd written and set the phone, and Mr Ehsan, aside.

On Friday, Rais Kaka and I were back in Old Dhaka, at Dhakeshwari Mandir. The morning started out clear and sunny, the air clean and fresh, but a thunderstorm during our CNG ride left us wet. We considered turning back at the halfway point, until the sun peeked out of the clouds again, glinting with the mischief of testing the strength of our resolve. We had tea and parathas at a teashop. Rais Kaka worried the street food would make me sick. I did, too, but it was too good to pass up.

'Baba,' Rais Kaka said as we walked around the front of the temple. 'Something is bothering you – what is it?'

I told him.

'Your father needs to know,' he said. 'Before it's too late. I've seen what money does. It's not worth suffering for.'

'You haven't seen his condition,' I said. 'He's not that robust man you knew.' I showed him a picture on my phone, taken a month before, on his birthday, my father holding a knife over a cake, my mother standing behind him.

'Old age, Baba,' Rais Kaka said, 'doesn't leave a person with too much.'

'I'll tell him,' I said. 'I have to at some point. I'm just—'

'I know, Baba.'

I hadn't planned anything else for the day, but I didn't want to go home yet, so I asked Rais Kaka where else he thought I should visit. This was, after all, his end of town. He was a proud Old Dhaka boy.

'Let's go to Tara Masjid.'

For a non-believer, my day had taken quite the divine turn, and fifteen minutes later we were walking into the mosque. Rais Kaka used to come for his Eid prayers here instead of Baitul Mukarram. His father preferred Tara Masjid's intimacy, and it was closer to home. We went inside and spoke with the imam for a few minutes. Rais Kaka and I took selfies by the star-shaped fountain out front, and then we walked ten minutes down the lane along the mosque to where his childhood home used to be. 'They should have given you a free unit,' I said as we stood before a multistorey apartment building.

'My grandfather built that house with his own hands,' Rais Kaka said. 'Three generations of ours were born in it.'

Walking back to the main road to catch a CNG home, it stood on the tip of my tongue to tell him I wanted to give him money. I wouldn't bring up the dowry, wouldn't say anything other than that we, my parents and I, were giving him a gift. I thought about it during the ride home, almost mentioned it at the long traffic light at Farmgate, and after lunch insisted he stay for tea and take an Uber home as late as he wished.

'Is there anything you need, Kaka? Anything for the house? For your son, for yourself?'

'Baba, what more can I need than... no, Baba, don't trouble yourself. You're here to do an important job – concentrate on that.'

'Tell me, OK?' I said.

For a moment I thought he would. 'Do you remember that time, Baba, you almost jumped off the second-floor balcony?'

'I do,' I said.

'You wanted to fly,' he said laughing. 'You used to put a towel on your back like a wing, and that day, Allah, would have been a

CHAPTER 15

disaster if your grandmother didn't catch you. I had just come back from market. I was giving the things to your bua in the kitchen. I heard your grandmother scream so loud my heart jumped to my throat.'

'I was a brat,' I said.

He looked at the pictures on the walls of the living room. 'Baba, I know this is none of my business, and your father did what he had to do, but...' He hesitated, and I gave him a nod. 'Why did you all leave so suddenly? It never made sense to me.'

'I've often wondered the same thing myself,' I said.

'You had everything. I would have left wherever I was and gone on being here with you all.'

'A lot of people left in those years,' I said. 'Even before that.'

He looked down at his lap. My explanation had not been satisfactory.

'My parents talked about how bad things were getting in the country quite a lot,' I said. 'They said it got bad after Independence and just kept getting worse. I never understood what that meant. And they'd never explain if I asked. I guess they wanted safety. For me. So... you can blame it on me.'

'They did the right thing,' he said. 'For your safety and well-being.' My guess was that he didn't really believe this but accepted it as the closest thing he'd have to an explanation.

'I made my own trouble in good time,' I said.

'I will pray for you,' he said. 'That you cross these trials with His hand guiding you.'

He refused take any other transportation home than the bus that had brought him here.

16

The art gallery and the musical program were at two different venues, the first in Baridhara, the second walking distance from me on Kemal Ataturk Avenue. Jasmine picked me up at six, and at seven we were the first ones at the gallery. We were early enough that the set-up crew was still laying out chairs and the curator was doing her final checks on the exhibits and their display cards. The works were a combination of charcoal sketches and photos, black and white and colour, in homage to photographers and artists I didn't know. Jasmine knew the curator. From their conversation I gathered that this was a debut and that the artist/photographer was related to a victim of the worst terrorist attack in Bangladesh's modern history at a bakery in Gulshan a year before. In light of that, the small shrine next to the guest book in the lobby made sense.

I remember receiving a message from a Bangladeshi friend that lived in another state: 'Are you watching this? Fanatics attacked a bakery in Dhaka.' For the rest of the day I watched the events as they unfolded, on MSNBC. One American pundit after another in the studios of the hourly talk shows dissected Islamic extremism in Bangladesh. There was one Bangladeshi guest and a few Indian ones, none of whom added much, who rehashed what had already been said a hundred times. Correspondents in Bangladesh provided real-time updates, and their assessment of the situation, its causes, its ramifications, were far more reliable.

CHAPTER 16

Thirty minutes after the scheduled beginning of the exhibition and opening, the rest of the guests started making their entrances. In total, it was about fifty or sixty people, invites only. The first people I recognised were Maisha and Gowhar Wasim, and after saying hello to them I spent several minutes in anguish that Tarek and Disha were going to arrive on scene next – though Disha hadn't said anything about an art gallery opening – nor was it her kind of thing.

Just before we took our seats, Asma Ferdous walked out of the elevator. I asked Jasmine if she knew her.

'Of course,' she said. 'Asma Apa is a legend. Everyone knows her. She's the best. Just don't piss her off.'

'I'd rather piss myself,' I said, causing Jasmine to flinch. 'Never mind.'

Anika, the artist, made an emotional opening speech. The victim of the massacre was a second cousin, as far as I could make out. She recalled what a graceful, spirited young woman her cousin was, the plans she had for her life, and how she wanted to serve Bangladesh after she completed her studies in England. She was a year away from finishing law school, and she wanted to practice human rights law, with an emphasis on rural women. She then moved on to her work. Over the next hour she went piece by piece, reflecting and explaining how each artwork and photograph came to be over a period of ten years. There were anecdotes that meandered for too long, but it was worth the time to hear her speak frankly about sexual exploits and feel the squirming in seats around the room. She cursed, made crass comments, bad-mouthed exes, men and women, and, despite the long-winded digressions, brought the stories back quite beautifully to the work she was explaining. I could not have guessed she was only thirty years old.

Over post-show refreshments Anika mingled with the guests, most of whom were family or close friends, and Jasmine made her way to her after the initial crush of people. She introduced me. I congratulated her, offered my condolences. Up close she looked even younger. She was barely five feet tall, had an apple-shaped face, childlike hands, which she used constantly when she talked, and a high-pitched laugh, which she let loose liberally.

The lobby had become rather cramped and stuffy, so I made my way back to the gallery. The charcoal drawings were exceptional, and were clearly meant to be viewed up close.

'They're lovely, aren't they?' I turned to my left to see Maisha standing before one of the photos.

'Up close, yes,' I said.

'How are you?' she asked.

'Not bad, you?'

'It's been a busy week, but next week I'll have some downtime.'

'That's great,' I said. 'Your food is fantastic.'

She gave a wan smile.

In the lobby, Gowhar and Jasmine were talking to a group, which included Asma Ferdous and Anika. The crowd had thinned out significantly in just the last few minutes. Some people were taking one last walk through the gallery.

'Jasmine told me you're going to Katerina's recital?' said Maisha.

'I didn't know her name, but we're supposed to go to a musical thing from here,' I said.

'You'll love it,' she promised. I sensed she wanted to say more. The uncomfortable silence lasted a hundred years, and then she said, 'See you there.'

Asma Ferdous had caught Jasmine up on our meeting, and Jasmine congratulated me on my expeditious work of finding the right people to talk to in Dhaka. Without mentioning names, I said I had help. Asma Ferdous hadn't named names either.

'How's Disha?' Jasmine asked me in the car.

'She was very drunk the last time I saw her,' I said.

'When?'

'Last night.'

'Those two,' she said.

'Those two indeed.'

'I just... I don't get it, no matter how well I know it.'

CHAPTER 16

'Why bother?' I said. 'It's not your problem.'

'Sorry?'

'I mean, their drama is their problem. Sorry.'

'Is that why you're involved?'

'I'm involved by blood.'

'That's the biggest bitch, isn't it? Blood. Family. People we don't choose, don't even want to be connected to sometimes, that we have to give a shit about.'

'I believe that's the best definition of family I've heard in my life.'

'My God, such a cynic! Writers are supposed to be romantic people, aren't they?'

'Are they? I wouldn't know. I couldn't tell you what romantic means unless you mean the capital 'R' kind.'

'No, I've read those white guys and learned nothing from their Grecian Urns and Tintern Abbeys.'

'They do make it sound so… perfect and attainable, don't they?'

'No, just unrealistic.'

We came to a stop in traffic and she rolled down her window to give money to a very old woman, hunchbacked and blind, led by her hand on the shoulder of a filthy young girl with the most stunning hazel eyes.

Katerina Estis was as Maisha had said: really good. She sang Tagore songs in Bangla and in Russian, which she'd translated, even though Russian was rather clunky with its offerings to Tagore's lyrics.

After the performance, we went up to the tea room on the roof. Gowhar and Maisha joined us.

'Are you all going to Junaid's place?' Gowhar asked.

'Right,' said Jasmine. 'I almost forgot.'

'The long ride from here to New Year's Eve,' I said.

'What else?' said Gowhar. 'Dhaka life hasn't become obvious to you by now?'

'I don't know,' I said. 'I've never lived Dhaka life like this before.'

'Lucky you,' said Maisha.

'Or maybe I've been missing out,' I said.

'On what?' said Jasmine. 'Drinking like a bloody fish, weekend after weekend, till you're sick?'

'On company,' I said.

'The company of freeloaders,' said Maisha.

'Freeloaders?' said Gowhar. 'What does that make us?'

'No, we are his actual friends,' Maisha said. 'I've known Junaid a long time. So have you. Not everyone that finds their way to him these days has.'

'He's a grown man,' said Gowhar. 'He can decide who comes to his house.'

'It's the freeloaders I can't stand,' Maisha said.

'They're all freeloaders,' said Jasmine. 'Every last one. They drink, they leave, they come back and drink some more, and not one of them returns the courtesy, ever.'

'Junaid doesn't care,' said Gowhar. 'He loves the attention.'

'He doesn't,' Jasmine objected. 'I know you're his good friend, Gowhar, but this is something I know very well.'

'Maybe he did when they were married because he couldn't avoid it,' Gowhar remarked with an eye to me. 'Your cousin is the one that loves attention.'

I shrugged.

'Watch out,' Jasmine jokingly warned. 'Nisar is super protective of his family.'

Gowhar didn't seem to take the point.

'She did – she loved it,' he insisted.

'OK, let's let it go,' said Maisha.

'Let what go?' Gowhar snapped. 'A week didn't go by without their fighting being a national affair. You never saw how miserable Junaid got.' His voice went up and his eyes were large.

'Disha wasn't any better either,' Jasmine said.

'Did she get suicidal?'

'Come on, Gowhar. Don't exaggerate.'

'Did she?' Gowhar demanded.

CHAPTER 16

'Junaid didn't get suicidal,' Jasmine said.

'Why won't you believe me? Maisha knows it too.'

'Let's not talk about people that aren't here,' Maisha said.

'We're not lying about them,' said Gowhar. 'At least, I'm not. It must have been more than a hundred times I had to talk Junaid out of getting in his car and driving it into a wall. And you know what he'd say every time? Every time, the same exact words: "Why won't she love me as much as I love her?" Because your best friend was too busy creating drama and enjoying it.'

'You're being an asshole, Gowhar,' said Jasmine. 'Stop right now.'

'You see, man,' he said to me, 'tell the truth around here and you're told to shut up.'

'If we need a lesson in truth and morality, Gowhar, it won't be you we come to,' Jasmine said.

Maisha looked as though she wanted to disappear into her cushion. 'Can we please stop?' she implored. 'Please.'

The server brought our teas. We listened to his instructions about how long to let them steep for optimal taste and enjoyment. I'd forgotten the kind I'd ordered and the teabag didn't look appetising. I dropped it in the pot.

'You're quiet,' Gowhar said to me. 'You don't have an opinion?'

'I didn't have any contact with Disha for years,' I told him.

'Now you do,' he said. 'What do you think?'

'Not enough to have an opinion.' I tried to get across with my tone that I didn't appreciate the badgering.

'Really?' he persisted. 'Your own cousin and you have no opinion – not one?'

'Gowhar, back off,' Jasmine said.

Maisha was watching him like an embarrassment run amok.

'She's my cousin,' I said. 'But she's her own person.'

'If you'd been here, you'd see how she didn't leave anyone a choice with her crap.'

I granted him that, more willing to agree with him than I showed.

'What's so special about their marriage?' I asked. 'Or about them? Are they really that important?'

Gowhar's face filled with his reply, enlarging his eyes, but he didn't – wasn't able to – get it out, the rush of words choking him.

'Nothing,' he puffed.

'Being there is what friendship is about,' said Jasmine.

'Once in a while, sure,' Gowhar was quick to say. 'Not every goddamn night. And day.'

'Oh, stop, Gowhar,' Jasmine said. 'Just stop.'

'I'm sorry I said anything,' said Maisha.

'OK,' Gowhar conceded, holding his hands up. 'Excuse the rest of us for not being so morally upstanding. I'm not saying anything else.'

We might all have sensed the temperature get too high too fast and felt out of breath. Disha and Gazi sucked the oxygen of ten people, and they didn't need to be present to do it.

Maisha checked her tea and took a sip. The rest of us followed suit.

'Morality,' I said, abandoning mine. The tea was so bad it didn't have a taste, and even made the water bland. 'I have no idea what it is.'

Gowhar arched his eyebrows. 'You don't?'

'Not a clue,' I said. 'As in a definition.'

'You're a writer and you don't know what morality is?'

'Writing has nothing to do with it.'

'The moral thing is the *right* thing to do.'

'No, not always,' said Maisha, looking up from her tea. 'A lot of wrongs are done in the name of doing what's morally right.'

'Right,' I said.

'Laws are moral,' said Gowhar.

'No, they're not,' Jasmine almost shouted. 'Laws are the furthest things from morals.'

'Then what is moral for you, both of you?' Gowhar asked.

CHAPTER 16

'I'm saying laws are not examples of morality,' Jasmine clarified.

'So you want a society without laws?'

'In this country the law is the party in power, that's it. Remember the eighties – remember *martial* law? Was that moral?'

'What's moral, then? Democracy?'

'Oh, no way,' I said. 'If that was the case every country on earth would be a dictatorship.'

'Just like this one,' said Jasmine.

'You're crazy,' said Gowhar, although it was unclear who he was talking to. 'OK, what about God? Is religion moral?'

'No,' said Jasmine. She looked to me.

'I strayed from religion too long ago to have a say,' I said.

Gowhar pushed himself up into a sitting position. 'If Bangladesh is a dictatorship, so is India, and so is Pakistan.'

'Many Indians and Pakistanis would probably agree with that,' Jasmine said.

'What does that make America?' said Gowhar. 'You know, that shining example of morality in the world?'

'You're the one who lived there,' said Maisha. 'You tell us.'

'We have a bigger expert among us who still lives there,' Gowhar said.

Jasmine gave me a sideways glance, a smirk couched in it.

'I'm not an expert on anything,' I said, pushing my mug aside. 'I live in America – doesn't mean I get it. I don't. I just bitch about it a lot. It feels better than saying nothing.'

'What about the American Dream?' said Maisha.

'The hoax of the ages,' I said.

'You don't believe in it?' she asked.

'It doesn't exist.'

'Without ambition, of course not,' said Gowhar.

'I guess that's my problem,' I said. 'I'm devoid of ambition. America or Bangladesh, doesn't matter. I'm hopeless.'

Maisha gave a soft, polite laugh. Gowhar had shifted to a position that had him on his side on the pillows, propped up on his elbow. He peered at his wife as though she'd done something out of character.

'Bangladeshis haven't done bad for themselves there,' Jasmine pointed out.

'No, they haven't,' I said. 'Compared to most of them, I'm definitely a shiftless loser. I aspire to none of the markers of life they do.'

'Like what?' asked Gowhar.

'I'm sure you could guess,' I said, 'having seen it yourself. What gets me is that Bangladeshis over there think they're white. You should hear them talk about Black people and Mexicans – they sound worse than the most rabid racists. But think about the Bangladeshi obsession with fair skin – that explains it.'

'They're all like that?' Maisha asked, with an endearing touch of awe.

'In my experience,' I said.

'I've seen it,' said Jasmine. 'Not only is it about skin colour, they think they're actually superior to Black and Hispanic people – like, as human beings.'

'My mother used to say when people forget where they come from, they forget who they are,' Maisha said.

Gowhar threw his wife a disapproving glance.

'Your mother would have been the worst of them,' he told her. 'She thinks poverty is a defect of character.'

'That's not true,' Maisha protested, but weakly.

'I didn't come from enough money or a good-enough family background,' Gowhar said, addressing me.

'She wanted us to be comfortable,' Maisha said.

'That's what you call it? She wanted us to be comfortable, and so put me down at every chance she got?'

'She gave us more than your parents ever did.'

'The competition, yes, of course. You want to know something more Bangladeshi than anything? That's it: competition. And in my mother-in-law's case, don't you dare cross the Empress of Bangladesh.'

'It's Mother of Humanity,' Jasmine said, 'and you have the wrong woman.'

CHAPTER 16

Maisha, despite being caught between hurt and insult, couldn't help laughing. Gowhar was not close to being amused. It took me a moment to remember where I'd seen the phrase Jasmine had used: on posters near the National Parliament, with the Prime Minister shaking hands with world leaders and kissing babies. She was the Mother of Humanity.

'See you,' Gowhar said, standing up. 'Maisha?'

'Don't worry about her,' Jasmine told him.

'See this, Nisar? My wife has all the protection of everyone; me, I'm the asshole.'

A long silence fell over us in his wake. I heard Katerina's voice at one of the tables behind me, and excused myself to go and offer her my compliments. Jasmine and Maisha, I sensed, could use the privacy.

The tables were at floor level, with people sitting around them on pillows of different sizes. Katerina was the centre of her table, surrounded mostly by Bangladeshis and one white European couple. I apologised for the interruption. Katerina gave me a warm, pretty smile, and we shook hands. She asked if I'd like to join them, and before I could protest she had made a space for me next to her.

'You know Jas and Maisha?' she asked.

'Just met them recently,' I said.

'They're lovely,' she said.

The European woman said something in German that made Katerina nod vigorously and smile. She spoke fluent German back and the woman agreed with her enthusiastically. Then the man said something. I nodded along with the English parts of the conversation around the table, tried to pay attention, made an attempt to understand – maybe pick something up I could latch on to – but after another minute or so I thanked Katerina, paid her my compliments again and went back to Jasmine and Maisha.

I busied myself with my phone, sending check-in texts to my parents, and one to Disha. They talked quietly a little longer, and then we all left.

17

There was a line of cars outside the entrance to Eternal Complex. Disha's was not among them.

'Are you going to ditch us now?' Jasmine asked me.

'I wasn't planning on a late night,' I said.

'Come up for one drink,' she said.

The first person I saw was Guru. With his customary smile, which was never accompanied with language, he held up a pinched forefinger and thumb to his mouth. I told him maybe in a few minutes, once I had had a drink and settled in.

The gathering was small. Everyone was in the living room – among them the crew-cut woman, her pockmarked male friend and the very drunk third of their party, who was very sober at the moment, and in an animated conversation with Majid Uddin, Tarek Bashir's plump-cheeked friend I'd met at Dhaka Club. He looked up when we entered, but didn't recognise me – not even when our eyes met and I gave him a nod – and went back to his conversation.

Maisha left us to go to the roof. I followed Jasmine to the kitchen, where the drinks were laid out on the counter, and a servant stood by – not as a server, but to make sure nothing the guests needed was overlooked. We took our drinks to the dining table.

'I feel like I'm in Dracula's castle when I come here,' I said. 'The mysterious host is never around, and when we do see him, he comes out of nowhere like a...'

CHAPTER 17

'Vampire?' she offered.

'Yes, but then I see Gazi's face, and it doesn't really fit.'

'Why do you call him by his last name?' she asked.

'I just started that way, and it stuck.' I'd also not once addressed him by his name when we talked, and neither, because of his nickname for me, had he used mine.

'So, if you're Jonathan Harker, am I Mina or Lucy?' Jasmine asked.

'Mina was Harker's wife... so...'

'It doesn't have to be exactly the same,' she said. 'More like an adaptation.'

'Either way, you don't want to get stuck married to me!' I meant it as a joke, but even to my ears it didn't sound funny.

'Are we feeling self-pitying, poor thing?' She patted my hand and leaned in. 'It's unbecoming.'

'My humour is what's unbecoming,' I said. 'And unnecessary.'

'I don't like too much funny,' she said.

'Who's up on the roof?' I asked.

'Tarek,' she said.

'You already knew that?'

'Sure. Maisha got a text from him.'

'What about my cousin? I texted her, but hasn't replied. It's become a habit with her. And what the hell is the deal with this love–hate thing between Tarek and Gazi? Are they friends, foes, rivals... what? I'm totally confused.'

'All of the above?' The start of a grin played on her face. 'Once they were good friends. And Tarek has been in love with Disha since Disha and Junaid first got together. Be glad you didn't see *that* version of the mess. Tarek married his wife to get back at Disha. I mean, she didn't care, and whatever message he was trying to send went nowhere. All he ended up with was a bad marriage, an affair and children he can't get away from.'

'And they're still married,' I said.

'I don't know, and I kept my nose out of it,' Jasmine said. 'But I do know that he loves his kids.'

My phone tickled my leg.

'Where are you?' a message from Disha asked. 'Come to the roof.'

'It appears,' I told Jasmine, 'my dear cousin is also above us.'

'I thought it was you,' I heard over my shoulder. I'd not made the turn in full, and Majid was standing over me. He pumped my hand heartily, and gave Jasmine a bow. 'Sorry I didn't say hello earlier. My memory took a moment to catch up. I knew the face – couldn't place from where.'

'It's fine. I forget names and faces all the time,' I said.

'I wanted to say sorry about the other day.' His jovial face grew dim, and he looked self-effacingly from me to Jasmine.

'Don't worry about it,' I told him. 'I have a lot to learn.'

'About Dhaka, no? I know someone you should meet. She's a journalist. Best in the country. Her name is Asma Ferdous. She knows Tarek. I'm surprised he hasn't told you.'

'I've met her,' I said. 'In fact, he did introduce us.'

'Oh good, good,' Majid's smile returned. 'Asma and my family go right back. She's famous in our circle for being the outspoken one – tells you why she isn't married.' He giggled.

'We saw her earlier this evening,' I said.

'Where?'

I looked to Jasmine for the name of the gallery.

'Yes, of course, she's a lover of art. She was writing a book, I think, about Bangladeshi artists. Maybe was a long time ago. I don't know.'

He stood there as if he had more to say – so much more that he didn't know where to begin – until laughter from the living room startled him. A woman's voice called his name. It was the drunk-sober woman. Majid's cheeks turned red, then expanded with a fleshy smile.

'The missus calls,' he said. 'And I must go. Newly-weds, after all.'

'I had no idea,' I said.

'Why would you? It's no problem. Come meet her.'

But she saved me a trip by making her way to us. She didn't recognise or remember me. She was also not as sober as before.

CHAPTER 17

'Hello darling,' he said, suddenly sounding very English, very formal – more so than the bow he'd given Jasmine. 'This is Nisar from America. This is Ruba.'

'Hi. You have to listen to this joke,' Ruba said to Majid, and pulled him away.

'Must be a hell of a good joke,' Jasmine said.

'You don't know them?' I said.

'Seen her here and around town.' In a whisper she added, 'Exhibits one and two of hangers-on-slash-freeloaders.'

'Them? I thought he was Tarek and Gowhar's good buddy?'

'That may be, but it doesn't change the fact. What do you think the age difference is? Best guess.'

'I don't know – I'd rather not gossip.'

'No need to be goody-goody with me.'

'I'm not. I…'

'Too good for Dhaka-style gossip?' she asked.

She'd missed all my attempts at jokes, and now I wasn't sure how to take her seeming playfulness.

'No, I swear,' I said. 'I'm not trying to be better than Dhaka or whatever.'

'Fifteen is my guess, on the low end. I won't be harsh. I'll say it was for love. Some of it.'

'And the rest?' I asked.

'You don't want to gossip now, do you, Nisar Chowdhury?' She clutched imaginary pearls.

I covered my mouth with a hand. 'Never me.'

'Dhaka is full of odd couples,' she said.

On the roof they were sitting on the ground by the fire pit and pool. The tarp had been removed, but the pool was still unfilled. The four of them didn't make for the ideal band of brothers and sisters, and no doubt tension hung over them like a cloud. But something unnatural in the air was keeping the façade and the decorum intact. Gazi was on the wall bench, quietly staring into the pool. Tarek was smoking, also not speaking.

Disha and Maisha may or may not have been talking, their voices were so low.

'Hi, boss,' Gazi said, breaking out of his trance-like state.

'Hey,' Disha said, jumping to her feet and rushing to give me a hug, and then Jasmine.

'Where have you two been?'

'Just downstairs,' Jasmine said. She, too, seemed to give the gathering a sceptical sweep.

'Have a seat,' Disha said, as if there were chairs to pull up to a table. I refreshed Jasmine's and my drink from the fridge by the bench in the wall and sat down next to Disha. 'You guys went to the opening, Maisha told me? I think Anika is super talented. She's a little fireball and a darling.'

'That new place in Baridhara?' said Tarek.

'Yes,' Jasmine answered, as if to shut him up.

Tarek momentarily went somewhere distant. Everyone except me seemed to have an inkling where he'd gone.

'I got the invite,' he said, sounding more like hadn't, and he begrudged being excluded. 'I can't stand galleries. That new art crap doesn't make sense to me.'

'Anika's work is more than just "new art",' Jasmine said. 'And it's not crap. It wasn't all about her work, either. She was paying tribute.'

The shrine in the lobby, the young woman's photo on the easel, came back to me more clearly than when I was standing in front of it. I wanted to say something, anything, but everything that came to mind felt hollow. I'd watched an event that had changed the city for ever from thousands of miles away while everyone around me lived through it.

'My God,' Disha said. 'Feels like it just happened.'

'It did just happen,' said Tarek, nearly cutting her off. 'It's only been a year – a little more.'

Disha lowered her eyes and head, as if she'd been shamed. The way she looked was how I'd feel if I'd spoken about that day.

'I was supposed to be there just an hour earlier,' said Maisha.

CHAPTER 17

'I got stuck in a bad traffic jam, and thank God my cousin who was supposed to meet me also cancelled. I don't know why. She got a headache or something. It's just God's will that saved us.'

'A traffic jam and a headache saved you,' said Tarek, again barrelling over Maisha when she was barely finished speaking.

Maisha moved over towards Disha, but kept her eyes on Tarek, apology and pity mingled in them.

'Where was God for the rest of them?' Tarek went on. 'Don't give me that God crap. Fuck him. Or her. God was the reason those people did what they did. A lot of good God is doing for this country, isn't he? Turning it into a den of fanatics.'

Maisha uttered a 'sorry', too quiet for Tarek to have heard.

Tarek had lost someone at the bakery siege, but not as a victim of the gunmen. A son of relatives on his wife's side was one of the gunmen, shot dead when paratroopers stormed the café.

'There was too much flaunting, too much showing, too much of everything,' Disha said, a remark even I found callous.

'What the hell does that mean?' Tarek demanded.

'I mean, this is still Bangladesh. It's not India, it's not even Pakistan. And suddenly everyone is going around in tight-fitting trousers and sleeveless shirts in broad daylight. This country won't be ready for that kind of lifestyle for another hundred years.'

'In a hundred years it will be an underwater annex of Saudi Arabia,' Tarek said. He watched Disha for a moment, then walked around to the other side of the pool.

'Underwater?' said Jasmine.

'The country is sinking every day. Didn't you notice? You're in Chittagong all the time – how could you miss it? And now there's the Rohingya coming in from Myanmar. Whatever will be left of the country will be underwater, and it won't take a hundred years. Give it twenty. Ten.'

'You're mixing two different problems: religious, fanatic mullahs and global warming,' Jasmine said. 'I'm having a hard time following the logic.'

'The logic is, it's all connected,' said Tarek. He fell quiet, as if he too was trying to unite the disparate ends of his argument, making the shift out of grief and anger to anger and logic. 'People are leaving their villages because their homes are already underwater, and the city has nothing to offer them – it can't. There's too many of them. The system is overloaded. But there's plenty of fanaticism to go around. Put the two together and you have the perfect terrorist cocktail.'

Their wounds were raw. It had happened in Dhaka, in their city, and that was enough for collective mourning, and outrage and protectiveness.

It was like America believing it was collectively attacked on 9/11, and the attack deserved nothing short of visiting collective retribution on the perpetrator – Islam – which required huge doses of patriotism that could be shown only through vengeful love of country.

We sat in tired silence, not even looking in each other's direction, until Gazi pushed to his feet and approached me.

'Boss, a minute?' He walked me towards the other side of the roof. 'I know we haven't had time to talk about business, but I wanted to say how grateful I am to you. Boss? Are you OK?'

'I'm fine – tired,' I said. 'And you don't have to thank me for anything. I just wish you and Disha would figure out… Forget it.'

'You can be honest with me, boss. I wish you would be.'

'You don't get tired of whatever you're doing? I'm tired of it and I just got here.'

'And who else is tired? All of them back there? Have they told you stories? Filled your head with more fiction?'

'I'm trying to understand where I fit in,' I said. 'You and me, we have a business relationship. I never wanted to get involved in your personal lives.'

'Boss, you fit in as Disha's family. You wouldn't get involved if it wasn't personal to you.' He lit a cigarette. 'You're lucky, boss,' he said, leaning on the balustrade.

'Why is that?' I asked.

CHAPTER 17

'You get to leave. This place.'

'What if I said you were the lucky one because you get to stay?' I said. 'Be home.'

He turned to me with a lonely smile and turned away again. 'I'd say,' he began, then paused. 'I'd say that we both have the same thing figured out. We both have no home.'

I was facing the others. Disha held her palms up as if to ask what was going on. I gave her a wink.

'There was something I wanted to ask you, about the property,' I said.

'Sure, anything.' He dropped his cigarette and made a full turn.

Disha looked our way again.

'Our house, can we leave it out?' I asked.

'Leave it out, as in you don't want to sell it?'

'Right.'

'I get it, boss. It's your home. Your family home. Its value can't be matched with money. I know the feeling.'

'I appreciate it.'

'I had a feeling you, or maybe Uncle, would consider that, and that's why I left the house out the first time. Or are you planning on living here, maybe staying more?'

'No, nothing like that.'

'I'm sure Disha would love to have family she can trust close to her. Looks like Jasmine would too.' He flashed me a wry little grin.

'I can't leave Chicago,' I said. 'Not right now. So, will you think about it?'

'Of course, boss. Anything for you.'

'Thanks.'

Tarek was getting ready to leave when we got back to them, and he was trying to get across to Disha that he would like her to go with him. Disha and Jasmine were comforting Maisha, who seemed to have broken down over something. Gazi left us and went downstairs.

'You need to go home, Maisha,' Tarek said. 'To Gowhar.'

'Tarek, get lost,' Jasmine told him. 'She doesn't need a lecture from you.'

'Disha, can we just go?' said Tarek. Disha didn't answer. He gave me a look which I evaded, going over and sitting on the bench.

The weather seemed to be taking a turn. It had only rained once all day, and the air was cooler. The difference wasn't much, but given how humid the nights had been, even half a degree came as a relief.

After another failed attempt at having his way, Tarek stomped off.

The party downstairs had tripled in size. I hadn't heard a single car on the street or voice come up to the building, but hordes of people were crammed in, wall to wall, drinks in hand, talking loudly over each other and the music, which was coming from a DJ booth that looked as though it had risen out of the dining room floor. I saw new faces. Majid and Ruba were gone, but Crew Cut and Pockmarked Face were there, as was Guru – and seeing him I remembered his offer. He was glad to keep his word. I insisted on paying him, but he produced his smile of magnanimity. I put the joint in my pocket for later.

Soon people were dancing. Disha, Jasmine and Maisha came down, Maisha's face puffy from crying, and Jasmine walked her down to Jasmine's car. Disha and I got drinks.

'This will sound crass, but I don't know how else to say it,' I said. 'Who is it going to be tonight?'

'Wow, that was low.'

'True. Forget it. Sorry.'

'No, you have a right to ask, to speak your mind,' she said.

'Nope, you're the one in the right. It was low and rude.'

'Tarek doesn't know what he wants,' she said.

'I never caught that from him – funny,' I said.

Disha poked me in the rib.

'I've done some dumb shit in my life,' I said, 'but he has me beaten. Not one, but two married women.'

'I'm not married.' Disha faced the dance floor, her back to me.

CHAPTER 17

'You were, and he was in love with you then,' I whispered in her ear.

She turned around. 'Don't believe everything you hear,' she said. 'Not even from Jasmine. She's a sweet girl, but she talks about things she doesn't know anything about. Did she ever say anything about her own life?'

'I didn't pry,' I said.

'But you were fine believing things she said about me?'

'I didn't ask, she just said it.'

'You're smarter than just taking whatever shit people tell you, Nisar. You're my brother.'

'And you keep giving me too much credit.'

The music seemed to have grown louder, as had the dancing guests. It must be nice to not have to worry about neighbours, I thought. Gazi would conceivably never have that concern.

'Can I ask you,' I said, 'since you've given me permission as your brother? What the fuck are you doing? What do you call it?'

'Nisar,' Disha brought her face so close her nose grazed mine. To anyone else we'd look on the verge of kissing. 'For an American, you sure are very old fashioned.' She grabbed fistfuls of my bearded cheeks and kissed them both. I took her wrists and lowered her arms to her sides.

'I don't know what that means, but OK, fair enough. Stop molesting me – in public, at least.'

She gave me a shove.

Jasmine walked in. I waved her over. She got a drink and joined us and the three of us took over an empty couch.

'Is Maisha OK?' Disha asked Jasmine.

'No,' Jasmine said. 'Poor thing, those two assholes treat her like a dirty rag.'

'She lets them,' Disha said.

'She's a grown woman.'

'She needs to throw both of them *out* like dirty rags.'

We watched the dancing for a while. I'd reached a point where I saw the couples grinding and twirling and laughing and wondered if they were the actual pair that went together or if they'd swapped with another. Disha's head was on my shoulder, and Jasmine's hand lay between her and me on the other side, touching my thigh. We were both working hard not to turn to each other.

'I love this song,' Disha said, shooting to her feet. 'Come, let's all dance.' She grabbed our hands and pulled us up.

'You're freakishly strong,' I said.

She and Jasmine threw off their shoes and started moving to the music as if they'd been dancing all along. I hovered at the edges. They were yelling at me to join. The music made no sense. It was a lot of bass with screeching prehistoric birds tearing through it at painfully long intervals. I was alone in my dislike of it. People were actually singing along to whatever was passing for lyrics if I really paid attention, which I couldn't. I held up my hands and walked back to the living room.

Minutes later, the chandeliers were dimmed, and roving dance club lights took over from the DJ booth. It was just one box-like contraption next to the booth, about four feet tall, but it was enough. I was no longer in Gazi's living room looking at his dining room, but in a bad flashback of a sweaty, armpit-smelling industrial hell some idiot or other I'd known in the past had dragged me to. I could see Disha and Jasmine. Their heads were close together like they were talking, and they stayed that way through the interminable blitzkrieg they both apparently loved and into the next one, which was noticeably worse – even to an ear as unschooled as mine – than the first mayhem of sound.

And then they were apart. Their heads sprang back, as if they'd come unstuck. Jasmine stormed off the dance floor, grabbed her shoes and walked out. Disha watched her, then watched me go after her. The confused look I threw her on the way out was lost to the lighting.

I caught up with Jasmine just as she was about to walk out of the Eternal Complex gate.

'Hey, wait!' I called.

CHAPTER 17

She kept going.

'Did something happen? What did Disha say?' I asked.

She was rigid to the point of shaking. She was upset, and she wouldn't look at me.

'Jasmine, you can tell me. Please?'

'I don't hide who I am.' She drew out the words, perfecting each syllable.

'That's great,' I said. 'I like that about you.'

'You don't have to say that. You barely know me.'

'Doesn't take long to see an honest person clearly.'

'I want to go home,' she said.

'Not like this, please.'

'How else should I leave?'

'Come inside? Five minutes?'

'I'm tired, Nisar. I don't think your cousin would appreciate it.'

'It's my house,' I said.

I lit the joint and passed it to her. She declined, and I apologised for not having anything to drink. She'd had enough alcohol, too, she said.

'I don't know how you guys do it,' I said, pulling a chair to a window. 'Every weekend, going at that rate, I'd be a zombie for a month after *one*.' Even though I'd been to two.

Jasmine was laying on the sofa with her arm over her eyes. She *was* tired. I felt bad for forcing her to stay, but I would have felt worse if she'd left upset. At the very least, I wanted to know, I needed to know, what Disha had said to her. If it had something to do with me, I wanted to clear it up.

'This Guru guy, what's his deal?' I asked, taking a long hit of Guru's generous gift.

Jasmine removed her arm and raised her head.

'Seriously,' I said. 'Does he talk? He homed in on me that first night at the party where I met you, and it's like he's my weed whisperer ever since. The moment he sees me, he smiles and offers me joints. Never takes money for them either.'

'Guru is probably one of the best people around,' Jasmine said, sitting up. 'And he's smart as hell. He used to teach economics at a university in England. Came back to take care of his mother and the family business when his father died, about ten, twelve years ago.'

'One would never know,' I said. 'Doesn't surprise me either.'

'There's a lot of talk in this town about what *isn't* true, but try telling the truth, and you're blacklisted. Guru's been around long enough to know silence works best.'

'Not when someone's talking shit about me. I won't stay silent.'

'You don't live here – you don't have to deal with the consequences.'

'The stock answer to everything Dhaka for an outsider,' I said tetchily.

'Outsider? You consider yourself an outsider?'

'I am an outsider,' I said. 'Even sitting here in this house I'm an outsider.'

'I'm sorry you feel that way,' Jasmine said.

'I'm over it,' I said.

'You have no idea how blessed you are, Nisar.'

'You all sound like you're serving some sentence here at times. Leave, if you hate it so much.'

'Hate what? I told you, I love Dhaka. And being quiet when it matters is a way of keeping the peace.'

'What's another way? Bottling it up? Letting people get away with it,' I said.

Jasmine walked over to me, took my wrist and raised the joint in my fingers to her lips. 'Guru's weed is also the best in the fucking country,' she said, exhaling a slow stream. 'Which way is the bathroom?'

I checked my phone while she was gone. Nothing from Disha. The party was still going on, but there was no way of knowing if Disha was still up there. I started writing a message to her, but erased it.

'This is a huge house,' Jasmine's voice came from the hallway before her. 'Don't you get lost or scared?' Her hair was up in a bun

CHAPTER 17

on top of her head, held there by some mystifying force of craft and physics.

'The second, yes,' I said, 'but not even that any more. Now there's sound and light day and night – not like it used to be when I was a child. There was nothing past the cemetery. We heard jackals at night. Remember that?'

'I didn't grow up in Dhaka. But Chittagong was even more undeveloped. So you were afraid of the dark?'

'Still am,' I said, my brain awash in Guru's best.

Jasmine sat down on the floor in front of me and clamped her arms around her knees. 'I don't want to cause trouble in the family,' she said.

'Too late for that,' I said.

'I'm serious. Disha adores you, I can tell. I was like that with my younger sister. I miss her.'

'I mean it's too late for you to make trouble. My family invented trouble.'

'All families invented trouble.'

'Will you please tell me what happened up there tonight?' I asked.

She observed me for a moment, as if reading my face for assurance she could trust me.

'She told me to mind my own business,' she said, finally. 'And not fill your head with nonsense. That's the long and the short of it.'

'Thank you,' I said. 'I'll let her know in my own way that I don't need babysitting.'

There was more, but I didn't know how else to get her to talk.

'There's nothing else to do here,' Jasmine said.

'I know, I'm sorry. After Gazi's lifestyle, my house is a mosque.'

'No,' she said seriously. 'You wondered how people do this every weekend. There's nothing else to do. You work during the week, and Thursday evening, as soon as the weekend starts, you start drinking.'

'That sounds completely depressing,' I said. 'No offence, but it does. And pathetic.'

'The truth is the truth,' she said with a chuckle. 'Unless you have the means to fly off to Bangkok for the weekend. People in the tri-state area call it Gulshan 3.'

'Tri-state?'

'Banani, Gulshan, both 1 and 2 as a single unit, and Baridhara. Then, for the bored and discerning weekender, Bangkok.'

I was laughing halfway through the list, the high making it a stupid, giggly cackle.

'How often do you go?' I asked. 'To Bangkok, I mean. Or, sorry, Gulshan 3.'

'Never. Can't stand it. All you see are the same Dhaka faces. What's the point? And since I'm not a freak shopper like some of the women that go on raiding trips like the world is ending, I might as well save the money.'

I wouldn't think a person of her wealth would talk of money as a factor. She was, in fact, the first person in Dhaka to have mentioned money in this way, suggesting that it wasn't available by the bushels, hanging from trees like year-round ripened fruit ready for the picking. In many ways, I felt more kinship with her than Disha – speaking of whom, there'd been a text from her, which I'd ignored, a misspelled mash-up saying, essentially, she was sorry and she'd leave me alone and away from her drama. I didn't answer it.

Jasmine waited for me to finish reading.

'You know, there was a time, for about three or four months, when I almost made the decision to stay back in the US.'

'Good for you that you didn't.'

She made a soft, breathy sound, distractedly, then stood up and walked back to the sofa. She was doing her best to keep her face averted. Her bun had come partially undone.

'Sorry,' she said.

'Why?'

'Nothing.'

'You can tell me,' I said.

CHAPTER 17

'It's nothing.'

I was interrupted by a car starting outside, and then another. A woman laughed, someone sneezed and a man spoke angrily to his driver – probably for falling asleep and not bringing the car around fast enough. I closed the window and went back to the sofa.

'Whatever you tell me, it stays right here,' I told her.

'I know,' she said. 'Doesn't sound like you're crazy about living in the States either.'

'There's an understatement,' I said.

'It's really not a bad country if it gets its act together.'

'And that is not happening in my lifetime,' I said.

'I find it so hard to believe you're such a cynic, Nisar.'

'I promise you, I'm not. I'm probably the most gullible person you'll come across on many things, most things, that I should be cynical or sceptical about.'

'Now imagine living in Bangladesh, year after year, with a dictator in power. No matter who it is, they're all the same. At least the army had the good sense to call it what it was and go all the way.'

'I vaguely remember the night of the coup,' I said. 'We were asleep and then the phone rang. My parents were suddenly out of bed, and next thing I knew there were people coming to the house – relatives, but still, it was the middle of the night.'

'We were visiting Chittagong,' Jasmine said. 'It was about the same there. My parents' friends in the army, in government, were panicked that they were going to be killed or jailed. I found it hypocritical when I thought about it later, because my parents talked about those same friends putting other people in jail while they were in power.'

Two more cars gunned their engines – one an SUV, taking its partying owners homeward, the other sounded like it held a couple in a whispered argument.

'I've been reading about these police killings of drug dealers,' I said. 'None of them really sounds like a kingpin.'

'Kingpin?' Jasmine said. 'They're little better than the frat-boy dealers in America. Probably better humans than them, but kingpins they're not.'

'And Dhaka police is no better than American police,' I said. 'They're scumbags everywhere.'

She sniffled, and brought out a tissue from her purse. She'd been crying the whole time.

'I was with this amazing man my last year in Houston,' she said. She blew her nose and dried her eyes and held the balled-up tissue in her fists. 'He wanted to get married. I wasn't sure – not about marrying him, but about my parents.'

'He wasn't Bangladeshi?' I said.

'American. Black. You can imagine the heart attack that would hit a Bangladeshi parent. I hadn't told mine yet. He, Esau, didn't pressure me, but he knew. I didn't post pictures on social media of us, didn't send any to my parents. In a way, I was worse than them.' Her voice broke as she continued. 'We had this huge argument one night. It was late. We'd been out. I did most of the arguing. He was a really calm, gentle person. I told him to back off and give me space. He did. The last time I saw him was the night of that argument. He left my apartment, and he... was pulled over for speeding. They saw the phone in his hand. He'd just called me and left a message saying he was sorry and he loved me. They didn't even *ask* him for his licence or insurance or anything.' She paused, took several breaths to fight the tears. They weren't enough. She excused herself to go use the bathroom. On the way she broke down, and I could hear her sobbing through the walls.

There was room enough in the house for her to have an entire floor to herself, but she wouldn't spend the night. I understood, and didn't insist. I could stay up talking to her all night, but instead walked her out to her car. She was going to Chittagong for two days and promised to be in touch when she got back.

CHAPTER 17

I went to the roof. I saw her car turn right on Road 23, then looked at Gazi's window. The lights were on. The music had stopped, and the last of the guests had left. The windows were open, and as I turned to go back downstairs, I heard laughter. I recognised the loudness of it, as if a caged flock of wild birds had been set free. I was tired. I could just as well have imagined it.

18

I wrestled with the decision to send the statements to my father. One part of my brain wanted to wring Mr Ehsan's neck for putting me in the position he had; another wished my father was there to take care of his guy his way; yet another didn't care what happened to him. I believed I'd given him a fair amount of time. The circumstances about his family and of his financial strains because of them smacked of embellishment. The kind favour-seekers dished out as prologue to claiming dubious blood ties, coming from the same village or serving our family for fifty generations. Mr Ehsan even had a leg-up where that was concerned.

I called my parents, gave my father a heads up that what he was about to see was not going to please him, then emailed the scanned copies of the statements with him on the phone.

I'd forgotten to ask my mother to stay calm, not to pour fuel on fire.

'He's stealing, oh my God,' she cried. 'He's outright stealing.' I heard nothing from my father.

'Did you go the banks?' he finally asked.

'I went to all three, but only met Mr Sadek at United City Bank.'

'He has to be reported to the police,' my mother demanded. 'Did you call the police, Nisar?'

'No, Mom, I didn't. I'm not getting tangled up with the police here. Dad, have you tried calling him?'

CHAPTER 18

'No,' my father replied. His tone was subdued. I feared an outburst. I hadn't considered shock. 'If he needed money, he could have just told me, asked for it.'

'You are going to press charges?' my mother wanted to know. 'Nisar, call the police. This man has to be arrested.'

'Will you let me deal with this?' my father said to her.

'Dad, the thing is, he was mixed up in some betting scandal,' I said. 'I haven't been able to find out if this is to do with settling those debts; but what he said to me was that he'd used the money to keep attention off our properties.'

'What attention?' my mother asked.

'What do you think?' said my father. 'Ehsan didn't do anything I wouldn't have authorised him to do. Thank God he did.'

The tale of the Anti-Corruption Commission questioning Mr Ehsan crossed my mind, but I held it back. It wouldn't make much of a difference. My father's faith in him was unshakeable – maybe because he had an idea of what it took to survive in a country like Bangladesh, because he knew that in Mr Ehsan's place he would not have been above doing the same, that compulsion often stood in opposition to will and survival trumped all else.

'Let me know when you talk to him,' he said.

My mother took the phone to another room. 'He'll divorce me and disown you before he says one bad word about that crook,' she fumed.

'Mom, it's fine. Don't stress out, and don't stress him out even more.'

My father used to pay people off all the time. It was an open secret in Dhaka. He wasn't alone. Jasmine's story about her parents' friends in the army was not an anomaly, it was rather the norm. Wealth worked in strange ways in Bangladesh. The few that had it had to spend it, giving it to entities that would scrutinise it to keep scrutiny of it at bay. That friend of my father's at the wedding was an example of how to do it wrong: he'd stashed most of his wealth out of the country, which was not unusual, but he'd overlooked pushing enough into the right hands at home. Added to that was his rotten luck of being rich during one regime and therefore paying that regime allegiance and bearing the brunt of the regime's fall, and, along with it, being targeted as illegitimate and illegal. I came home from school one day to be introduced to the mayor of Dhaka North, who was sitting in our living room with my father. On the coffee table before them was a bottle of Chivas Regal, along with two glasses, an ice bucket and two stacks of money. I shook the mayor's hand, answered his questions about school, then went off to get changed for tennis at Dhaka Club.

I left Mr Ehsan a message telling him of my conversation with my father.

I walked to Gourmet Bazaar. I'd been writing more or less steadily, but what it was amounting to was unclear. They were mostly notes, anecdotal jottings, about my trip so far. I'd strayed completely from the outline. It was proving difficult to stick to an outline I'd made years ago with no physical connection to Dhaka – being here was a timely wake-up call about the book itself, what I thought it was going to be, what it needed to be and how, no matter which way I tried to direct it, it was going to become the story *it* wanted to be.

An hour or so into working I received an email from Asma Ferdous. It was an invitation to a book launch that evening. An editor of the country's leading English paper had co-authored a book with a Dutch architect on the architectural history of contemporary Dhaka. She thought it would be a good place for me to meet people that could help with my book – or, barring that, at the very least I could get an expensive meal and top-shelf liquor for free. On a more serious note, she said she was impressed that a Bangladeshi writer who no longer lived in Dhaka was so interested in writing about the city. Her encouraging words were heartening and terrifying. If she saw the paltry mess I had so far, she'd reconsider.

She ended the message saying there was something she wanted to discuss with me, and she'd rather do it in person.

CHAPTER 18

I thought of asking Jasmine to go with me. I hadn't seen her since the other night. When I texted her, she wrote back that she was still in Chittagong and would be gone for a few more days. I hadn't mentioned the book launch, and said I was checking in to see how she was. 'You're very sweet,' was her reply. 'See you soon?'

'I look forward to it,' I sent back.

The book launch started at eight, with cocktails at seven. I stepped out of the elevator five minutes after seven and breathed a sigh of relief at not being the first one there. The lobby area outside the auditorium had the buffet set up on one side and the bar on the other. The food would turn out to be as Asma Ferdous promised: rich, with expensive offerings from steak and lobster to Thai, Chinese, sushi and Bangladeshi fare. The open bar was already flowing. Asma Ferdous was talking to a man about half her height – she was about five foot nine – with a shiny bald head, glasses and a Karl Marx beard. Asma looked like a teacher towering over her student and lecturing him about why what he was being punished for was wrong. She saw me making my way over and waved.

'Glad you made it,' she said. 'This is Masood Bhuiyan. Masood, this is Nisar Chowdhury. Masood is editor of the *Dhaka Gazette*.' We shook hands.

The editor asked what I wanted to drink and ordered a red wine. I was bringing out my wallet to leave a tip for the bartender when both of them asked what I was doing and started laughing when I told them.

'Still getting used to Dhaka?' Asma said. 'Don't worry.'

'Where in the US are you based?' Masood asked.

'Chicago.'

'I was there for about a month right after finishing my bachelor's at Pepperdine,' he said, 'staying with family and friends. If I had my pick of cities in the States to live, Chicago would be in the top five.'

'He's too much of a Dhaka boy to live anywhere else,' said Asma.

'Speaking of which,' said Masood, 'you're writing a book about Dhaka, I hear?'

'I'm trying,' I said, sounding more dispirited than in the throes of challenging work.

'That's great,' said Masood. 'Would you be interested in writing for the *Gazette*?'

'Yes,' said Asma, 'since you're here, since you're writing about Dhaka, and Masood is always on the lookout for good talent, even if it is for a short time, so why not?'

'We're in Panthapath,' said Masood. 'Here's my card. Let me know a good time and I'll send a car. We can talk and go from there. I'm really interested in knowing more about your book.'

I thanked him, and he excused himself to go talk to someone that had called his name.

'Was that what you wanted to talk to me about?' I asked Asma.

'Yes and no,' she said. 'I think you'll bring some good, fresh energy to the *Gazette*. The young people working there are phenomenal, but they could also use the help of some new blood. Especially,' she stage-whispered, 'with the English. Masood doesn't have that kind of time, and I don't have the patience.' After a pause she said, 'There was something else, but I can't tell you here. I would have told you the other day, but I wasn't sure. I had to think about it. Maybe you know it already. Maybe not. I believe you should.'

I was intrigued, and a little wary.

'Let's meet tomorrow?' she said. 'I'm going to be in this area around four. We can go next door to Cuppa Joe. That way you'll have time to think about Masood's offer too.'

'I really appreciate the offer,' I said, 'but I'm going to decline.'

'Sleep on it,' Asma said.

'Thank you, but I can't.'

She nodded. 'I can understand and respect loyalty to family,' she said.

I didn't know what to make of the remark. 'The decision is entirely mine,' I told her. 'My hands are too full for the short time I'm here. I'm sure I'm passing up a good opportunity, and again, I'm grateful for your faith in my work.'

CHAPTER 18

'Give me tomorrow?' she asked.

I said I would. The pull of curiosity was too strong.

The high point of the event was the editor of the Bangladesh *Star Tribune* lambasting the destruction of the city's ecosystem to build what he called 'more unnecessary monuments to men's egos'. In comparison, the two authors were wet leaves, and like sodden refuse they sat mooning at the audience while one of the guest speakers rained on their parade. The editor did, in his concluding remarks, thank the authors for their valuable contribution. He looked for more ways for Dhaka and Bangladesh to celebrate architectural achievements, which was part of Dhaka's legacy, and be responsible actors in the global community. Throughout his speech, the quips, jabs and coded swipes flew unrestrained, arcing over the audience, splattering invisibly on every ear, no matter if they wanted to hear them or not, embarrassing everyone in the room but him.

I ran into Mr Sadek at the bar. 'Good to see you, young man,' he said, giving my back a hearty clap and shaking my hand.

'It's good to see you, too, Uncle. I just wanted to thank you again for your help. I've sent the statements to my father. It couldn't have happened without your assistance.'

'Any time, any time,' he said. 'Next time you talk to him, your father, tell him to get that fellow off the account. I'll make sure it's done. You can become a co-signer instead. I'm sure your father will be much happier.'

He had more confidence in my father's ability to let go of Mr Ehsan than I did, but his idea was one that I'd been mulling as well. Maybe it was time to gang up with my mother on my father and make him see the light.

Drink in hand, I turned to head back into the auditorium just as the elevator dinged and out walked Disha with Tarek Bashir at her side. I waited a moment – just long enough for her to see me – and smiled. Her eyes grew larger than their natural shape in recognition, and I nodded that I was going inside.

Disha made no haste in getting to my table. She knew everyone, and people flocked to her like fans at a red-carpet event. She was a star making her way from the limo to her grand entrance, showered in adoration and love.

And it was Tarek Bashir that manifested that love, trailing a step behind her, stuck on her with his eyes, mind and heart, the picture of a longing that would remain unfulfilled. It was hard not to feel sorry for the guy. The mechanics of their relationship, if it could be called that, that I'd seen the first night were nothing. Tarek was never in charge. Disha was too far out of his reach, his capacities and his endurance. I had no interest in knowing if they had a sex life, but my guess was they didn't – or if they did, it was fleeting. While Disha was surrounded by friends and acquaintances and colleagues, Tarek stepped out of her shadow and came over to our table. I gave him my chair and made my way to my cousin. She was in a burnt-orange Dhakai sari, her hair in a classically Bengali bun at the back of her head, large loop earrings and very little make up. When she called me 'jaan' and reached her arms out of the throngs to hug me, my body went warm, and I felt the heat from my cheeks in my eyes. Plenty of eyes were on me, too – until now a nobody, in the arms of one of Dhaka' highest profile and talked-about women.

Disha took my hand in a way that shot eyebrows through hairlines. She wanted a drink.

'You're getting around nicely,' she told me while we waited at the bar. 'Why should I be surprised? Good looking, smart. You know there are women here that would tear you apart like that,' she snapped her fingers.

'Is that good?' I said.

'For them, yes; for you, absolutely not.' She looked so good it took me back to those times in our childhood when she could crush my heart and drive my hormones batty in the same second.

'Look who's talking,' I said. 'Queen of Dhaka. I feel like I'm hogging you, keeping you away from the adoring masses.'

CHAPTER 18

'You're the one wasting yourself, hanging around with your old cousin,' said Disha. 'Besides, don't be fooled by the congeniality you see here. Everyone here puts up with each other because they have to. Professionally, and through that, personally.'

'Sounds godawful,' I said.

'It is,' Disha said, 'and it's the price to pay for a way of life that some people can't get around.'

'You mean like being born into it?' I asked.

'Yes.' Disha's expression clouded with seriousness. 'You know how that feels. If you lived here, you'd eat, sleep, breathe, work and die with it. It's the only way.' She waved to someone with the smile of a beauty pageant contestant, only hers was genuine.

'And you like it?' I asked.

'I like what I do and how I do it,' she said.

'And heading a PR firm was what you wanted to do?'

'What I wanted to do was have something of my own. Not go to my grave building someone else's castle. Abbu didn't want me to spend my life at it. He told me that, and he told me I was free to pursue whatever I wanted any time. What's more satisfying than pursuing what's already your own?'

I couldn't argue. It added a certain perspective to the task I was in Dhaka to accomplish.

'So, my jaan, don't you want to mingle?' said Disha, tilting her face and smirking. 'It all depends on what you like.'

'What're you talking about?' I said.

'You asked me if it was good that you'd be picked off like ripe fruit. I'm telling you it's up to you. Speaking of which, is Jasmine here?'

'No,' I said. 'She's in Chittagong. Speaking of which, please let me fight my own battles.'

She handed me my wine and clinked her glass to it.

'She's too broken for you,' she said, almost flippantly. 'I'm just looking out for my little brother.'

'Your little brother is a grown-ass man. Thank you, big sister, but I can manage.'

Thinking we were leaving the bar for our table I started towards the auditorium, only to feel Disha's hand hold me back by my arm.

'Were you going to tell me that you were coming here?'

'I didn't know till this morning I was. Don't look at me like that – it's the truth. Why would I lie to you?'

'You had all day to tell me.'

'You're not going to split hairs over that, are you?'

'I absolutely am. I have to know where my little brother is at all times.'

'Good luck with that.' I had a view of our table through the open doors of the auditorium – a straight shot, in fact – and saw Tarek Bashir staring at us. 'Let's go, before your boyfriend thinks we're having incestuous relations.'

'He's not my boyfriend,' Disha snapped.

'OK, well, your date then. At least tonight. OK, OK. Tarek. How's that?'

She threw him a look. It broke his stare. He started saying something to Masood Bhuiyan, who held up a hand to tell him to wait while he finished with the person he was talking to.

'I'd be careful with that Asma Ferdous character,' Disha said.

'Why is that? She's a journalist. A pretty damn good one.'

'I'm sure that's what she wants you to believe. She tried to ruin my life and Junaid's life for years.'

Out of respect for the openness Asma had shown me, I didn't tell Disha what I'd learned about my uncle, Disha's father, and Mohammad Gazi.

'Don't worry,' I said. 'I won't reveal any deep, dark Chowdhury family secrets. They're all for me to expose when the time is right.'

'Everybody knows all there is to know, my jaan. No secrets here.' Despite the casual sarcasm, she'd spoken a glaring truth. We were on our way back to the auditorium when Disha stopped and turned to the elevator, which had just delivered Gowhar and Maisha Wasim.

Disha and Tarek had taken a table with the Wasims, a gathering that I was happy to stay clear of. Maisha was in good spirits, as far

CHAPTER 18

as I could tell, while Gowhar looked gloomy, making me wonder if he was having one of his 'God's Eyes' moments, and he was bookended by Tarek in his brooding mood. Disha and Maisha were chatting away.

Gowhar noticed me and waved. He shot to his feet, all smiles, just as quickly as he'd been sunken, and came over. 'I wanted to apologise,' he said. 'For the other night.'

'Don't worry about it,' I said.

'You want a drink? I'm going up to the bar.'

'No, thanks, I'm good. I'm going to leave soon.'

'Come have a cigarette with me before you go.'

Seeing me leave the room with Gowhar, Disha held up her hands asking where I was going. I gestured I'd be right back. Maisha threw Gowhar a suspicious look, which he didn't see. Tarek turned to her for the first time since they'd sat down. It was as if Gowhar was doing them the courtesy of leaving the room so they could finally talk to each other.

'Did you think any more about what I said?' Gowhar asked when we came out of the hotel. 'About God's Eyes?'

'I can't say I have,' I said, trying hard to keep a straight face. God's Eyes. I had a literal image of eyes wearing horn-rimmed spectacles staring down from the sky. A billboard along an American highway portending the End of Days while those eyes watched and judged.

Gowhar shrugged somewhere between disappointment and indifference. If there were these eyes of God watching from somewhere, up or down, they'd missed the staggering gap in lifestyle between the kind of people that could go to places like the Westin and the ones that loitered just outside its doors in destitution, from the rickshaw-pullers to the beggars, with an ash-heap of nothing in between.

'You're thinking about it, though, I can tell,' he said.

'How's that?'

'You're a thoughtful guy. I see how you look at people, how you watch them, how you're affected by them. That's what makes the difference. That you're affected. Others, they look and then they look away.'

A boy and a girl of about ten and eleven with filthy hair and ragged clothes begged us for money. Gowhar yelled at them, then scolded the doorman for allowing hotel guests to be accosted so easily. The doorman shooed the kids. But I'd made eye contact, the minutest move for my wallet, which had arrested their hopes.

'They get spoiled that way,' said Gowhar, as the boy and girl ran off with the money in their hands.

'It's no big deal,' I said.

'You give money to bums in America?' he asked.

'Sometimes,' I replied.

'You ever ask them if they'll use it for food or drugs?'

'Not really. I used to, but only because others made it sound like I had to. I couldn't care less. Drugs are the least of that country's problems.'

My pocket was having seizures from Disha's texts. 'Where did you go?' 'You ok?' 'What's he saying to you?'

I didn't write back.

'How's it going with Junaid?' Gowhar asked. He'd finished one cigarette and lit another. 'He's not a bad guy, is he?'

'Not that I've seen,' I said.

'That's all that matters. That and what God's eyes see. Everyone else can go to hell.'

'You believe in heaven and hell?'

Gowhar patted my back like a child's, and didn't answer. 'You're too smart a guy for me to debate,' he said.

'No, I'm not. It was a legitimate question.'

'If there's a hell, it's right here – we're standing in it. Heaven is the way *out* of it.'

Of the many times that I'd had conversations touching religion or walked away from one after getting nowhere with a zealot, or the zealot hitting a wall with me, this was the most concise and brilliant conclusion I'd heard.

CHAPTER 18

'I don't go in for the man-made brainwashing bullshit,' Gowhar went on. 'I look at what people do. Their actions. How they live. Me included. I live a shit life. I know it, my wife knows it, my parents, my in-laws, my employees, my servants, everyone knows it.'

'What's a shit life? I mean, what defines it?'

'Acceptance that it *is* shit. Each one is different.' He took a last drag and crushed the cigarette with his heel. 'Tarek and me, Junaid, we were all the best of friends. Then we were colleagues. Ventures to make money we talked about when we were young. We thought our friendships would make those relationships strong, we'd be like the musketeers, rule Dhaka, rule Bangladesh, do good, make money and spread it, give it away. Lots of dreams, and not enough actions to hold them up. What did we do instead? Backstab each other, cheat each other, then put our marriages on the line, too.'

'No offence,' I said. 'But no one I've met has a marriage that looks... healthy.'

'See? That's what I mean,' he said, with a glint of appreciation in his eyes. 'You're damn smart. More than you realise.'

'I'm sorry,' I said. 'That was rude.'

'No,' he said. 'But then, what does healthy look like?'

I didn't take the question seriously, but he'd asked it with a composed expression.

'I have no idea,' I said. 'I'm the last person to know.'

A car pulled up, and out of it climbed Majid Uddin and Ruba.

'Always late, you two, always,' said Gowhar.

'And still we won't miss a thing,' Ruba quipped. She could be drunk, or perhaps not – it was hard to tell. Her eyes had a permanent glazed slowness about them. She blinked in slow motion, especially when she moved from person to person, which enhanced the appearance of being drunk or high. Majid shook my hand, and Ruba, having forgotten that we'd met, introduced herself again.

'You don't remember Nisar?' Majid said to her. 'From Junaid's? He's his neighbour, the man Junaid bought the land from.'

'Oh,' was all Ruba said.

'See you both inside?' said Majid.

'Unfortunately,' Gowhar muttered. Majid gave him a sideways glance.

'Theirs looks like a healthy marriage,' I said, after they'd walked inside.

'Love at first sight,' said Gowhar. He was not joking. 'Tells you something about how we judge what we see before knowing the truth, right?'

'I try not to,' I said. 'Judge, that is.'

'Everyone judges, my friend, everyone. I judged you; you judged me when we met. It's what people do. It's human.'

'What's the news on your Porsche?' I asked.

He beamed, like a new parent that had been waiting for just this question to bring out the pictures.

'Very soon, not long now, and then we'll all go and look at it up close.'

The book launch was over by ten. I didn't see any indication that Asma had passed on my decision to Masood, which was confirmed when he said on his way out that he looked forward to working with me.

'You got a job?' said Disha.

'Don't believe everything you hear,' I said.

'Seriously, Nisar, you can do much better. I can introduce you to a hundred people tomorrow.'

'I'll keep that in mind.'

'What are they paying you?' said Disha.

'For God's sake, will you stop?'

'I'm only looking out—'

'Well, look elsewhere,' I snapped.

'Negotiate hard. That organisation, that whole bloody empire, can afford whatever sum you want.'

'Everyone is the head of an empire,' I said.

'Why is that surprising?' asked Disha.

'I guess it shouldn't be,' I said.

CHAPTER 18

Stragglers crowded the bar, drinking and being obnoxious. Majid Uddin was the only one among us not drinking alcohol. Ruba had done a championship job of catching up with and exceeding us. There was an iciness between her and Disha, which they navigated by not speaking to each other. Ruba and Maisha got along well enough. Tarek and Majid talked at length for a while, just the two of them, and Gowhar found people he knew among the obnoxious bar crowd. I was grateful he didn't ask me to join them.

'Don't get mixed up, jaan,' Disha said, out of the blue.

'Mixed up?' I said.

'I know these people, you don't.'

'OK, Mom, what else should your little cub know?'

'Just trying to protect you.'

'Thank you, and now stop. Really.'

Disha never talked about her mother. Her parents hadn't been married long. Her mother left her father a few weeks after her third birthday, which ruined birthdays for her for several years, and she refused to celebrate hers or attend parties for others'. By the end of that year her mother had remarried. My uncle thought it was important for Disha to have a relationship with her mother when she was young, but Disha's mother had disappeared. She changed her name, first and last, and kept herself unlisted in her new home away from Bangladesh. I picked up these pieces from conversations I overheard between my parents and their relatives and friends over the years, paying them little more mind than I did any family matters. Disha said nothing about her mother to me when we met in Chicago, and I hadn't had the presence of mind to bring her up based on what I'd unintentionally heard. Perhaps because of the absence of a mother in her life, Disha's own maternal instincts were overdeveloped – it was as good a layperson's guess as any. That was why she was such a compelling presence for us male cousins. She was a figure of authority without being an adult. She was one of us, only better. She knew what went on in our dirty little brains and she didn't mind what hid there. I never talked about her in any other way with my male counterparts than as our cousin. We boys had an idea we might kick each other's asses or hold each other in disgust, or both, if we confessed our unclean desires for own flesh and blood. I'd gone the route of simplifying my feelings down to a crush. It was the most innocuous option.

The mothering routine, however, lost its charm fast, if charm was even the word for it.

'Don't be so cruel, jaan, it's only love.'

'I can think of a few other ways you could show love,' I said.

'That would be your way, not mine.'

'Then let's try respect,' I said.

'Love and respect go hand in hand,' said Disha.

'Not always,' I said.

She touched my face. 'You're way too young to be so—'

'I'm not too young to be anything.'

Tarek joined us. He was ready to leave.

'You go ahead,' Disha told him. 'Nisar and I have things to talk about.'

'Like what?' Tarek wanted to know.

'Like family stuff, Tarek,' she snapped.

He looked me up and down as if for the first time. I gave him a shrug. Disha wanted to be with Gazi, and she was using me to get rid of Tarek.

'By the way,' I said to Tarek, 'thank you for the intro to Asma. She's great.'

'I figured I owed you one,' he said.

'Why?'

'I did get you stuck with Gowhar and Majid. Since they proved useless, you know, with your book.'

'Yeah, that was stupid,' Disha said.

'Why?' said Tarek.

'Because you didn't have to lie. If you wanted him to meet your friends, you should've just said it. If you wanted him to meet your

CHAPTER 18

friends to dish out dirt on Junaid, you should've been smarter about who you introduced him to.'

Tarek looked wilted. He checked the periphery. It was bad enough I was witnessing the dressing down; too many other people were within earshot if they chose to listen.

What I found remarkable was Disha's demeanour. It had gone from 'quiet companion of chauvinist pig' to the Disha that I recognised, whom a team of men like Tarek Bashir would not be able to dominate, not even in their dreams. In fact, after the first dinner I had with them, this had been the trajectory. Whatever was going on that night was, it seemed, a one-time occurrence – or some play of power dynamics between them. It was her off night, and his turn to be on.

'Don't talk to me like that,' Tarek hissed.

'Don't lie to me,' said Disha.

This caught Maisha's and Ruba's attention. They were at the bar with Gowhar and Majid, and the foursome came over. They knew the sound of brewing trouble.

Downstairs, Tarek got in his car and left without goodbyes, without another word to Disha. Majid and Ruba asked what the rest of us were up to. I was ready to go home, and I wanted to walk. After some fussing and offering of rides, Majid and Ruba left. Maisha was standing to the side, looking as though she was waiting for her ride, which wasn't her husband, or like she'd been stood up, which was closer to the truth. Gowhar asked her something quietly in her ear. At his touch she flinched. She threw off his hands and refused to accept whatever he was saying, and he stood back and regarded her helplessly.

'Don't walk,' Disha whispered. 'Come with me. We're going to the same place anyway.'

'Goodnight,' I said in Gowhar's and Maisha's direction.

'I'll call you tomorrow,' Disha said to Maisha.

'You're not worried about her?' I asked Disha in the car.

'There's not enough worry in the world that can help that poor girl.'

We got out at the Eternal Complex gate. Disha let her driver go for the night. It was interesting that she no longer cared that her driver was bringing her to Gazi's place at all hours. Driving herself to meet Gazi that afternoon might have been a case of nerves and secrecy. It could have been about showing him her independence, even though he was well aware of that already. I was with her tonight, and the driver knew I was family, and perhaps that eased the concern. But Disha was not concerned. She was, if anything, different in every way. To give myself credit for the smallest contribution to the change would be arrogant, and yet I couldn't help thinking my presence had had an effect. She was alone in Dhaka as far as family went. She didn't engage in frivolous relationships in the name of family. The legion of relatives we had in the city meant nothing to her. We had that in common, and she shared that quality with my father as well – he was clannish when it came to family. Hatfield or McCoy, he'd take up arms for his immediate blood kin any day, but relatives outside those bounds were as good as strangers. And like strangers, they had a way of showing up when in need of money, or the scent of an inheritance touched the air and lured them like bloodhounds. I'd seen instances of this. Out of the blue people would appear on our doorstep, claiming they were family and naming my grandfather and great-grandfather as proof. My father derailed their plans in one move. 'Proof of what?' he'd ask. Everyone in our village knew our family. It didn't take being kindred to know our names going back generations. These favour-seekers were contemptuous beings, and my father treated them accordingly. Disha was wired the same.

'Hi, boss.' Gazi had come out of Eternal Complex just as I was walking Disha to the entrance. 'Will you come up?'

'Not tonight.'

'He's being a bore, and unappreciative,' Disha said.

'Him? The Boss?' said Gazi.

'What's with this "Boss" stuff?' said Disha.

'It's between us,' Gazi answered with a smile.

CHAPTER 18

'Isn't it, boss?' she asked.

'I guess so,' I said.

I left Disha with him and felt their eyes on me until I was inside the house.

Much later, unable to sleep or read or write, I went to the roof. Gazi's light was on, and the windows must have been open because I was able to hear their argument. Disha's voice carried like a theatre actor's. She was reaching for the furthest seats in a large house – every last ear could hear every syllable. I didn't want to. I took in a few lungfuls of air. There was a scent of burning leaves. A train passed through the Mohakhali rail crossing. From the direction of the airport came sounds of trucks making their night-time runs. A nightwatchman's whistle made its piercing shriek. I had always found it comforting, a final goodnight assuring me all would be well, and I could sleep in peace.

My sleep didn't last long. The night guard knocked on my window half an hour after I'd got into bed. I must've been sleeping pretty deeply, even having a dream, because the sleep hung on for several minutes and I kept dozing off after telling the guard I'd be right out. For the first few minutes I thought the knocking was part of a dream, as were my exchanges with the guard, until my phone started vibrating. Gazi's name was on the screen.

'Boss, I'm so sorry to wake you. I asked your guard to knock before calling. I'm sorry, boss.'

'What's the matter?' I said. 'Is everything OK?'

'Boss, can I come in?'

Gazi was wearing the clothes I'd seen him in earlier. He didn't look like he'd been to bed. His phone and cigarettes were in one hand, clutched tightly, as if he was holding the hand of a small child, and with the back of the other hand he kept wiping his face.

I couldn't decide if he was a child or the most arrogant bastard under the sun. My night guard was standing guiltily to the side. I could use him as a proxy, channel my frustration with Gazi through him, give him the dressing-down I should give my selfish neighbour, and add a dash of reassertion of my authority by shouting at him to remember whom he worked for – and it would do nothing. Gazi would apologise some more, tell me not to scold the poor guy, ply the calm out of me, but he wouldn't change. Men like Gazi didn't know how to not put themselves first. They were incapable of not getting their way.

'Boss, I've disturbed you,' said Gazi. 'I'll leave you alone. I didn't know what else to do, where to go.'

'What would you do if I wasn't here?' I asked. 'I mean, what is it that you think I can do?'

'You're right. I don't know.'

'What happened?' It was a pointless inquiry. I could tell him myself what had happened.

'It was my fault, boss. Mine, as always. I say the wrong thing, do the wrong thing; it's always me.'

'What did you say?'

He gave me a look as if I'd asked him the weight of the moon.

'Doesn't matter,' he said, and sniffled.

'Is Disha still up there?'

'She drove off.'

I was asleep, and the air conditioning was running; I hadn't heard her car.

'She's not picking up either,' Gazi said.

'I'm sure she's fine,' I said. I couldn't care less right then. No wonder their friends got sick and tired of them. 'Either you come inside or go back home.'

'Boss,' my neighbour said, sinking tiredly into a chair, 'you're the only friend I have.' He leaned his head back and closed his eyes.

'You can sleep in the guest room,' I said. He gave me a dazed, battered look.

'I'm good, boss,' he mumbled. 'You're a good friend. Thank you.'

I said nothing. He was soon fast asleep.

I found some coffee in the kitchen and set a pot on to brew. My father's insistence on keeping the house stocked, the appliances up to date had its upsides.

CHAPTER 18

I was debating whether to send Disha a text when her message came in: 'Whatever he tells you, don't believe him!'

'If I didn't give a shit about you, I would've shut you both out by now,' I wrote, and then erased it. I tried again: 'You two are worse than spoiled brats.' I didn't send that one either. 'He's right here, blubbering like a pathetic asshole. Come get him, then leave me the fuck alone.' That one, too, didn't make the cut. The one I sent was: 'You OK?'

'I'm fine!'

'OK. I'm going back to sleep.'

I poured myself some coffee and stood drinking it in the kitchen. I was not ready for Gazi yet. I drank a second cup, then poured one for Gazi. When I went back into the living room, Gazi was gone.

I called Asma Ferdous the next day and asked if we could just talk over the phone.

'Not even one cup of coffee?' she said dejectedly.

'I have a pretty busy day – I'm sorry,' I said.

'Have you reconsidered?' she asked.

'My decision is final,' I said.

'It hasn't even been a full twenty-four hours,' she chuckled.

'Sorry, and I really do appreciate your help,' I said.

'Are you at home?' she asked.

'Yes.'

She took a deep, dramatic breath and launched into her tale. She spoke without a pause for the next twenty minutes. It was as if she'd waited years to unburden herself of what she told me. At the end of it, I was on my feet, pacing. Asma had told her story in a near monotone, with perfect journalistic calm.

'This is a lot,' I said, unable to find other words. 'Why did you want to tell me this?'

'Disha is your family – I thought you should know. I'm surprised she hasn't told you.' I was not. I found out something new about my cousin every day, it seemed.

'I guess I should thank you,' I said.

'Is there any chance you'd talk to your cousin?' she asked.

'Talk to her about what?' I said.

'About going on the record. Maybe bringing Gazi on too.'

'On the record?'

'His, and her, reputation took big hits from this. And still the full truth is not known.'

'I thought you didn't want to do anything with information like this about Gazi any more? And why, all of a sudden, is all this so important to you?'

Asma cleared her throat. There was the sound of traffic in the background I hadn't heard before. It sounded as though she'd started the call indoors and taken it outside.

'It's not all of a sudden,' she said, with a note of resentment. 'I'd forgotten about it. And then seeing your cousin, hearing Gazi's name again, brought it back. They suffered no consequences. I thought I was past it, but I guess not.'

'So this is personal?' I asked.

'Nisar, life is personal. Journalism is personal. You can think whatever you want of me for thinking that, but there are things I've learned in my career, and that's one of them.'

'I'm not thinking anything of you. I just want you to accept and respect my decision. About the job and about this.'

She called out to a CNG, they bartered and she got on. The tinny revving of the CNG drowned out all other noise for a moment.

'If you change your mind—'

'I won't. And please don't ask again.'

19

While I waited for Rais Kaka on Friday, I texted Mr Ehsan. Last time I'd settled on a simple thank you for his prompt communication, keeping questions about the vagueness of it for another time. I didn't expect him to have anything new to tell me. My purpose was more to keep him on his guard. Ten minutes later, he wrote back: 'Be patient. All is well.'

Rais Kaka was heavy with the burden of something he didn't immediately share; I figured it was the situation with his son and didn't pursue the matter. We kept our outing short – nothing from my must-visit list. We took the quick CNG ride to Hatirpool and went down by the water.

'You used to be close with Disha's father once, didn't you?' I asked.

'Very close.' He grew sad. 'I went to see Disha many times over the years, but I never did. She didn't want to see me.'

'Why?'

'Let it be. She's busy.'

I had brought up Disha's father because of a family story from during the war that involved my uncle and Rais Kaka.

In the days after the crackdown in Dhaka by the Pakistan Army in March 1971, my uncle and his friends were stopped at a checkpoint on what is today Kemal Ataturk Avenue, and were ordered to get out of the car so they and the vehicle could be searched. My uncle refused. He cursed at the soldier. He dropped a slew of names, among whom were army officers that were close friends of the family. The soldier wasn't having any of it. He pushed his semi-automatic in my uncle's face and reached his hand through the window and grabbed his hair. My uncle, as the story went, backed the car away from the checkpoint, then sped forward and ran the soldier over.

The family was terrified, for my uncle, and for themselves. They feared countless scenarios, every one ending in the army massacring them. The neighbourhood back then was nowhere near as busy, but still someone could have seen something. My uncle's car, his face, were well known. He had no choice. He had to leave town.

Rais Kaka accompanied him. They went to Sylhet, where they stayed with relatives until the end of the war.

'Such a long time ago,' Rais Kaka said, with fond recollection. 'He was a good man. Helped people. Everyone. I couldn't believe my ears when I heard he had…' he couldn't finish. He touched the back of his hand to his eyes to wipe away the tears. 'Baba, listen now. Something you should know. I've eaten your family's salt. It's the only family I had before I had my own. I don't want your father to get the wrong idea. I know Ehsan Shaheb has his trust more than anyone else.'

Aware that Mr Ehsan had been difficult to get hold of, Rais Kaka had paid Mr Ehsan a visit at home.

'I didn't get past the doorman, of course, with my own name,' Rais Kaka said. 'And so I had to mention your father. It worked. Ehsan Shaheb came down after some time. He was not happy to see me. I think he thought your father had actually showed up. The doorman was a little slow. I couldn't think of anything else, so I said you had sent me. I hope you don't mind, Baba. Please don't.'

'You did me a huge favour,' I said.

'So, he asked me why you sent me,' Rais Kaka went on. 'I said you hadn't been able to get him on the phone and you were wondering what was going on. He said he's been busy. And then he yelled at me for stepping out of my bounds. I no longer work for your family,

CHAPTER 19

and he threatened to call the police. I apologised and said he should contact you, and then I left.'

His eyes filled with tears again.

'You *are* this family,' I told him. 'When was this?'

'Three days ago. Baba, he looked like a prisoner. Like he never leaves home. Like he's afraid – or maybe ashamed.'

'Let's go,' I said, getting to my feet. 'What's he going to do if I show up – jump out of a window?'

'Baba, he looked like a man who would do exactly that.'

The doorman at Mr Ehsan's building was a different one from Rais Kaka's visit, and so didn't recognise him. He saluted me and let us through when I told him Mr Ehsan was my lawyer. I told Rais Kaka he could wait downstairs if he didn't want to face Mr Ehsan again, but he wouldn't leave my side.

A young boy-servant answered the door. Past him, through the opening he'd made, I saw a middle-aged woman in a sari peek around a corner. Mrs Ehsan was my guess, and I pretended I hadn't noticed her, and instead asked the boy loudly if Mr Ehsan was home.

'Ji...' the boy began, looking a little terrified. He might've been given instructions to not let anyone in that wasn't expected. I realised how it must seem to Mrs Ehsan – two strange men showing up at her door in the middle of the day asking for her husband, and I mentioned my father's name, and then mine, more gently.

'If he's not home, I'll come back,' I said. The boy looked over his shoulder.

'Let them in,' said the woman. 'Go tell Shaheb.'

The apartment was well, but carefully, furnished. Any trace of overt wealth was humbled by the ordinariness of the furniture. There was no flat-screen TV on a wall. Instead, where one could have been mounted, there was a framed picture of Mecca at night. Past the living room was the dining room – a plain dining table covered in a simple white cloth. The boy ushered us towards seats. I said we were fine, in a hurry, and he needed to go get his employer.

Rais Kaka took note of the place with the suspicion and critical eye of a detective in the home of a man living far beyond his means, and possibly not honestly.

Ten minutes passed before we heard footsteps. Mr Ehsan came out of a part of the apartment past the dining table and stood before me like a long-hunted man too tired to run any more. Rais Kaka had described him accurately. He was dishevelled, his punjabi wrinkled, a tea stain the shape of a large teardrop in the centre, over his sternum. He gave Rais Kaka a resentful look. He scratched the stubble on his chin, and gestured weakly to the sofa.

'Are you sick, Mr Ehsan?' I asked. 'Your texts make no sense; they're barely full sentences.'

He stared impassively at me.

'I've been a little ill, yes,' he said. 'Blood pressure and cholesterol.'

'Well, how am I supposed to know that if you don't return my calls or texts?'

'No, you wouldn't,' he said. He sat down. I noticed pictures of his children on the table next to the chair.

'If you're not going to be available any more, I need to know,' I told him. 'If you need some time off, fine. I wouldn't even know this much if I hadn't come here today.'

Mr Ehsan said nothing, just stared at the floor. He couldn't meet my eye. If he was hoping I'd send Rais Kaka out so he could open up to me, he was wrong. I was past trusting him. I was on the side of everyone who over the years had warned my father about him.

'I went to the banks,' I said, when it became clear we could be sitting in silence all afternoon. This didn't move him either. 'I met Mr Sadek at United City Bank,' I went on. 'I got the statements and I've sent them to my father.'

'Good,' he said with an air of defiance. 'You know how to do everything – then what else do you need me for?'

'You work for my father, Mr Ehsan. If you don't want that to be the case any more, then say so, and I'll make sure he knows it. Better yet, tell him yourself.'

CHAPTER 19

'I've done nothing wrong,' said Mr Ehsan. 'I don't know what you are suggesting, but I don't appreciate being talked to in this way.'

Rais Kaka shuffled in his seat. He'd been glowering at Mr Ehsan and looked ready to lunge at him.

'Do your job, and I won't,' I said.

'You don't know anything.'

'You're right, I don't. That's the problem. And right here, right now, I want you to be honest with me.'

'Honest? How have I not been honest? Why don't you just say what you have to say? Instead of leaving me threatening messages.'

'I didn't want to, but you also left me no choice.'

He held his stare on me. 'They were insulting and not worth my time, and still I did what you asked and replied.'

'I had no idea what you were talking about,' I said. 'What if it had been my father?'

'It wasn't,' he snapped. 'I know my place, and so should you.'

I could hear Rais Kaka's elevated breathing.

'I'm sure you resent that I just came over like this,' I said. 'But you left me no choice.'

'You seem to have your spies working for you pretty well,' he remarked, taking a swipe at Rais Kaka.

'I'm the only one you're dealing with, Mr Ehsan, and my father. Tell me this: what happened with this Premier League betting business?'

Mr Ehsan didn't flinch.

'Premier League?' he said. 'As in cricket?' He seemed honestly perturbed. 'That's what your threats were about?'

'They were not threats, Mr Ehsan.'

'Then you must have a different definition of threat from everyone else.'

'Before I tell my father and he's the one that has to ask you, I want you to tell me the truth: did you use our money to do anything illegal? And did you get questioned by the Anti-Corruption Commission for it?'

'Who has been filling your ears with poison, Nisar?' He leaned forward like an interrogator suspicious of every word coming out of a suspect's mouth. 'Tell me. You really think after all the years I've spent with your family that I would do that to your father? And you come in here, to my home, to make such a blatantly offensive accusation? I saw you when you were a boy, in shorts, screaming and running around.'

'Then explain to me why you were making such big withdrawals all of a sudden,' I said. 'Dad is really upset, and he refuses to believe you would cheat him.' I ignored the other comments. Nothing he could tell me could endear me to him, I wanted that to be clear.

'Cheat him,' he said, releasing a long exhale. 'This is what I have to hear after a lifetime of service.'

'We can clear it up right now,' I said.

'I did nothing with the money your father didn't do when you still lived here,' he said. 'Nothing he told me not to keep doing.' He smoothed his moustache proudly and waited for me to further challenge his integrity.

'So then what was the problem sending him the statements?' I asked. 'Why were you being evasive about it? Can you understand how that seems? If you needed money, you should've just asked for it. And these explanations you're giving, they don't make any sense. Mr Sadek says you should be taken off as co-signer on all the accounts. I think that's worth considering.'

'Do as you please,' said Mr Ehsan, waving dismissively. 'You're a grown man. It's yours, all of it. You don't know how things work here.'

'I don't,' I said, 'and I don't care. Dhaka can fuck itself with how it does things. I want you to do what my father pays you to do the right way.'

'You are in my home,' Mr Ehsan said coldly. 'Mind your language. I work for your father, not you. Whatever it is you came here to accuse me of, you've done it. What else do you want me to tell?'

'So you can account for all the money you withdrew?' I asked.

CHAPTER 19

'No,' Mr Ehsan replied. He gave his punjabi a smoothing stroke, which helped nothing. 'Your father is still a well-known and well-respected man. People do things for him that they don't for everyone else. That's what the money kept alive.'

I caught a glimpse of Rais Kaka's hands out of the corner of my eye. They were clenched.

Mr Ehsan stood up. 'I won't stand for this treatment from you any more.' He strutted to the door and threw it open.

'Let's go, Baba,' said Rais Kaka, patting my knee. 'It's a waste of time here – you have bigger things to worry about.'

Mr Ehsan wanted badly to put Rais Kaka in his place. Rais Kaka walked by him without giving him another look. I wanted to have the last word. Threatening to get the police involved felt cheap. He would probably mock me. Tell me to go ahead. Then watch me eat crow when I got nowhere.

Out in the hallway, I held Rais Kaka back. I wanted to hear if Mr Ehsan said something, to his wife, to the servant boy – anything that would show his true mind. Nothing came from the other side. Rais Kaka flicked a wrist at the door and gestured for us to leave.

My father said less than a dozen words to me and handed the phone to my mother when I mentioned my visit with Mr Ehsan and what I'd learned.

'He's the most unreadable person I've ever met,' I told my mother.

'Now you know,' was her answer. 'This is how it's been ever since that man came into the picture. Your father just won't hear it.'

'What more do you want me to do?' my father yelled in the background. 'Send a family man to jail for a few thousand dollars?'

'You see?' my mother said to me. 'I don't know what to say, Mom.'

'There's nothing more to do or say. Finish what there is to finish, then come back and live your own life.' She said this calmer than I'd expected, and yet it left me pondering and out of sorts the rest of the night.

20

I tried to process what I'd learned from Asma Ferdous by writing it down. There were several points during our call that I had the impulse to take notes, but I didn't want to interrupt her flow by asking her to stop while I readied myself. She spoke meticulously, with great detail, as if reading from extensively kept records. Writing it out helped calm my nerves as well, before broaching the topic with my cousin.

Disha was having dinner with Tarek at a Korean restaurant by Gulshan Club and asked if I wanted to join them when I texted her. I said I'd rather see her alone. She told me she'd come over within the hour.

Gazi's windows were dark. It was early still. He didn't get home till late on weekdays. I'd somehow missed a text from Jasmine. She had tickets to a fashion show the day after next and wondered if I'd like to go. Local designers, she added, as if to perk my interest further. I wrote to her that I would be delighted. I took a long shower, ate dinner and read over the two single-spaced pages I'd written. I was glad I did, as I was unsure I'd be able to repeat the account to Disha without some anchor, depending only on my powers of recollection, harried by shaky nerves.

Some years ago, Gazi was on a trip to Thailand. His parents joined him for a few days of it, because, as Asma told it, they were in the car with him when it happened. They'd gone out of Bangkok for the day and were returning to the city late at night, Gazi behind the wheel,

CHAPTER 20

and the car struck a tuk-tuk, instantly killing the two passengers, while the driver survived. Gazi didn't stop. He fled the scene. He'd been speeding, but the tuk-tuk driver, like the drivers of CNGs in Dhaka, knew his city, and was too seasoned in its mad traffic to lose his bearings. The driver noted the licence plate, make and model of the car. It took the police no time to arrive at Gazi's hotel room. He and his parents were taken in for questioning, and that was when the story took its bizarre turn. According to Asma, Gazi made a 'deal' with the authorities. In exchange for a handsome fee, he was let go and in his place a fall guy was, essentially, bought. This man was one of countless prisoners rotting in Thai jails with no hope of seeing a lawyer or the light of day. Whatever his original crime had been, he now had the additional charge of two murders on his head. Gazi had his freedom, his clean record, and nothing keeping him from going back to Bangladesh. As far as Asma was aware, the Thai man was still awaiting execution for Gazi's crime.

I opened the bottle of wine Disha brought and drank the first glass in three gulps. Disha sipped hers, stretched out on the sofa with her feet up and sandals off and didn't interrupt me once, not even to cough or sneeze or so much as clear her throat.

'You're finished now?' she said when I brought the bottle over to refill her glass.

'I think so,' I said.

'Sit here,' she said. 'Close to me.' We drank without speaking for several minutes. 'Do you believe it?'

'It's more like, how do I even process it?' I said.

'I told you about that bitch Asma Ferdous.'

'You've told me a lot of things.'

'What does that mean?' She looked at me incredulously.

'It means, I don't know from one day, from one hour to the next, which part of what to believe from you – or your... Gazi.'

'You're going to believe some hack reporter out to get me over your own flesh and blood?' She laid her head back and covered her eyes with her arm.

'If there's no truth to it, then that's it,' I said. 'If there is, well, there's not much *I* can do about it. Except that Asma is trying to leverage my connection to Gazi, and you, to write about it.'

Disha sat up slowly, taking her time, and set the wine glass down. She'd let her hair down when she came in, and it was draped over one shoulder, long enough to pool into her lap. 'You can do whatever you want with what I'm about to tell you,' she said with cool abandon. 'Asma Ferdous, the bloody *New York Times*, I don't care.'

I followed her gaze to the wine bottle and emptied it into her glass.

'It wasn't his parents,' she said. 'Asma Ferdous got that part wrong.'

'I don't understand,' I said.

'His parents were not with him on that trip,' Disha explained.

'Asma has the wrong information then,' I said.

'No. It's not her fault. It's the information that was given out. By Junaid, and his parents.'

'They gave out false information?' I said.

Disha nodded.

'Why?'

'So Junaid wouldn't be alone in answering questions, if they ever came up.'

'And did they? The questions, I mean. Did anything come up?'

Disha's extended stare was her reply.

'Right,' I said. 'Why should they? The whole case was bought out and closed shut.'

Disha turned to me. 'Are you so clean, Nisar, that you think everyone else is here for your judgement?'

'I'm clean of vehicular homicide, if you want to get specific.'

She raised clenched fists to indicate how frustrating she was finding me. 'You watch too much TV, little brother. It was an accident. He didn't set out to kill those people.'

'He fled the scene. That's the crime. Then he bribed the police and put the blame on another man.'

CHAPTER 20

'Are you going to go interrogate the Thai police next?' she said.

'I'm not interrogating anyone, Disha.'

'You used to call me Disha Apa.'

'Please don't deflect.'

'I'm not.' She rearranged herself, dropping her feet, assuming a professional, officious pose. 'If Asma Ferdous wants dirt on me, she can have the spine to come to me. Tell her that. I know what journalism is, and I know that what she does isn't it. None of it is in this country. They're all mouthpieces for whoever is in charge.'

'I don't want to tell anyone anything,' I said. 'I thought it was the right thing to do to tell you what I heard. Since you and he are – I don't know – rekindling or whatever again. It doesn't matter. I'll tell Asma she can do her own digging. Also, Jasmine seems to think pretty highly of her.'

'Jasmine is her own person – I couldn't care less who she likes,' Disha said, sounding a little hurt that I'd privilege Jasmine's assessment over her sentiments.

I could hear our breathing, mine at a higher rate than Disha's. She put her hand on the back of my neck. Her palm was warm and damp.

'Don't be mad,' she said. 'I know I'm a mess.'

'Everyone is a mess,' I said.

'It was me. I was with him on that trip.'

I poured what was left in my glass down my throat. My heart had been calming down, but now started on its frantic dance again.

'It was one last attempt,' she went on, 'at saving our marriage. It was a months-long trip we had planned. Bangkok was the first stop. That night we had a huge fight. I know – what else is new? He left the hotel. And he was gone almost all night. Didn't answer his phone, didn't return texts. Finally, when he showed up, he looked like he'd seen the dead climbing out of their graves. Nisar, if you saw him…' Her voice caught. 'He was terrified, like a little boy. He was crying so much I freaked out. I didn't know what to do. He didn't want me to, but I didn't see any other option: I called his father. He got on the next flight to Bangkok.'

'Then the part about his parents being there isn't altogether false,' I said.

'His father was the one that…' Disha trailed off.

'Made the arrangements?' I offered.

'Junaid was torn up over the whole thing. Really, you have to believe that. He wanted to contact the couple's families. He wanted to tell the truth. He wanted to reach out to the other prisoner's family too. But his father warned him not to. Guilted him, like he did all his life, into doing what he wanted. Junaid was too shaken up to fight back. He didn't have the strength. And he was terrified.'

'Of his father?'

'Of him, of going to jail, of everything. On top of that, our marriage was falling apart. Can you have the tiniest bit of sympathy?'

'It's not my place to have any feelings either way,' I said.

'What is it that you want from me, Nisar? What is it that you think I owe you? Is that it? Besides honesty, what else?' She got up and walked to the windows facing the driveway.

'Does anyone else know?' I asked.

'What do you think?' she said, scoffing. 'In Dhaka? They just don't know the blanks I filled for you. Because it's over. That's how everyone prefers it.'

'You too?'

'Doesn't matter.'

'I think you did the right thing,' I said, after a brief silence. 'Not talking to her. Both of you.'

'Yeah,' she said, 'thanks.'

'Come here,' I said. She stayed at the window a moment longer, then made her way over.

'Don't interrogate me any more, please,' she said, sitting down.

'This is not an interrogation, but did you know Rais Kaka came to see you?' I said.

'I don't like him – I never have,' she yawned.

CHAPTER 20

'He was close to your father,' I said.

'Good for them. You can like him all you want.'

I almost blurted something I was glad I didn't: that it was she who I had a hard time liking as much as I wanted to, all the time, without doubt, with all my trust, with the heart and mind of the boy that put her on a pedestal.

'I do. I don't think you understand how much he's done for our family,' I said, knowing full well it wouldn't make a difference.

'Good for him and good for our family.' Disha closed her eyes.

I was exhausted, and the wine had me dozing off fast. I leaned my head back, and was soon asleep.

I awoke to Gazi's car pulling up to Eternal Complex. Disha's head was on my lap; she was fast asleep. I didn't disturb her, and set my head back down and closed my eyes. A dream came and went, making no sense. Light filtered through it, until the brightness cut through my sleep, and I woke up with a start and an achy, stiff neck.

Disha wasn't there.

She wouldn't be anywhere else in the house, but I still checked the bathroom, guest room and even my bedroom – where I finished my search, undressed and crawled into bed.

My father would have done no less to protect me than Mohammad Gazi had done to save his son.

I spent the morning trying to read and then write, but Disha's story made both impossible. No matter how I reasoned it, Gazi had killed a man. Then, by his choice or not, he'd relented to an outcome that was almost worse than the crime. He could've gone to the police on his own. He could've confessed, overridden his father, had a spine, done the right thing – no matter what it cost him.

It was stupidly righteous of me to think so reductively, as if the threat of a long prison sentence, and possibly execution, in a foreign land, wouldn't turn my conscience to corruption of whatever stripe it took to get me out alive.

I ate a small breakfast and drank a cup of tea to clean out the cobwebs left by the wine, and then took a walk across the way to Eternal Complex.

Gazi's servant let me in, and said he was on a phone call. My mouth went dry, and my throat felt parched. I asked for a glass of water.

'Boss?' Gazi startled me. I'd been standing by the window, unmindfully searching the sky, thinking of the last time I'd looked out to find God's Eyes. 'This is a surprise.'

'Why?' I said. 'Is it a bad time?' I had asked the question not as a courtesy, but to deliver a jab of sarcasm with my tone. If he could show up at my place at all hours, wake me up, pull me into his quandaries, so could I.

'Not at all,' he said amiably. 'Have you had breakfast?'

I said I had. I didn't move from the window.

'Are you OK?' he asked. 'You seem a little—'

'I'm fine,' I interrupted him. Everything flooded my mind – Asma's story, Disha's corroboration. I saw not one but two Junaid Gazis, the second behind him, a few steps away, off to a side, challenging me to speak my mind. Nothing I had to say would touch him. He was not ashamed or afraid. I was the one burning and quaking, brimming with so much principled outrage I couldn't stand being in my skin. 'I actually came to thank you,' I said. My heart was beating fast. 'I confronted Ehsan. Don't worry, I didn't mention your name. I didn't mention any names.'

'I'm sorry, boss, that you had to go through that.'

'He didn't confess to anything,' I said. 'My father, he'll still believe him before he believes me.'

He brought out his pack of cigarettes and lit one. 'You can fire him,' he said.

'Is that what you would do?' I asked.

'I wouldn't have to,' he said, releasing smoke. 'My father would have him in prison long before that.'

'Prison? My father won't do that. He's made that clear. Besides, what would be the point?'

CHAPTER 20

Gazi did a minor double-take. 'He'd be held accountable,' he said, mechanically.

'And then?'

'And then... make him answer...' his logic seemed to deflate as he spoke.

'By what?' I kept on. 'Torture?'

Gazi nearly laughed at this, but seeing I wasn't joking pressed his lips. 'You're a better man than that, boss.'

'I'm sure it could be arranged,' I said. 'Powerful men like our fathers can make anything happen, can't they?'

'Boss,' he grinned, 'you've been in Dhaka too long.'

'Maybe I have. But I'm not saying this lightly. How many men are there in Dhaka, in all of Bangladesh, that could challenge men like your father? On anything?' I let some moments pass, then added. 'Or mine?'

Gazi snuffed out his cigarette. 'Not many,' he said.

'We get away with things our guards and servants and drivers wouldn't,' I said.

'Meaning?'

'Meaning, it's not easy just wanting accountability.'

'You're in a philosophical mood today,' he said. 'As far as your Mr Ehsan is concerned, besides letting him go, I don't know what else you could do.'

I could have thrown our relationship out of sorts right then, altered its contours, pushed it through a one-way door for the rest of time. I imagined our places reversed. He was the one asking me, without compunction, if the Bangkok story had happened the way Asma and Disha had told it. They'd said their piece. He could say his. This was his chance to clear his name.

The scene played in my head. I saw myself enraged, lambasting Disha, threatening to ruin Asma, my composure up in smoke long before Gazi was finished, my guilty conscience no more needed to be left to guessing, as he continued sitting there with equanimity if, our roles back to their places, I had taken the fight to him.

'He put me in my place,' I said, shaking my head clear. 'No one seems to want to take responsibility for what they do. Everyone's too wound up trying to keep their name and integrity clear.'

'You drive the conversation, not him,' Gazi counselled.

'I don't know,' I said. 'It's more trouble than it's worth.'

He lit another cigarette. 'Is there something you're not telling me, boss?' he asked.

'I feel like I'm always the one not being told everything,' I said.

'Boss, whatever you want to know, all you have to do is ask me.'

'Is it really that simple? Do I really want to know more than I do? I'm just running an errand for my father and trying to write a book. I didn't ask to be involved in anything else.'

'You can't walk away from it either,' said Gazi. 'Because you care.'

'Why – because Disha is my cousin?'

'Because you love her.'

'That's not always enough,' I said.

'The way you love her it is,' Gazi said.

'The way I love her?'

Gazi fixed me with a look that could have been a trap. Had it been one, I would have had no escape.

'Are you really saying what I think you're saying?' I asked.

'I know she's easy to love in more ways than one.'

'Disha is my cousin – she's my sister. It's sickening that you'd even mention something like that!'

'Then what other reason do you have for not liking me as much as I do you?'

21

I left Gazi's place thoroughly disoriented. He'd kicked my legs out from under me. I hadn't considered that the confidence with which I'd gone to throw him off was never on solid footing to begin with – how flimsy it was in its ill-conceived umbrage. He didn't stop me when I stood up and walked out, sullen, pouting, dejected, tail between my legs; nor did he sit there puffed up by his win, pleased with himself, as I would have done. When I closed the door behind me – and for a moment before it shut – I saw him sitting still in his chair, not looking at me, as though I'd never been there at all, with only his sincerity, the same probity with which he'd struck his blow and sent me on my way.

I fired up the joint Almas had left while I was getting ready, forcing my train of thought to stay on Jasmine. I had a good high going when her car pulled in.

Jasmine looked gorgeous in a light-pink sari and matching blouse, with a string of honeysuckle clipped to her hair, and virtually no make-up. Against the sea of Dhaka's women whitewashing their faces with foundation, hers was a natural wonder. It also made me think of how similar she and Disha were, in so many ways, from their appearance to the turns their lives had taken. The horrific end to Jasmine's relationship and Disha's experience in Bangkok with Junaid had stark differences, but also shared elements that only the two of them would understand – including the need to push past the events and move on.

The fashion show was at the International Convention City Bashundhara, a massive complex of buildings the size of small stadiums. I joked with Jasmine about being seen with me at such a large affair, giving Dhaka ideas about us, and she said with complete seriousness: 'If you have no problem, I love the idea.' I was glad we were in the car and she couldn't see my expression. For the next three hours, the fashion show was not the only attraction that held my attention: it was seeing faces I hadn't seen for years – since I was thirteen years old in some cases – relatives, friends, acquaintances. It felt like a reunion.

'I shouldn't be surprised,' Jasmine said at one point. 'You're Disha Chowdhury's cousin, after all.'

My cousin's name brought back our last meeting, its pall still hanging over me. We hadn't spoken since then, neither of us so much as sending a text. I didn't appreciate her sneaking off, to which I was sure her excuse would be that she didn't want to wake me.

'Small things to be thankful for,' I said.

'What's up?' she asked after the show was over and we were standing outside. 'You've been – what's the word? – brooding.'

'I don't know how to brood,' I said. 'Nothing's up.'

She didn't buy it, but she was respectful enough to accept it. There lay a foundational difference between her and my cousin. Disha would pester me to death. She'd claim her right as my big sister, demand openness, force me to tell her something was up, even if there wasn't.

Jasmine waved to someone over my shoulder. Before I could turn, a hand clapped my back.

'Hey,' said Gowhar.

I so wanted to tell him never to do that again. Jasmine saw my irritation.

'Hi, Nisar,' said Maisha. 'Did you like the show?'

'I did,' I replied. 'Actually quite a lot.'

'This is one of theirs.' Maisha spread her arms to indicate what she was wearing: a long shirt, between a punjabi and kameez, and

CHAPTER 21

flared, pantaloon-like slacks. Up close the get-up looked a little comical, like a clown costume, but still Maisha wore it well.

'It's beautiful,' I said.

'I think it's a little ridiculous,' Gowhar commented.

'That's because you have no taste,' Jasmine retorted.

'Look at it!' said Gowhar.

'You can be such a prick, Gowhar,' Jasmine said. 'Maisha, you look stunning. Forget him.'

It was too late – Maisha's spirits had been dulled.

'Forget me, that's right,' said Gowhar, and then, turning to me, 'Are you going to Junaid's tonight?'

'I have to go home, and he's my neighbour,' I answered. 'Not sure I'm up for…'

I stopped, seeing Gazi coming out of the auditorium. I hadn't seen him before then. He lit a cigarette and waved at us but didn't come over. He stood by the metal detectors at the entrance and talked to people, as if he was the star of the evening. I didn't blame him for not wanting to be in my company after our last conversation. I waited for Disha to make an appearance next, but she wasn't there. The next face I looked for was Tarek's, but he too was nowhere to be seen.

Gowhar went over and the two of them talked for a long time. I got the feeling Gazi had one eye on me – a prickly sensation on my neck that told me I was being watched. I'd been right in the past on several occasions and had caught the person staring. But when I finally looked, I found Gazi standing with his back to me, encircled by people like a fan club. Gowhar stood outside the circle for a few minutes, then came back to us.

I met some more people from the past, caught up, exchanged updates and information, and looked to Jasmine to make our exit.

'Coming over?' Gazi was standing at the top of steps down which we'd just made our way to Jasmine's car, sporting a winning smile.

'Maybe,' Jasmine replied.

'Boss, you?'

'I won't be too far away if you need me,' I said.

'Always the funny guy, boss,' Gazi said. 'I'd love to see you both. Please come. Sorry I couldn't talk to you here.'

Outside the convention centre grounds, the traffic was murderous. We were stuck feet away from the main entrance for half an hour, but the time didn't go idly by. When Dhaka's wealthy citizens went all out, they went all out. No extravagance was too much. Not even hiring private security goons to clear traffic for them. I'd seen these hired hands around my neighbourhood: big men, with walkie-talkies and scowls, flanking the vehicles of their employers like the Secret Service, thrashing rickshaws and pedestrians and anything or anyone else that got in their way. In Dhaka, something was always in the way – just as was the case of the SUV ahead of us.

'I don't know whether to laugh or be outraged,' I said.

Jasmine was not as engaged as me with the fiasco, which included two 'traffic clearers' terrorising a line of rickshaws and CNGs that was supposedly holding up their boss' car. They weren't, but it was easier to pick on poor drivers of rickshaws and CNGs than the actual culprits, all of which were other cars equal to or higher than the status of the hired hands' boss.

'I know that was a lot to unload on you last time,' Jasmine said once we'd finally cleared the jam and had been driving for a while.

'I'm glad you did,' I said. 'I appreciate it. I'm sure it's... I can't imagine...'

She gave a smile and touched my hand. I left it flattened on the seat, and a moment later she took hers back.

'Sorry,' she said under her breath.

'Don't be, please. I'm...' Everything I could think to say was lame or insulting. 'Your company has been one of the best parts of this trip. And believe me, there have not been many good parts to speak of.'

'That doesn't sound too good,' she said wryly.

'No,' I said. 'It doesn't. But I hope the sentiment is clear. Thank you, in other words.'

CHAPTER 21

Jasmine let me out at my gate and said she wasn't in the mood to go up to Gazi's that night. I didn't blame her. She was also tired from her trip. There didn't seem to be anything going on up there anyway, but it was early. We said goodbye, and I started walking into my house, then changed course and headed towards Eternal Complex.

He was alone, sitting in a dimly lit living room, smoking, with the windows closed.

'I'm happy to see you, boss,' he said, as if he was expecting me. 'Sorry about the smoke.' He stood up, opened the windows, and sat back down. 'Drink?'

'I'm fine, thanks,' I said. 'Where is everyone?'

'Probably still at the convention centre or stuck in traffic. Or maybe they're not coming.'

'That's unusual, isn't it?'

'I don't know, boss, I'm just the provider. They come and go as they please.'

'Must be tiresome,' I said. 'Is Disha coming?'

'Your guess is as good as mine, boss. But I'm glad you're here, and it's just us,' he said, switching gears. 'I've been thinking about your request.'

It took me a second, and then I remembered.

'About the house?' I said.

'Thing is, boss, my father makes the very last and final decision, and he is a very hard man to dissuade when his mind is made up about something.'

'And his mind is made up to keep the house in the deal?' I said.

'I'm sorry, boss.'

'Would it be possible for me to speak to him?'

'I would never let you suffer through that,' he said.

'I don't mind – I suffer through my own father's behaviour over things like this all the time these days.'

'Which is why you don't need mine to add to it,' Gazi said.

Sometimes a silence holds more than words, and sometimes there's no need to look into someone's face to know what they're saying is a lie. Gazi had presented me with enough conundrums to create a spectrum just for him; and even then it was never clear where on his spectrum he was – he could be genial in the morning and glum in the afternoon, vanished in the evening and a jovial, entertaining host by night's end. But those were masks. That much I had determined. And those masks hovered just beyond the borders of the spectrum, making the one he was wearing at any given occasion undeterminable, especially if one saw him in fleeting glimpses, like a movie watched haphazardly, or slides of photos showing a different expression from frame to frame.

Keeping the house, denying my request, was not his father's decision but his own. He wanted it all.

'I've been curious about this,' I said. 'I tried asking you before, but why didn't you buy us out the first time around? Why this gap?'

'Also my father's doing,' Gazi replied, as though he'd been expecting the question. 'I was not part of it; I wasn't even in Bangladesh at the time. And you didn't exactly ask me this before. You wanted to know why I wanted to buy *all* of it.'

'Right, yes,' I said. 'The questions are related.'

'But my answers have not been satisfactory, I know.'

'I'm not a business-minded person,' I said. 'I'm just following the orders my father sent me with.'

'That's not entirely true, boss, is it now? You have a personal attachment too.'

'Maybe it was a passing thing.' I'd said this on a whim, in the moment, for something to say.

'I don't believe that, boss. You seem to me like a more deliberate man than that.'

'Maybe I'm not.'

'It pains me to see you in pain.'

It was the most earnest thing I'd heard him say. It didn't matter that he'd said it to me. I would have felt the same had I been a third wheel, an interloper, a silent witness.

'OK, well, then that's that,' I said.

CHAPTER 21

'Boss, wait.' Gazi dropped the cigarette – his third since I had arrived – into the ashtray, and hunched forward. He let out a long sigh. 'I've meant to tell you this for some time. Please don't think I've been dishonest. It was for her sake.'

'Disha's?' I asked.

He nodded. 'I promised her, but I owe you complete honesty, too. Disha asked me to make the offer.'

'I would be surprised, but...'

'I know.'

'She actually told you to make the offer you made?'

'Well, not literally, no. She just wanted me to think it over. And you know when your cousin says something she does not mean it lightly.'

'So you two were in touch before I was anywhere near the picture?' I said.

'Only because she contacted me about this. It was more a strong suggestion than a request. She mentioned it only once and left it alone after that. And hearing from her, after such a long time, I... just crumbled. I never stopped thinking about her, wanting her. If this would make her happy, it would make me happy. Boss, don't blame her. Be angry with me all you want.'

'I don't want to be angry. Not at you and not at her. Not even at Ehsan. I felt bad about last time. I didn't mean to come in here and harass you. Then seeing you at the fashion show, it looked like you were mad at me.'

'I was out of line myself. It was insulting what I said. I'm sorry.' Before I could return the apology, he said, once more changing course, 'You know, I've been thinking, ever since I met you. You should be here. This country needs people like you. Honest, good people.'

'Thank you, but that's an overstatement,' I said.

'You don't understand, boss. We lost so many of the good ones – look at what we're left with.'

'Yourself included?'

'Public Enemy Number One.'

'I'll take your vote of confidence,' I said.

'Boss, if you don't believe anything else I say, know this, from the bottom of my heart: I would never lie to you. You could ask me anything. Everything I've told you has been true. No matter what else you hear from whoever else, you'll always get the truth from me. So… will you tell me the truth in return?'

'Sure. About what?'

'What did you really come here to talk about the other day?'

'I told you,' I said. 'I wanted to thank you for the tip on Mr Ehsan. I'm sorry the conversation got so heavy. I know I contributed to it too.'

He dragged on his cigarette and crushed it in the ashtray. 'Everything I've done,' he said, 'I've done with a clear conscience. Losing Disha is my only regret. All other mistakes can go to hell.'

'I don't know how you do it,' I said, pushing to my feet. 'I'd go crazy. The way people talk in this town, constantly. And I've only been here a month.'

'You accept it,' Gazi said. 'It's better than trying to dispute it.'

'Even if it's a rumour?'

'Boss, especially if it's a rumour.'

22

I was awake when Jasmine's text came in. She couldn't sleep either. I asked if she wanted to talk. I could call. It was I who could have used a listening ear. And yet, what I wanted to air would be too big a betrayal to two people at the cost of my need to vent.

'Any chance you're in the mood to come over?' she wrote.

She'd left the door open for me. Her living room was lit by only one floor lamp in a corner. There was a similarity between her and Disha's decor I found disorienting at first but got past as soon as she came out. She was wearing silk pyjamas, her hair down and brushed to a sheen, her face washed and scrubbed.

'Can I get you something?' she asked.

'I'm good for now,' I replied.

We sat next to each other on a long sofa like two strangers in a doctor's waiting room.

'Thank you again for the invitation tonight,' I said.

'I'm glad you weren't bored to death,' she said, turning her head at an angle that made her hair cascade off her shoulder.

'No, I was entertained, really. By the show and the social scene.'

'Dhaka is full of entertainment, that's for sure.'

'Can I ask you something?' I said. 'Maybe I know the answer already, but you're really the only other person, other than Disha, that I can... well... talk to honestly.'

'I'm happy to hear you can be honest with me,' she said, smiling appreciatively.

'I know you take care of your family's business,' I said, 'but if you didn't have that, would you live here? In Dhaka? In Bangladesh? I mean, I know you love Dhaka, but still, I just… I don't know… do you ever think about living somewhere else?'

'I'd live right here,' she answered without hesitation or thought. 'Absolutely. This is my home. I can't imagine living anywhere else.'

'What about that time when you were in the US?' I regretted my question immediately after asking it. 'Sorry, I mean… you said you might have stayed back… God, I'm so sorry…'

'It's OK. That was a different time in my life,' Jasmine said. 'Esau was open to the idea of living here. We never had the chance to really, you know, talk about things to that point.'

'I'm sorry,' I said again.

'Don't be.' She took my hand. 'You have the softest, most comforting hands. And long fingers, like a piano player's.'

'Sometimes I wish we'd never left,' I said.

She held on to my hand with hers closed firmly around it. My fingers were limp, refusing to reciprocate. 'Why?' she said.

'Because I wish I could feel like where I live was really my home,' I said.

'You don't feel like Chicago is home?'

'By decisions I didn't make it is. I love the city. My life happened there. But being here I feel – I don't belong there or here. And I really wish I did.'

'What does belonging mean to you?'

'I don't know… knowing it, really knowing it, like you do: that this, where I am, is it. Home. I was born here. I'm going to die here.' I made a move to take my hand out of hers, but she held on.

'Just for a minute, please,' she said. She laid her head on my shoulder.

'I'm going back soon,' I said. It was as if an outside force had blown the words into me, then pushed them out in my voice.

CHAPTER 22

'OK...' Jasmine raised her head. 'When?'

'I mean, I haven't set a date yet, but it's probably going to be soon.'

'I'm sure it's a relief.' She put her head back down and pushed up against me.

'Relief? From what?' I asked.

'Oh, you know, Dhaka crap. Your life is over there.'

'Yes, it is,' I said.

Her scent was the pomegranate fragrance of her soap, and shampoo, and a natural hint of her skin that I couldn't name.

'If you stayed back,' she said, 'then...'

'I can't. My parents need me.'

'If, if you did, then... maybe something wonderful would have happened and you'd feel like this really is home.'

'Jasmine, I do think you're wonderful,' I said – again, something I wouldn't have done if I'd been thinking straight.

'So are you,' said Jasmine.

'You've made my time here really beautiful,' I said. My breath was catching in my throat; I felt a constriction in my chest.

'Now you're just being silly.' She lifted her head again.

'I'm serious,' I said. 'I think if I lived here I'd...'

'You would what?'

'I'd want to see you all the time.'

'You'd give me a kick in the ass and throw me out!' she laughed.

'Not a chance,' I said.

'I'd get on your nerves in a week, and then you'd find someone else. And believe me, you would *not* have a hard time of it.'

'Right,' I said. 'You and my cousin are convinced that for some reason Dhaka women are lining up for me.'

'They will – she's right.'

'Well, they'd be disappointed.'

'Why do you say such stupid things?'

'Because I wouldn't be interested,' I said.

'Oh, I see. Mr Hard-to-Get *and* Hard-to-Please?'

'No,' I said. 'Because I'd want to see only you.'

She came closer. I moved back. 'Am I really that bad?' she asked.
'No,' I said.
'I can imagine something, can't I?' she asked.
'Yes,' I said. 'So can I.'
'I like the thought of it,' she said. 'It's a very nice thing to think.'

But there was no discomfort, no awkwardness, and we sat together as two people with a long and complex history, of many cycles of ups and downs, back once more to equilibrium. I hadn't been so at ease in someone's company in years – and a relative stranger at that.

'I have something for you,' I said, bringing out my phone. She read what I pulled up on the screen.

'This is…' she began, 'I'm not sure what it is. Is this part of your book?'

'The beginnings,' I said. 'I know it's lousy right now, but it gives you an idea what I want to do with it.

'Going all the way back to Dhaka's founding,' she said. 'That's ambitious.'

I'd hoped for more enthusiasm. Now I felt embarrassed.

'I'm thinking fiction is going to have to be my way,' I said, taking my phone. 'I'm not a historian, and I don't have the kind of fortitude needed for writing *The Big Book of Dhaka*.'

'You're good at what you're good at,' she said. 'It's enough.'

At some point we both dozed off, and when I woke up to sunlight peeping from behind a panel of lace curtains, I saw Jasmine stretched out on the sofa.

She opened her eyes moments later. 'Are you going?' she asked.

'It's morning,' I said. 'I have some things to get done.'

'Thank you again for coming over,' she said.

'I'm glad I did.'

'Did you mean what you said?' Jasmine asked. 'About wanting to see me all the time?'

'Cross my heart,' I said.

She smiled sleepily. And drifting off again said, 'I wish you would stay…'

23

I took it as some small progress that Mr Ehsan was returning my texts, even though his replies brought my frustration back full circle. 'What is your schedule like tomorrow?' I asked, trying to plan our visits to the banks.

'Might be busy,' was his reply.

'When are you free this week?' I followed up.

'I'm not free,' he responded.

I decided to call. The phone rang several times. I waited for voicemail to kick in, tiredly dreading leaving a message.

A woman, sounding out of breath and knowing exactly who was calling, said, 'Sir, hello, yes, this is Mrs Ehsan.'

'Hello,' I said.

'He's here, sir, right here,' she insisted, as if I'd disputed the fact. 'Take it!' I heard her say with the phone held away. 'Take it right now, Ehsan, or...' The phone changed hands.

Mr Ehsan came on so quietly I had to ask if he was there three times.

'I'm taking an Uber to your place,' I told him. 'I don't have time to leave things hanging. We'll go to the banks today and get you off the accounts. Hello? Mr Ehsan?'

Mrs Ehsan spoke forcefully in the background, her inflection leaving no need to hear her words.

'Fine, OK, fine. But I can send car, no?' Mr Ehsan said demurely.

'No, I don't want to sit here wasting time,' I told him. 'I'll be there soon. And Mr Ehsan, don't go anywhere. This is more important than anything else on your list today.'

It was not yet six in the morning. The roads were still empty, and a CNG scooter ride to Mr Ehsan's place took no time.

I heard raised voices. Mostly Mrs Ehsan's. I waited for a pause to press the bell. Thirty seconds later she was still talking. I pushed the button once. A hush fell inside. Seconds passed, then the lock turned and the door was thrown open.

Mrs Ehsan was a diminutive woman with limp hair and lines at the corners of her mouth and eyes. She stepped aside to let me in, as if she'd summoned me to settle their dispute. 'Sir, come.'

I wanted to tell her not to call me sir, but the time did not seem appropriate.

Mr Ehsan was standing in the middle of the room, like a prisoner in a kangaroo-court proceeding. He was wearing the same clothes as last time. They were filthy, and he too could use a wash. After I stepped inside, Mrs Ehsan crossed her arms and looked at her husband, angry, exhausted, at her wits' end.

'I'm ready if you are,' I said.

Mr Ehsan looked from me to his wife and to me again. 'One minute,' he said, and went inside.

Mrs Ehsan and I stayed in our places. Several times I thought she would speak, and once or twice I wanted to thank her. 'Give your father and mother my prayers and gratitude,' she said softly. 'We will always be in their debt. For everything.'

Her husband came back out with his hair hurriedly combed and a bush shirt and baggy trousers barely buttoned. He was no longer the immaculately sartorial man I'd met my first day. That effusive man, full of charm and a sense of the history he'd had with our family, was gone.

We didn't talk during the drive – not even in the traffic jams that formed as the city shook off its slumber and thronged the streets. At the banks, Mr Ehsan kept his head down, his mouth shut, and

CHAPTER 23

complied. I'd notified them in advance what was happening; they had most of the paperwork ready, and the processes were fairly straightforward. I hoped as we went through the steps that Mr Ehsan felt every shred of shame and embarrassment possible for how he'd tried to lie and manipulate me. I couldn't stop being furious at how gullible he thought I was.

I should have felt lighter, more relieved as his name came off the accounts, but I couldn't shake the nagging sense that he still had the upper hand. It was the figure he was making of himself – that something so terrible was being done to him, that I was the one who should be ashamed. He was a man who believed he was being disgraced and condemned for wrongs he hadn't committed, and he was taking wrongful public persecution with honour.

Mr Sadek's assistant greeted me at United City Bank and said he would like to see me in his office.

'Is everything going OK?' he asked. 'Sit, sit. Have something. Tea, coffee?'

'No, thank you, Uncle,' I said. 'This is our last stop. I can't thank you enough for telling me to do this.'

'Yes, yes,' he said, distractedly. 'Get that man as far from your affairs and your family as you can.'

'Maybe this isn't something you can answer,' I said, 'but do you know anything about this Premier League cricket scandal?'

'Ah, yes.' He laced his fingers and rested his chin on his hands. 'Big mess; could have been bigger. But this country has too many people with too much power, and most of it was swept away. Why?'

Before I could answer, his eyes widened.

'Oh my God,' he said, muttering the words, one at a time. 'Good God, I hadn't thought about it for one second. The withdrawals, the urgency...' He sat back. 'My God, if I had had the first idea...'

'I don't think there's any way to prove it,' I said. 'And he refuses to give straight answers.'

Mr Sadek rubbed his forehead. 'I know you don't have time to get involved with the police and all, but...'

'I heard he was questioned by the Anti-Corruption Commission,' I said.

'Pointless,' Mr Sadek sighed. 'All talk and no action. The action that does happen is useless – politics and sham. As you can tell. He clearly didn't suffer any losses, any repercussions. I don't know what happened to this country. We fought for it, and now we have to fight with it.'

'I'm going to tell my father to let him go,' I said.

'Yes,' he said. 'I don't see another way.'

We shook hands, and I walked back out to the main floor. Mr Ehsan was not where I'd left him. The associate that had helped us told me he was downstairs.

I saw the car, the driver leaning listlessly on the hood. Mr Ehsan was in the back seat. The driver opened the door for me.

'I thought you had left,' I said, getting in next to him. 'You shouldn't have just walked out without me.'

'I couldn't keep sitting up there,' he said. The driver opened his door to get in, but Mr Ehsan told him to wait outside. 'Is there anything else you want from me?' he asked.

'I wish you hadn't given me this runaround,' I said.

'It was your neighbour who told you,' said Mr Ehsan – not as a question but as truth he was certain was indisputable.

'What are you talking about?' I said.

'I did the cricket betting,' he said, assertively. 'And I suffered the consequences. But it was my money I used. As God is my witness. Let anyone say what they want. I never touched your father's money unless he told me to. Ask him that. Ask anyone that. You are his son; you are a young man; you are doing what you feel is right by your father: fine. I've done my part from day one.'

I didn't believe him. He was a lawyer. He could spin words, twist plots, sway minds, reach hearts.

'It's the worst thing in the world,' he said, looking out of his window, 'being taken out of your house in your T-shirt and pyjamas,

CHAPTER 23

not given the time to put on your shoes, while your wife watches helplessly. I hope you never have to know.'

I said nothing. Also, I'd heard no mention again of the daughter that needed round-the-clock medical care. Not seen or heard sign of her at his apartment. Didn't spy a single crease of worry anywhere near his face. She could be at a hospital, sure, but his credibility with me was too low, and I wasn't ready to grant any more concessions.

'My wife has suffered,' he went on. 'A lot. Because of me. I know this. But that's no longer enough.'

'Did you mention my father's name to them?'

Mr Ehsan kept his face averted. I thought he hadn't heard me, as I'd kept my voice low, and I was about to ask again. I couldn't make myself believe him. I hoped for my father's sake he was telling the truth, even if whatever damage could be done was done. I didn't want to be trapped in the car with him any more and opted to walk home.

'You keep the car,' Mr Ehsan said as I was getting out.

'No,' I said, closing the door.

24

'You proved yourself the real boss,' were Gazi's first words upon hearing of Ehsan being booted off the accounts. We were on my roof, him smoking a cigarette, me finishing a joint, our cups of tea empty on the table beside us.

'Maybe,' I said. 'I don't want to be. I'm not like you.'

Gazi looked at me with the hint of a grin. A light breeze was making the hem of his punjabi flutter.

'I mean, it's not for me to be anyone's boss,' I said.

Gazi blew a final plume of smoke and tossed the cigarette into the darkening day. The sky was a whirl of burning orange and shades of purple, the street below filled with the noise of evening: students getting out of classes, rickshaws and scooters, snack vendors and hawkers. An argument between two drivers from the direction of Road 23. The sonorous beggar courting God.

'You'd make a hell of a boss,' Gazi said. 'What's Uncle going to do? Fire Ehsan?'

I hadn't spoken to my father yet. 'That's up to him,' I said. 'What will you do with this house if your father doesn't agree to let us have it?'

Gazi looked pained. 'That makes it sound so harsh, boss,' he said.

'Well, I don't know how else to put it.'

'Boss, I'm really sorry. For everything.'

CHAPTER 24

The word had no meaning. It had been used and overused to the point I didn't know in what context he said it any more.

'Sorry has nothing to do with it,' I said, perhaps too officiously. 'It's business. Isn't it?'

'I meant about dragging you in between me and Disha.'

'I really don't care about that any more,' I said.

'But you do,' said my neighbour, with a passing glint in his eyes. It was dark now, and for a moment his eyes actually glowed. 'You're the kind of person that cares, more than you know.'

'I didn't realise you had me figured out so well.'

'It's not hard to see goodness in good people.'

Gazi was an exceptional wordsmith. I may be the writer, but he knew how to maximise words, each one chosen carefully, artfully, placed strategically, leading to a sentence that most, including me, could not refute. He was a champion flatterer when he wanted to be, and it worked. I could have reciprocated. Offered him a compliment in return for his. I wasn't sure he'd believe me, and he would be too respectful to say to my face that I was lying.

25

On Thursday I met up with Jasmine at Butlers Chocolate Café. It was the first time I'd spoken with her or seen her since the night at her place, and initially we were both awkward. I didn't speak out of turn, didn't try to minimise what we'd shared or dismiss it. Whatever could have happened between us had circumstances been different was speculation. I preferred to think our friendship, because I believed we'd forged a good one, would last.

Our small talk fell into a lull. We looked our separate ways for some time. I watched people come and go, groups sitting around tables and in booths in conversation and laughter, the outward shows of all-is-well that we put on in public, and when I turned back to Jasmine, I wanted to take her hand in mine. It would contradict how I'd been with her the last time, and so I clasped my hands together and kept them to myself.

In the couple hours that we were there, Jasmine introduced me to people whose names I'd never remember, but some of whom I'd seen at Gazi's parties. There were greetings and good cheer, questions asked about life and work and children, recent travels and events shared, and fond wishes imparted. It would be wrong of me to think such niceties fake, but I would be lying if I said I found them completely sincere. I could only be present and appreciate the genuine fondness I felt for Jasmine, and understand the feeling to be mutual.

CHAPTER 25

Around the time that we were thinking of leaving to go to Gazi's, Gowhar and Maisha walked in.

More small talk ensued. Gowhar bought a round of beverages, and we spent another half hour being like the other happy patrons around us.

Gowhar was bristling with childlike excitement. His Porsche had arrived. He'd been to Savar to receive it that day, and he showed us the one-hundred-plus photos he'd taken of it.

'It's even more gorgeous than the pictures,' he said. 'And that engine... It's like flying on a cloud.'

'You're a lucky guy,' I told him. 'Not everyone gets to have the hobby they want.'

'This isn't a hobby,' Gowhar said. 'It's—'

'Life,' Maisha finished for him. 'It's life for him.'

Gowhar made to say something, but instead he smiled. It was the first and only time I'd seen him smile at his wife. The two of them attracted more people to stop by our table. New names and faces entered my brain, and out they went as soon as they were gone.

I sent Disha a text telling her we were at Butlers, and she wrote back saying she was headed there herself and was about to send me a message to see if I wanted to meet her. When she got there, we ordered a round of beverages, and Gowhar's photos made another appearance for her sake.

We stayed late at Gazi's. The early November evening was perfect for sitting on the roof, even though that was the popular end-of-night spot regardless of the weather. I drank my fill with full acceptance of the torture the hangover would visit on me the next day, and I wished Guru had been there with his generous offering. Tarek and Disha were icy with each other for a while – Tarek had been absent for several days because he was with his children. At the same time Maisha kept breaking my heart with her mooning gazes at Tarek, and I wanted to tell her to let him go – he who hadn't given her as much notice all night as he would a mosquito before swatting it.

Despite my perception of being an outsider, I felt a peculiar sense of belonging – or maybe I wanted to feel it so badly that I convinced myself it was true. I'd been around them a very short time, but our time together had been more intense than many friendships I'd had over the years. I'd seen the many moving parts of their lives that I hadn't with people back in Chicago, whose stories of love, marriage, heartbreak and loss I'd known from the beginning, and once or twice had a hand in sparking. There was an informality here that didn't exist there. And that informality was the line between the façade and the real. Perhaps my comparison was unfair, but it was true. Regardless of the inner workings, I would never understand, and would rather not. The best I could do was be quietly in gratitude to these people.

'You look sleepy,' Jasmine said, catching the glaze that must have come over my eyes.

'I'm relaxed,' I said. 'Feeling good.'

'Before he leaves,' Gowhar said, 'why don't you all come out to Savar tomorrow? What do you say, Nisar?'

'Sure,' I said. 'I'm not leaving yet, but—'

'You have to see this car in real life,' he said. 'You can stay at the rest house; we'll spend the night, come back Saturday.'

'I'm in,' I said. I looked to Jasmine, who, after a moment's thought, nodded. 'Disha?'

'Savar, for the day?' said my cousin. 'Sounds a little boring.'

'What about you?' Gowhar asked Gazi. Disha's eyes darted to him.

'If Boss is in, I'm in too,' Gazi answered, looking not at me but at Disha.

'Tarek?' said Gowhar.

'You and your fucking cars.'

'OK, then it's set,' said Gowhar. 'We'll get there by late afternoon. You don't need to bring anything. It's all there.'

26

The morning of our trip I made calls to the banks for safety. Mr Sadek's confidence and assurances notwithstanding, I wanted them to know I hadn't let my guard down quite yet. Mr Sadek took my call. He told me Mr Ehsan had not shown himself since the last time he was there with me, and that Mr Sadek had left strict instructions with all his employees and staff to alert him the moment he did.

Next, I called Mr Ehsan. With the mess put to rest, my anger abated, I wanted to offer an olive branch.

He didn't answer. After several rings, his wife did.

'Sir, he left Dhaka,' she said, with a finality that suggested he was gone for good. 'I told him he should,' she added.

'Call me Nisar, please,' I told her. 'For how long?'

Mrs Ehsan didn't answer the question. She launched instead into a sort of history of my family as seen by her. How her husband had been given a lifeline by my father, my mother's many generosities towards her and their children, the roof over their heads, including their current home, possible because Shahriar and Amina Chowdhury had offered them the dignity their own families had not.

Before the day I went to their home, I'd never seen Mrs Ehsan.

'I hope,' she said, her voice drenched in remorse, 'you can ask your father and mother not to abandon us. In their place I would, but I pray they don't.'

A fleeting impulse passed through me to ask what she knew about the betting and the money. It wouldn't be fair to put her on the spot. And I had had enough of my share of it. I left my regards for her husband, and then I looked forward to clearing my mind with the day away from business of any kind.

We were delayed by a few hours, and it was early evening when we reached Gowhar's family's rest house. He gave us a full tour, strutting like a proud connoisseur of the finest things in life. The centre of the tour: the Porsche. We stood looking at it as though it was an ancient and rare artefact in a museum. It was a beautiful piece of machinery, no doubt, and I wondered, between the Porsche and the other cars in his collection, where in Bangladesh he got to drive them to their fullest potential.

We ate dinner out on the lawn sitting at a circular cane table, and then moved on to drinks. The lawn was sprawling, encircled by mango, jackfruit, banana and lemon trees. I was reminded of my father's family's tea estates in Sylhet, the winter vacations we spent there. The air, too, was similar, without the grime and dust of the city. I could also see stars, and a quarter moon was rising above the tops of the trees.

After one round of drinks Disha, Jasmine and Maisha went their way together, and we sat back, watching them walk into the deepening night, their voices trailing off.

Gazi was staring in the direction the women had gone. I was getting sleepy. The food, the drinks, the fresh and clean air were working their magic.

'It's spooky as hell out here,' said Tarek.

'You're an embarrassment,' Gowhar chuckled.

'Fuck you!' said Tarek. It was banter, and Gazi and I treated it as such.

'Why did you come if you don't like it?' said Gowhar.

'Because…' Tarek began, then shot me and Gazi a look.

'You can leave any time,' Gowhar told him.

'Don't tell me what to do, asshole.'

CHAPTER 26

Gowhar let out a soft laugh.

'He calls me an asshole! He has no shame about—'

'About what?' Tarek demanded, pushing himself to his feet. 'Go ahead, say it. About what?'

'About ruining a friend's marriage—'

'Go to hell, Gowhar. Go. To. Hell.'

'Guys, please,' said Gazi.

'You're one to talk,' Tarek turned on him. 'Disha and I were doing just fine. After all your bullshit, all the years, year after year, finally you were gone – but no! You just couldn't stay gone. Who the fuck do you think you are, Junaid? I've known you all my life, and you've never been anything but a fucking prick.'

'Takes one to know one,' Gowhar said.

Tarek flung his glass into the dark. It crashed on the paved driveway.

The women reappeared from the darkness of the lawn.

'You all make me sick,' Tarek said. 'Starting with you,' he told Gazi.

'Fine,' Gazi said. 'Now calm down and have a seat. OK?'

'What's going on?' Maisha asked. 'Gowhar, what happened?'

'Shut up,' Gowhar snapped.

'What the hell is your problem?' Jasmine said to him, then went after Maisha, who had run off into the house.

'What's going on?' said Disha. 'Nisar?'

I help up my hands in surrender.

A piercing scream stunned us into silence, and we all turned.

Maisha was in the driveway; Jasmine was next to her, trying to get her under control. There was scuffling, indecipherable exchanges. Maisha's footsteps scrambled to the nearest car, which was Gazi's, and she climbed in and slammed the door.

'Maisha,' Gowhar yelled, banging on the glass. 'Come out. Don't be a bitch!'

'I don't want to be here,' Maisha cried. 'I'm going to sleep in this car if I have to.'

The rest of us were in the driveway by now – all except Gazi and Disha, who seemed to be wrapped up in a quarrel of their own. I walked towards them, getting close enough to hear the tail end.

'I don't want to be with Tarek, I want to be with you,' Disha was saying.

'You could've fooled me, and half of Dhaka city,' Gazi retorted, very unlike himself.

'Junaid, this is why,' Disha hissed. 'This is why we've been hopeless, and why we'll always be hopeless.'

'Thank you,' Gazi said, 'for that enlightening perspective.'

'Go to hell, Junaid.'

She swept past me in a windy blast. She went to Gazi's car and got in on the driver's side.

'What're you doing, Disha?' Gazi went after her. Disha turned the ignition and started the car.

Gazi thought fast and got in the back door on the other side, next to Maisha.

'You're all crazy,' Tarek shouted.

'Nice job,' said Gowhar.

'Fuck you and fuck your Porsche, Gowhar.'

Disha gunned the car. Before the rest of us could get into Tarek's car and go after them, Gazi's car was out of sight.

Tarek drove much too slow and with a delicacy I found disconcerting given the situation, although in his place I would not be doing any better. There was no sign of Gazi's car – not for miles. Tarek finally picked up speed, shifting in his seat with urgency at last. Fifteen minutes later we were slowing down again.

A crowd was gathered on the side of the road. There was a groan from Gowhar, a deep, animal growl at the approach of danger, and Tarek veered the car in the direction of the crowd. I was the last of us to recognise Gazi's car, which lay next to a truck. One side of it was crashed against a streetlight, and the windshield had completely shattered as Maisha Wasim was thrown out of her seat on impact.

CHAPTER 26

Traffic thundered by. Tarek and I were feeble against the crowd, insanely attempting to control them, trying to ward them off, make them scatter. We berated them, shouted threats, warned the police were on their way.

Gowhar was being held back by Gazi with help from Disha, although he wasn't putting up a fight. To the contrary: he'd turned to stone; only his mouth fluttered with his breathing, his eyes blank with shock.

27

The ambulance took Maisha's body to United General Hospital in Gulshan, and we spent the rest of the night there. Most of those hours were a blur. I was trying to comfort Disha, as was Jasmine, and Gowhar was catatonic outside the room where his wife's corpse awaited the medical examiner's release. Tarek and Gazi were standing quietly in a corner.

Gazi looked at me when Tarek stepped away.

'Boss,' he said, laying a heavy hand on my shoulder. 'I'd finally convinced her to stop, so I could take the wheel. That's why we pulled over. Maisha wanted to stretch out on the back seat – she was feeling ill. We were... me and Disha got out to switch places. Maisha was still inside. She'd crawled over to the back. The truck just... it came out of nowhere, and rammed the car right up into the pole.'

Disha and Jasmine were looking at us. I left Gazi and went back to them.

Maisha's parents barred all of us except Jasmine from their daughter's qulkhwani prayers and from visiting them. I didn't know Maisha well enough for it to matter to me, but I wished she'd had more peace in life.

A few days later her card fell out of my wallet. I remembered that day two months ago when she'd called on me. The mark on her neck I recalled with a sense of shame, as if I'd walked in on

CHAPTER 27

her naked, seen her in ways I had no right to. If my first guess had been correct, if what I noticed had been a birthmark, I'd be able to recall that moment with less shame, more grace. That was it – that was all I was permitted to feel about her. And hope her end had been quick.

28

There was silence all around. No one called anyone; no one went to anyone's place or met up outside. I'd spoken with Gazi once, and that had happened when we met by chance on our way into our respective homes. We chatted briefly. He told me he was ready to finish the formalities before he left town for several days the following week. It was a cold, disconnected exchange, during which he did not once look directly at me. And when we were done, he walked off without a goodbye or a handshake. He had also not called me Boss the entire conversation. Whatever was my part in causing him offence, I'd never know, and if it was by association to Disha, then I couldn't blame him. My cousin was not in my good graces either.

The next afternoon, I heard cars pulling up outside Eternal Complex – two of them, within minutes of each other. Tarek Bashir bolted through the gate and into Eternal Complex. Behind him went Gowhar Wasim.

I came out, went as far as the entrance and stopped. I didn't want to get involved any further. Because of that, I would only learn what happened after it was all over.

Gowhar was the one that came pounding on my front door. His face had the same look I'd seen not long ago. He couldn't get a word out without choking and coughing. I followed him to Eternal Complex and up to Gazi's roof.

CHAPTER 28

Tarek was standing by the reflecting pool, staring into it. I looked for Gazi. Gowhar gripped my arm so hard I winced. Gasping and heaving, he led me to the pool.

Gazi was on the roof when Gowhar came up to him. I wondered if he'd been looking at Disha's building, the green lights over the sign, or if he'd been sitting at the bench in the wall facing the pool, as was his preference when up there. The latter was likelier, and the former left for me to speculate.

'I just wanted to talk to him,' Gowhar kept saying. 'You got in the way,' he said to Tarek.

Tarek said nothing. He didn't move, and when he did, it was to walk to the other side of the roof and light a cigarette.

Gowhar's account had it that he and Tarek, both vying for Gazi's ear – for what precisely I was unable to discern – got into a scuffle. Gazi got between them. Their tussle intensified, and Gazi lost his footing at the edge of the pool. Where he now lay.

'Tarek?' I asked. 'Is that what happened?'

His eyes bore through me. He didn't break his silence.

Muhammad and Saira Gazi did not want fanfare. Junaid Gazi was buried in a quiet ceremony at Banani Graveyard. Disha and I were there. I asked the Gazis if I could be among the carriers of their son to his resting place. Mrs Gazi nodded, but I got the feeling she didn't fully understand what she was agreeing to. Mr Gazi took my hand in his and placed it on one of the handles of the takhta, then took the one on the other side, by his son's head. The other two bearers were long-time servants that had travelled with them from Rajshahi, where they lived – older men that had looked after Gazi as a boy. Both were sobbing all the way to the grave, through the burial and long after the last clods of earth covered Junaid.

In the week they spent at Eternal Complex, I saw them about half a dozen times. I didn't ask, and Mr Gazi didn't share, what was going to happen to their son's apartment, or to the building.

'We can finish things,' Mr Gazi said to me the first day, unable to speak more than a few words at a time.

'Uncle, it can wait. I've told my father what happened. They're both very upset. They want you and Auntie to know how sorry they are.'

'He's a good man. So was your uncle. He was a friend to me when no one else was. He helped me.' He fell silent for a while, then said, 'We were family. Family always stays family no matter what happens.' After another pause, he said, 'My son mentioned you want to keep your house.'

'We talked about it,' I said. 'But, Uncle, we don't have to do this right now.'

'He was adamant,' Mr Gazi went on as if I hadn't spoken. 'Of course, it's your house. It's all yours. I don't even know what possessed him to buy everything from you. But I stopped standing in his way long ago.'

I couldn't look him directly in the face for a long time – it was Gazi that stared back at me: just how he'd look thirty years from now. It was the same with Mrs Gazi. Her son had her bearing, her quiet presence.

'Thank you, Uncle,' I said.

'If there's anything else I can do for you, please…' His hand touched my shoulder the way his son's had so many times.

Mrs Gazi didn't leave her son's room until the day they left. Disha spent every day with them. Contrary to everything I'd heard about her and Gazi's marriage, I saw with my own eyes much her former in-laws still had affection for her. There was no acrimony. They barely spoke, and when they did it was to recall a fond moment, a childhood anecdote, the times filled with love and memories Disha and Gazi had shared.

Rais Kaka came by for his Friday visit. I handed him a cheque for five lakh takas and told him I wouldn't take it back. He could burn it for all I cared. He stared at the cheque. I knew he wanted to say something, anything that would preserve his dignity. I took the cheque, folded it and tucked it into his shirt pocket.

CHAPTER 28

We didn't go out. Before he left, he paid his respects to Mr and Mrs Gazi.

A few days later, Disha called to say she was having a difficult time sleeping at night, or during the day, or any time, and wanted to stay with me.

'Are you sure?' I asked.

'I understand if you don't want me to...'

'No, that's not it. I'm asking for you, with his building being right there.'

'That's what I need, jaan,' Disha said. 'To be close to something about him a little longer.'

After we both spent a sleepless night sitting up in the living room, staring aimlessly at the TV so as not be completely by ourselves, she asked if it was too soon to visit the cemetery.

'No,' I said.

The earth on the grave looked fresh, and it had been recently watered. Three sticks of incense burned at the centre. A framed picture of Gazi leaned on the headstone, the ghost of a smile playing about his mouth.

'He was trying to calm me down,' Disha said. 'I wasn't listening. I was mad at him, at Gowhar, at Tarek, at the car. At everything I could be mad at. Except Maisha. It was the kind of anger I felt only with him. He knew what it looked like and sounded like, and he knew how to talk me down.' She blew her nose and dried her eyes. 'I pulled the car over and walked away, and he came after me. I don't know how long we were talking, but it wasn't long.' She stopped again to swallow. Two thin, transparent streaks rolled out of her nose. 'That truck was going like lightning. It had no lights, and it was weaving all over the road. The car had no chance. It looked like a little toy car, and Maisha, she just flew out of the windshield like she was... like she was trying to fly away.'

We stood at the grave until Disha got a hold of herself as best she could.

'Come,' she said. She led me by my hand to the other section of the cemetery, the side on which Sheikh Mujib's family is buried. 'You wanted to see him before you left,' she said.

Rajib Hussain Chowdhury. I said my version of a prayer for my uncle and touched the headstone.

Outside, I put Disha in her car, telling her I'd see her at home, and then I went for a walk. I walked for a long time. I walked until I felt faint, and then I walked some more. I thought of nothing. I put one foot in front of the other and kept going. I heard no traffic, no horns, no police whistles, no profanities from drivers, no tinkling rickshaw bells, no human voices in conversation. Nothing.

In spite of their 'damaged reputation', the Gazis never left Bangladesh. They didn't leave Dhaka. They stayed, they battled, they prospered. They accumulated wealth, name, fame, infamy. For those that grumbled or even openly cried that they 'owned' Dhaka, the claim would be both simplistic and accurate. I wouldn't know which to agree with, which to deny.

My journey to Dhaka was supposed to have nothing to do with Junaid Gazi beyond the parameters of business. I went for a reconnection, and through my book, a way of reclaiming the voiceless exile's – because I hadn't had a vote in our move to America – sense of home. But home isn't just one thing. It isn't a country, a city or a place of dwelling. Home is a going away, contained in loss, obscured by the brushstrokes of memory.

I want to believe the friendship Gazi offered me was sincere. I find it difficult, because I'm not sure what I returned was friendship. I was swept up in his charm, compelled by his authority, spellbound by the ease with which he drew people in. It was more that I made him a study than I was interested in creating a bond. Gazi had been handed an empire and envisioned it as a force of decency, if not good. Its baggage was not his making, its history out of his control. His door was open to friends and detractors alike. Both sat under his roof and took him apart for better and worse. Gazi was

CHAPTER 28

the quintessential survivor of those of his echelon in Dhaka. This city, ancient, glorious, damaged, risen again, requires the spirit of a warrior. Gazi may have been the best of its kind to take it on its own terms, and, when he took it to task, leave it speechless. I, on the other hand, in a mere few months, was defeated. It could only exist for me in going away.

My last Friday outing with Rais Kaka was to Lalbagh Fort, that remnant of Dhaka's days as the capital of Mughal Bengal. It never became the fort it was designed to be, and for nearly four centuries since the abandonment of its construction has been the site of a single mausoleum, a graveyard of one. Pori Bibi's final resting place commands the centre of the grounds. Destroyed by her death, her father, Shaista Khan, never finished the fort. If it's true that people sometimes see their beloved departed souls come for them at the time of their death, I thought about whom Gazi might have seen in those final moments when life crept out of him, spreading around his head in its red halo. We inherit the lineage we're born into, with its history and its contradictions, both the very beautiful and the very ugly, neither of which we have a hand in being able to change, and the past beats on, louder sometimes than the present, clearer than any visions of the future.

END

ACKNOWLEDGEMENTS

Thanks, above all, to my agent Kanishka Gupta, and to Will Dady for giving the book a home at Renard Press. It's quite the privilege to see the book begin this new journey into the world after its initial publication in the Subcontinent by Hachette India. I wish I could thank by name each and every person who has worked on it and supported it so far, and my gratitude in advance to everyone who will guide its way forward once again.

ABOUT THE AUTHOR

NADEEM ZAMAN is the author of the novel *In the Time of the Others*, a nominee for the 2019 DSC Prize for South Asian Literature, and a collection of stories *Up in the Main House and Other Stories*. His fiction has appeared in numerous journals around the world. Born in Dhaka, he lives in Maryland where he teaches in the English Department at St Mary's College of Maryland.

A NOTE ON SUSTAINABILITY

RENARD PRESS feels strongly that there is no denying the climate crisis, and we all have a part to play in fixing the problem.

We are proud to be one of the UK's first climate-positive publishers, taking more carbon out of the air than we put in. How? We reduce our emissions as much as possible, using green energy, printing locally and choosing the materials we use carefully; we calculate our carbon footprint and doubly offset it through gold-standard schemes; and we plant a tree for every order we receive via our website to give back to the planet.

Find out more at:
RENARDPRESS.COM/ECO

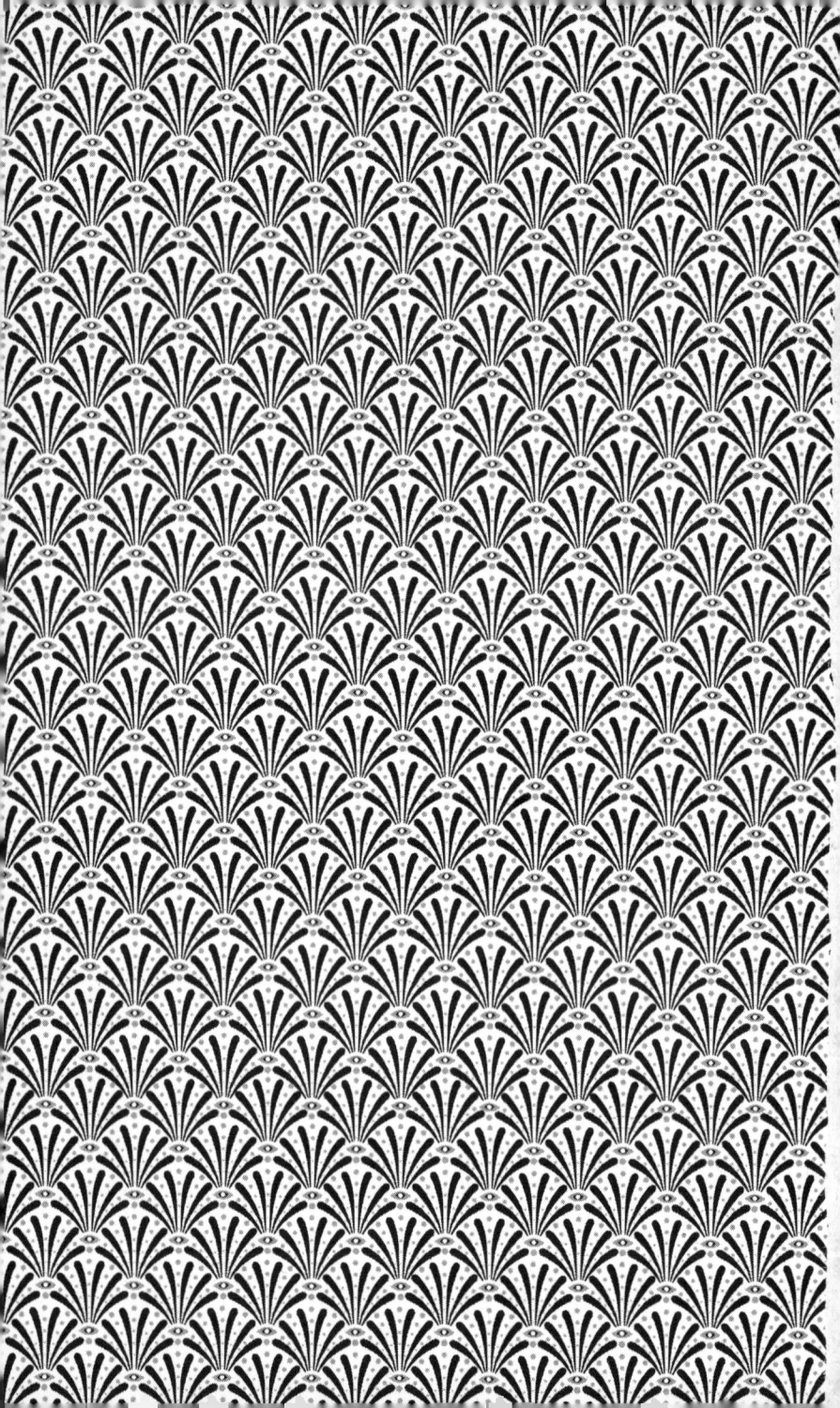